HOME OF THE BRAISED

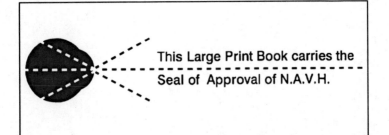

HOME OF THE BRAISED

JULIE HYZY

WHEELER PUBLISHING
A part of Gale, Cengage Learning

GALE
CENGAGE Learning·

Farmington Hills, Mich • San Francisco • New York • Waterville, Maine
Meriden, Conn • Mason, Ohio • Chicago

LIBRARY OF CONGRESS CATALOGING-IN-PUBLICATION DATA

Hyzy, Julie A.
    Home of the braised / by Julie Hyzy. — Large print edition.
        pages ; cm. — (A White House chef mystery) (Wheeler Publishing large
    print cozy mystery)
    ISBN 978-1-4104-6875-8 (softcover) — ISBN 1-4104-6875-5 (softcover)
    1. Paras, Olivia (Fictitious character)—Fiction. 2. Women cooks—Fiction.
3. Murder—Investigation—Fiction. 4. White House (Washington, D.C.)—
Fiction. 5. Washington (D.C.)—Fiction. 6. Large type books. I. Title.
PS3608.Y98H66 2014
813'.6—dc23   2014008358

Published in 2014 by arrangement with The Berkley Publishing Group,
a member of Penguin Group (USA) LLC, a Penguin Random House
Company

Printed in the United States of America
  1 2 3 4 5   18 17 16 15 14

For Patrick Smith, who I am very lucky to be able to call my friend

ACKNOWLEDGMENTS

In *Fonduing Fathers,* Ollie spent a great deal of time outside the White House, following a cold trail that ultimately led to discovering the truth about her father's murder. Here, in *Home of the Braised* (Thank you, Kathy K. Grow, for the title suggestion!), Ollie's back in the kitchen most of the time, but hasn't forgotten her promise to Gav. I hope that as you read this adventure, you remember that none of Ollie's stories would be possible without help from some truly great people:

First, my awesome editor, Natalee Rosenstein. I'm extremely fortunate to be able to work with her, and her fabulous assistant, Robin Barletta, at Berkley Prime Crime. Thank you both for all your wonderful help and support. An unsung hero I've recently had the pleasure to meet is Stacy Edwards, the fabulous production editor who guides my manuscripts through the many steps required before publication. Thank you, Stacy! Thanks, too, to copyeditor Erica Horisk who catches inconsistencies, and offers spot-on suggestions. I'm also very happy to be working with Larry Segriff at Tekno Books LLC, who is simply one of the nicest people on the planet.

Thanks much to my enthusiastic agent, Paige Wheeler, and all the great folks at Folio. And to my friend Matthew Clemens, who "spitballed" an idea or two that made it into this story.

Big hugs to my blog sisters, the Cozy Chicks (cozychicksblog.com), and friends at CozyPromo, as well as to reader Sue Gilot who was kind enough to "introduce" me to the incomparable Grandma Mae some years ago. Grandma Mae, you will be missed.

To my friends and especially my family: Curt, Robyn, Sara, and Biz. Love you all. You guys are my rock — my life — and I cherish our times together above all else. A special thank-you to Curt, Sara, and Biz for pre-screening all my books, catching more than a few "Oops!" moments, as well as a few misplaced modifiers.

Thanks, too, to you, my wonderful readers, who keep asking when the next Ollie story or the next Grace adventure is due out. Your e-mails make me happier than you can ever know. I am a lucky, lucky woman indeed.

CHAPTER 1

I'm of the belief that there are precious few moments of absolute clarity in our lives and that, when we're granted one of these deliciously pure bursts of comprehension, we'd best act on it. Quickly, decisively, boldly.

Special Agent in Charge Leonard Gavin — Gav — shared my attitude. We'd made the decision, we both knew it was right for us. There was no good reason to wait.

Unfortunately, however, bureaucracies don't care a whit about the courage of one's convictions.

"What do you mean, Ollie?" Cyan asked. "Yesterday you told us that you and Gav were getting married in three days. How can it be off now?"

Cyan, Bucky, and I were in the White House kitchen which, considering the number of hours I spend here in my role of executive chef, often feels more like home to me than my apartment does. Cyan had worn her emerald contact lenses today. I think of all her choices, this was my favorite. With her red hair and spunky attitude, the combination suited her. Now her bright-green eyes gleamed with worry.

"You seemed so sure," she said. "What happened?"

My two assistants had come in to work about a half hour after I did, and had immediately picked up on my mood. It's not that I was morose — it wasn't my style to whine or feel sorry for myself — but I was considerably less upbeat than I had been the day before.

"You forget what life is like in the Washington, D.C. area," I said, striving for levity. "The wheels of justice turn slowly. Except in this case, we're dealing with the wheels of the justice of the peace. They've ground to a halt."

Squinty-eyed, Bucky regarded me, his arms folded across his chest. Shaped a bit like a slim bowling pin, with freckles across his bald pate, he hadn't been officially titled as such, but I considered him my next in command. An absolute genius with flavor combinations, he spoke his mind freely, and often. That character trait had been difficult to get used to at first, but I'd come to ap-

12

preciate it. And him.

"What are you telling us?" Bucky asked. "That your plans are delayed? By how long?"

I pulled in a deep breath and let it out again. Bucky and Cyan were not only coworkers, they were my good friends. There was no point in hiding my disappointment from them. "It looks as though —"

"Good morning," Virgil said as he blew into the kitchen. With one of his fat cookbook binders tucked under an arm, he precariously balanced used bowls and utensils on a stainless steel tray. "What is this? A kitchen conference? And I wasn't invited?" He rolled his eyes as he dropped his load onto the countertop. One of the bowls teetered and toppled onto its side, sending a whisk somersaulting into the air. As the batter-laden utensil spun, it shot pale firework patterns onto everything in its path before splatter-crashing onto the floor.

"Good morning, Virgil." I chose to ignore his jab about gathering without him, but I didn't care to continue my tale of wedding woes with him in the room. Experience made me reluctant to share personal information with the newest member of my White House kitchen team. He'd been a thorn in all of our sides since he'd started working here. The First Family had shocked us all by bringing a personal chef into the White House to cook their daily meals, a task that, until then, had always belonged to the executive chef — me.

When Virgil had first started, he'd mistakenly believed he was hired to take over the executive chef position. He'd been sorely disappointed to discover that wasn't the case. To be honest, I'd been fearful for my job the first few weeks he'd been here, too. I'd been under the misguided notion that he was cherished and valued by the president and his family.

As we'd gotten to know the Hyden family better, and as we'd gotten to know Virgil better, we'd begun to realize that he was not nearly as beloved as we'd first believed. He'd made more than one misstep, and several big ones. Despite his many blunders, however, Virgil remained on staff. On *my* staff. That meant he remained my headache.

I tried mightily to maintain a cordial working relationship, although I couldn't help but believe that the effort was one-sided. "No conference here, Virgil," I said. "Bucky, Cyan, and I are catching up on plans for the Durasi dinner next week."

I decided to change the subject. If there

was one thing guaranteed to engage Virgil's attention, it was talking about himself. "How was breakfast upstairs?" I asked.

"Wonderful, as always."

Up to this point he hadn't made any effort to clean up the mess he'd made. In fact, he looked like he planned to ignore it.

I pointed. "You're not going to leave that, are you?"

He turned to me with an impatient stare. While he might be considered good-looking by some, I didn't see it. It's a well-known phenomenon that the more you like a person, the more attractive he or she becomes. I'd come to the conclusion that the reverse was true as well. At this point I knew Virgil too well to see him as anything more than a glowering diva in my otherwise marvelous kitchen.

"Let the cleanup staff take care of it," he said as though we hadn't had this conversation a hundred times before.

"Their job isn't to follow you around with a mop," I said. "We clean up after ourselves here. As much as we can."

Again the baleful glare. With a dramatic sigh worthy of Norma Desmond, he started picking things up. One by one he hurled the spatula, the bowl, the whisk, and the rest of his gear into the sink, each piece clattering louder than the one before. When I pointed again, he even wiped down the side of the cabinet and the floor where the whisk splatter had hit.

"We really should let the cleaning people tend to this kind of thing. It's job security for them," he said. "Don't you understand that?"

"What *you* need to understand is that this kitchen will be run the way I want it run." I folded my hands in front of my waist. "How many times do we need to go over this?"

This time he didn't answer. Thank goodness.

Bucky, Cyan, and I shifted subjects, this time returning to the earlier discussion about the Durasi state dinner. We'd gotten word first thing this morning that the Durasi president had agreed to peace talks with President Hyden and that they would be held here. Not only that, but to signal the beginning of negotiations, there would be a state dinner held in the Durasi president's honor to welcome him and his advisers next week.

State dinners, with their myriad updates, extensive guest lists, and exhaustive details, were usually months in the making. This time we had mere days to get everything together.

If it all went well, however, the extra effort to scramble would be worth it. As far back as I could remember, relations between the United States and the Durasi had been strained, and that was putting it mildly. We'd maintained troops there for years under a long-standing arrangement approved by the United Nations. There had always been unrest in Durasi, and the prior administration's resentment of the United States was well known.

By all accounts this chance for future peace negotiations, starting with this welcoming dinner, could be the defining moment in President Hyden's career. Stakes were high, and tensions were even higher.

My staff and I were determined to serve a spectacular meal in this sparkling venue, knowing that world leaders were always in better spirits when they were comfortable and well-fed.

"As far as we know, there are no cultural dietary issues, is that right?" Bucky asked.

"That's correct," I said. "We're waiting on a final word from Sargeant, though."

"How is he going to balance his new position as chief usher with his sensitivity director responsibilities?" Cyan asked. "They haven't hired his replacement yet and both are big jobs. Especially the chief usher position."

"You know Sargeant," I said. "He'll get it done."

Bucky looked like he was about to say something disparaging about our newly appointed chief usher, but I interrupted him. Peter Everett Sargeant, III, and I had experienced problems working together in the past, but this new reporting structure gave us an opportunity to start fresh. Plus, he and I had recently forged a tenuous truce. I wasn't yet at the stage where I'd want to hang out with the man during my off hours, but I appreciated the newfound respect he'd shown for me. The least I could do was return the favor.

"He's going to need all the support we can give him," I said.

"Ollie, you are too forgiving," Bucky said. "Think about all the aggravation Sargeant's caused you over the years."

I hadn't forgotten. But people change, often when you least expect them to. Sargeant and I had faced death together, and since that frightening day, he'd been kinder to me. Not by a lot, but enough to notice. He was definitely more approachable. "He's the chief usher now," I reminded Bucky. "Which makes him our boss."

Virgil rolled his eyes at that. "I still can't believe they selected Sargeant for that position. What were they thinking?" I was about to chastise him for questioning the president and First Lady's decision, but he waved a hand as though he couldn't be bothered to care. "Does anyone know if the chocolate shop staff is in today?"

"I saw one of them earlier," Bucky said. "They're busy coming up with ideas for the Durasi dinner, too. Why?"

"I have an amazing chocolate dessert planned for the family tonight. I want to make sure they haven't forgotten." Virgil headed for the door, speaking without bothering to face us. "If anyone needs me, that's where I'll be."

The moment he was gone, Cyan nudged me. "Okay, back to the wedding. What happened?"

I told them about how, after Gav had proposed the day before, we'd gone directly to the Moultrie Courthouse to fill out a marriage application. According to the courthouse website, our license would be ready in three business days.

"Except now," I concluded, "even though the license will be ready, it looks like there aren't any openings for weddings for eight weeks."

"Oh, that's not so bad." Cyan clasped her hands to her chest and let out a romantic sigh. "What's eight weeks when you're in love?"

Bucky held up both hands. "What's the problem?" he asked. "In this day and age, you should be able to find a willing officiant on the Internet . . . like that." He snapped his fingers. "I can't believe you didn't think of that yourself."

"We did, actually," I said. "In fact, we searched out a few last night."

"And?"

How to explain? Even though Gav and I weren't the most traditionally romantic people in the world, we'd both had the same reaction to the "Wedding Officiant" ads we'd encountered online. One after another, we'd rejected them (those who weren't already booked solid for the next three months, that is) for coming across too eager or too flashy. Although I knew that legally, standing before a judge wasn't any different than standing before one of the "Get married today!" agents, it sure seemed as though it would *feel* different.

"Choosing an officiant from an online ad didn't sit well with us," I said. Uncomfortable explaining myself beyond that, I shrugged. "Plus, most of them have waiting lists, too."

Bucky and Cyan didn't know why Gav and I intended to keep our engagement as short as possible. They didn't know that Gav had suffered heartbreaking loss in the past. He'd been engaged twice before, both women dying tragically before they could be wed. Despite the fact that he wasn't superstitious by nature, Gav believed he'd been cursed by some implacable wedding fates.

The man constantly worried for my safety. As a Secret Service agent, it was his nature to see danger lurking around every corner. Now that we'd made the decision to get married, his panic would skyrocket.

The fact that I'd developed a habit of getting into trouble while working at the White House made the waiting all the worse.

"I know," I said, putting on a cheerful face. "Even though eight weeks feels like forever right now, I'm sure someday we'll look back and this will be nothing but a minor blip." I thought about how tough this time would be for Gav. For both of us. "All I can tell you is that the sooner we say our vows, the happier I'll be."

CHAPTER 2

On the ride home on the Metro that evening, I thought about how my life would change once Gav and I were actually married. We hadn't had much chance to talk about it — seeing as how we'd only made the decision the day before — and I looked forward to making future plans with him. For the first time in my life I'd met someone who understood my curious tendencies and who loved me for who I was.

I stared out the window at nothing as my train trundled through one of many dark tunnels on its trip to Crystal City. Another thing Gav and I hadn't discussed yet was where we'd live. Gav had a tiny apartment with a gorgeous view of Washington, D.C. My apartment was a little farther out, but it was larger and my neighbors were nice.

My knee bounced with impatience, both because I'd been thrown by this wedding delay and because of the upcoming Durasi dinner. Bucky, Cyan, and I had pulled major events together in the past, but nothing quite like this.

As much as I hated to admit it, this eight-week delay could prove to be a godsend. How could I even imagine getting married in the midst of organizing and executing a major White House dinner? I sighed and reminded myself that things work out for the best sometimes, even if it doesn't always feel like it. This might be one of those times.

I clapped my hand to my forehead, remembering that I hadn't even called my mother yet. I'd planned to do so as soon as we'd filed the marriage application, but the news of the unexpected delay had thrown me. Gav and I had been so disappointed that I'd decided to wait until I was cheerier again. This afternoon would have worked, but the day had gotten away from me. I'd call her tonight as soon as I got home. For sure.

My train pulled into my station and as I disembarked and made my way up into the warm evening air, my cell phone rang. Gav.

"Hey," he said when I answered, "you busy?"

"Never too busy for you."

He laughed. "That's a lie. You're going to be far too busy for me over the next week,

23

I'm sure of it."

"This Durasi dinner *will* keep us flying, no question about it."

"That's all anyone is talking about. Lots of interesting fallout from that decision."

"Fallout?" I asked. "That doesn't sound good."

"I'll tell you about it later. But for now, are you up for an adventure?"

"Always," I said. "What's going on?"

"I'll meet you at your apartment and explain on the way."

"Almost home right now."

"Good. See you in twenty. Meet you out front."

"Wow. You're not wasting any time," I said.

"Not a second more than necessary. I can't wait to tell you my idea. I hope you're as excited about this as I am."

I speed-walked to my building and made it upstairs to my apartment without being waylaid by the elderly doorman who was busy signing for a package and didn't notice me scurry by. I changed clothes, brushed my hair, and made it back down to the lobby in less than fifteen. James's eyes lit up when he spied me. "Ollie," he said. "You got a minute? What's the read among the staff at the White House on these peace negotiations?"

James was a sweet man and a kind soul. I hated to brush him off, but at that very moment I noticed Gav pulling up outside.

"Sorry," I said. "Gotta run."

"That's all right, honey. I'll catch up with you later."

Of course he would. James knew that I was privy to a lot of secrets working at the White House. He also knew that I never shared anything that wasn't already public knowledge. But that didn't stop him from trying.

Gav was just starting to get out of the car when I pushed through the apartment building's glass doors. "Where are we going?" I asked. "And what's with all the mystery?"

"I'll explain when you get in."

As he and I settled ourselves and buckled up, I stole a glance to the backseat to make sure Gav had brought his cane. Even though he was walking much better now than he had been immediately after a recent skirmish, there was no mistaking how much he hated assistance getting around. We both knew that his dependence on the cane was temporary, but the angry set of his jaw whenever he used the device told me how much this infirmity taxed his patience.

25

He didn't seem bothered in the least at this moment, though. Behind the wheel, with a sly grin on his face, Gav was more animated than usual. He restarted the car and set off, making me wait for enlightenment. I could tell he was enjoying this.

"I got a call from a friend of mine this afternoon. His name's Evan Bonder."

"You've never mentioned him before," I said. "At least not that I remember. Did you?"

"Probably not. I only hear from him occasionally."

"Okay," I said slowly, in an effort to prompt him for more.

"Evan Bonder used to be in the Secret Service," he began. "We were good friends and, as I mentioned, still keep in touch from time to time. He called me today for a favor and I didn't think anything of it until after we'd hung up. When I remembered, I called him back." He took one hand off the wheel to gesture vaguely into the air. "It's not like that was the first thing that came to mind. I mean, neither you nor I expected there would be an eight-week backlog on marriage ceremonies."

"And with that, you have officially lost me," I said. I was more amused than angry. Whatever thoughts were careering through

Gav's head, they'd lifted his spirits exponentially since yesterday.

He reached to grab my hand, the lines in his usually serious face creasing into a deep, genuine smile. "Evan," he said taking his eyes off the road long enough to give me a pointed look, "is a minister. And he said he would be delighted to perform our ceremony. Assuming you're willing, of course."

"That's wonderful," I said. "Wow. What a change from yesterday, huh?" Though not displeased, I was unprepared for this news. Questions raced through my brain so fast it took me a moment to latch on to one. "What kind of minister is he?"

Gav gave a sheepish shrug. "I don't remember. Nondenominational, maybe? He left the Secret Service because he had a profound calling to serve others. He said he wanted to help those on the fringes of society's fabric to find a way to weave themselves back in."

"Poetic."

"Evan is different. Always was. He's a decent guy. What do you say?"

"Are you kidding? This is great news. I'm all for it." I'd been willing to say "I do," three days from now if the court had been able to provide a presider. There was no need to think twice. But I did have one requirement. "I'd like to meet him first. I assume that's where we're going?"

"Your deductive skills do you well." Gav pointed at me. "This is why you should have been a Secret Service agent instead of a chef."

I laughed. "I'll stick to the kitchen, thanks." A moment later, I asked, "Why did he call you? You said you remembered that he was a minister after you hung up. You mentioned he needed a favor?"

For the first time since I'd gotten in the car, Gav's mood shifted. "That part has me concerned. Even though Evan chose a vastly different path than the rest of us did, he maintains a connection with a few others in the service. There are men and women who have had problems with one or more aspects of the job. Beside counseling the fringe folk, he tries to help his former comrades-in-arms as well."

"Sounds like a great guy."

"He is." Gav's lips were tight for a moment, then he went on. "Evan called me because he's run into a problem that he thinks is too big to handle on his own. He wants some advice, and he suggested we meet tomorrow morning. At first I agreed and we planned to meet around ten. Then, when I thought of him as a possible offi-

28

ciant, I suggested we stop by tonight."

"Isn't he going to mind my being there? If this problem involves members of the Secret Service, or is otherwise confidential, he may not be comfortable confiding in you with me hanging around."

Gav took my hand again. "I may never have mentioned Evan to you, but I definitely mentioned you to him. From the start, actually." He laughed. "I complained to him mightily about this little upstart chef who was giving me all kinds of grief. It was Evan who first called me out on it, accusing me of protesting too much."

"You mean, back when you first came to the White House for those bomb classes?"

Gav nodded, smiling as though he was reliving those first days. "When I'd heard that you'd broken up with Tom MacKenzie, I told Evan. He warned me that I'd better make my move or be eternally sorry I'd hesitated." He gave a soft chuckle. "Even if he hadn't pushed, there was no way I wasn't going to try. I think having his blessing — no pun intended — made it easier, though. Evan knows about you, knows you're in my life, and knows that you can be trusted. It'll be fine."

"I didn't know that you talked about me with your friends."

"Only with friends who matter."

I had a feeling I was going to like this Evan Bonder.

The sun was beginning to set as the quiet settled over us. We traveled a few more miles before I broke the silence. "I haven't yet told anyone — beyond my staff, of course — about our plans. I've been meaning to, but nothing's gone right. Not until now, at least."

"You still haven't called your mother, you mean?"

"No, I haven't," I said. "I meant to yesterday, but after we heard about the delay, I was too disappointed to pick up the phone. I'm dying to call her right this minute — she'll be so happy for us, you know — but I also think it may be better to wait until I get home tonight."

He kept his eyes on the road. "When you're alone and I'm not around to overhear? Is that it?"

I acknowledged his observation with a mischievous grin. "I'm liable to get mushy and sappy. I'm not sure I want you to see that side of me."

He made eye contact. "I want to know every side of you, Olivia Paras," he said. "Not just today. Forever." Returning his attention to driving, he added, "But I under-

30

stand. You'll let me know if she disapproves, right?"

"She won't," I said, "but why? Will that change your mind?"

"Not a chance. I'd work that much harder to win her over."

"Don't worry. You already have."

We made it to DuPont Circle and entered the roundabout. Halfway through, we took a right then traveled awhile longer, making several more turns, bringing us to a section of the neighborhood that was congested with tight, battered buildings. Where parts of Washington, D.C., were gorgeous this time of year — fragrant with flowers and energetic with busy, bustling crowds — this area was the exact opposite.

There were more abandoned storefronts than there were viable businesses. A barber shop and a consignment/resale store were closed for the night, secured behind accordion-style metal grates fastened shut with padlocks the size of my hand. Two liquor stores were open for business, their neon beer signs blinking plaintively in the approaching dusk. Five young men loitered outside one of them, while an old man shouted from across the street, demanding that the youths get out of his sight.

"It doesn't seem like the best of neighborhoods," I said.

"Rent is less expensive here. And this is where many of those fringe folk live. It's where Evan needs to be."

As we cruised up the block, there were fewer pedestrians on the street. It seemed the farther north we went, the quieter it became.

"Ainsley Street," I said aloud. "I don't know that I've ever been up this way before."

"Parking might be a challenge," Gav said. He wasn't kidding.

As he found and then maneuvered into a tight spot, I caught sight of a tall, bare-chested man heading our way. Even in the waning light, I could tell that he carried a very large wooden staff, which he used as a walking stick. With his scraggly white beard and white dreadlocks that bounced in the wind, he kept up a pace I'd consider brisk for a man his age. I put him at sixty-five, maybe seventy. His expression was one of manic determination. If he'd been wearing flowing robes rather than ragged jeans and shabby sandals, he could have auditioned for the role of vengeful God.

"How far does Evan live?" I asked.

Gav pointed up the block. "See that two-story tucked in between the apartment buildings? He's in there. Calls it the Ainsley Street Ministry. Clever name, huh? The first floor is his meeting area and where people can hang out if they want to. It used to be a dry cleaner, and I swear you can still smell the chemicals. Evan lives in the apartment directly above."

The bare-chested man slowed as he spotted us, watching and giving us a wide berth as Gav put the car into Park and shut it off.

"Let's let him go on ahead before you get out." Gav spoke quietly, even though there was no way the guy outside could hear us.

I didn't need the warning, but I appreciated it nonetheless. I smiled at the man as he passed, hoping he'd perceive me as nonthreatening. His eyes met mine and for a brief flash, lost their distracted wildness. Without warning, he stopped. He turned to face us, then took a step closer. I got a better look at him. Long and lean, he had a narrow nose that had likely been broken once and never reset properly.

He waved his free hand at me, making a motion as though to move us along, as though telling us we'd taken the wrong parking spot. A second later he started jumping up and down in place. He never got more than an inch off the ground, owing to his age maybe, but the man was clearly intent on making a spectacle of himself. Still jumping, he stared at me, shaking his head and mouthing, "No, no, no, no."

He expected a response from us, that much I could see. I got the impression he wanted us to drive away and never come back. When we didn't comply, he waved his staff in the air and shouted again, loud enough for me to hear him clearly through the closed windows, "Go away. Get away. Run before they see you!"

He spoke with a bit of an accent, one I couldn't place. Eastern European, I thought. He brought his face right up to the glass between us, coming almost close enough for his crooked nose to touch the clear pane. Close enough for me to see the dirt in his pores.

"Get. Out. Now. Don't you understand?"

As much as I knew I should, I couldn't tear my gaze away. His expression shifted and he stared at me with panic and fear.

"Gav, we have to help him," I said. "But I don't know how."

"He may be high." Gav shifted in his seat, as though to open his door. "I'll see if I can get him to move along."

"No." I grabbed Gav's arm, even as I maintained eye contact with the peculiar stranger. "You're still healing. We don't know what this guy is capable of, and we don't want to risk you ripping your stitches."

Gav relaxed enough for me to know that he wouldn't do anything rash. I let go and leaned toward the window. I sensed that the wayward man was waiting for acknowledgment from me.

"Thank you," I shouted back. "We understand."

He studied us a moment longer, then stepped away from the door, nodding as though his mission had been accomplished. He pivoted, lifted his staff in the air, and took off running down the street.

CHAPTER 3

I twisted to watch the man's swiftly departing figure. "I wonder what spooked him."

"We'll never know," Gav said. When I turned back, he opened his door. "At least the coast is clear, now. You ready?"

Gav took two seconds longer than I did to get out of the car and when he didn't grab his cane, I pointed. "You forgot something."

He scowled at the apparatus stowed behind the driver's seat. "Not this time. It's enough that Evan knows I was hurt. I don't need him feeling sorry for me."

"He's your friend; he'll understand." When that didn't sway him, I added, "You're supposed to use the cane for another couple of weeks. Doctor's orders."

He wagged a finger. "Doctor's *suggestion.*" Gav took a breath, walked a few steps away from me, then turned. "See? Like new. I don't need the cane. And I don't need Evan to pity me."

"If you say so."

Gav and I fell into step together, heading north. I pretended not to notice his occasional wince.

There were few trees on this street, and the scrawny ones that remained cast ghostly shadows on the evening sidewalk. As we made our way closer to Evan's storefront, I asked a couple of questions, discovering that Evan was younger than Gav by a few years and that he'd been married once. That union had ended right about the same time Evan had started his new career. His wife apparently hadn't shared Evan's vision about ministering to the disenfranchised. She'd tried to talk him out of giving up their successful life, and when she'd failed to convince him, took off.

"That had to hurt."

Gav stopped about four feet from the building. He kept his voice low. "When she left, he fell apart. I worried for him. I thought he might give up his dreams for this ministry in order to win her back. But his calling was strong. Once she was gone for good, however, he made his peace with the situation. It seemed to me that once free of her constant nay-saying, he was able to create the life he'd envisioned. It hasn't been easy, and it took him a long time to get settled, but Evan has done well. He seems happy."

"Seems?"

Gav's mouth curled to one side. "Evan keeps a lot to himself. Every so often I get a glimpse inside, but he can be hard to read."

"And you have no idea what kind of trouble he needs your help with?"

I'd expected Gav to laugh at that. Instead, his eyes tightened. Like when he didn't use his cane. "I guess we're about to find out."

The building was old, its first-floor façade reminiscent of an old-fashioned bookstore — the kind you might expect to see in London, with leather-bound first editions proudly displayed in the front windows. This was different, however. Shabby.

The door was set back a few feet from the sidewalk, centered, and painted shiny black, as were the frames surrounding the bowed, mullioned windows that flanked it. The window glass was covered with faded, water-stained butcher paper, taped three-quarters of the way up. There was enough of an opening to allow light, but not enough for someone of even Gav's height to see in.

There were no signs out front, and no welcome mat. The small walkway to the door was paved with tiny, cracked tiles, which wore a patina of grime.

"How long has it been since you've been here?" I asked.

Gav didn't answer. He grabbed the knob and pushed at the door. It opened easily, and I half expected an overhead bell to tinkle and announce our arrival. I kept behind him as he strode into the wide, dimly lit space. It was silent, stuffy, and . . . empty.

Gav stopped about a quarter of the way in, rotating in place as though to ensure he hadn't missed anything. "This is odd."

Built in the early part of the last century, the building felt echo-y and smelled like a musty antique store. I looked up at the high, tin ceiling. Someone had painted it white a very long time ago. Cracks and water marks stained the corners. Everything about the space was sad and lonely. This was where people came to find help?

I caught a whiff of the cigarette butts before I saw them. Spilling out of freestanding chrome ashtrays, the kind that were oh-so-popular in '60s fashion-conscious homes, there were way too many butts than could have been collected in a single day.

Under the graying scent of cold tobacco, I detected yet another familiar smell. Human and warm, it reminded me of body odor, but overwhelmingly sour and stale. Rotten

39

eggs, maybe.

I reminded myself that people on the fringes of society — people like the wild-eyed man we'd recently encountered — didn't always have access to conveniences we took for granted, and didn't always shower regularly. Body odor shouldn't surprise me. It didn't really. But the scent in here contained something else.

I struggled to shake off my sense of unease.

Gav was feeling it too, I could tell. His gaze darted to the corners, then around, then back toward the door we'd just come through. "Very odd."

The scarred wood floor creaked as we walked around and waited for someone to show up. Faded posters from last century's blockbuster movies covered the walls from waist to about eye height. Behind them, the paint was crimson and cracked. Higher up, AINSLEY STREET MINISTRY had been hand-lettered unevenly across one wall.

Behind the posters, chunky white lines slashed up and down the red walls. These were straight plaster-cracked lines, leading me to believe that large pieces of built-in furniture had been ripped out at some point. To our right, a dozen folding chairs were set up in a circle, and to our left was a sad attempt at a library — four weather-beaten, pressboard bookcases crammed with distressed paperbacks. The overhead fluorescent fixtures flickered and buzzed. Otherwise the place was utterly silent.

Gav met my gaze. "I don't understand this," he said. Raising his voice, he called, "Hello?"

No answer.

"Strange," he said again, making his way to a large bulletin board on a tripod. "Evan is always here. And when he goes out he leaves a note."

I stood behind him, reading the advertisements that promised help and understanding. That offered solace in the form of church services and food.

Gav looked around. "Evan?" he called again.

When there was still no answer, he started for the back door. "There's an apartment this way. Evan lets people stay here from time to time. It's not much: a kitchen, a bedroom, and a small bathroom. Maybe he's busy back there and can't hear us."

Gav's words felt as empty as this building. There was no one here. We both knew it. "Could Evan have simply forgotten to leave a note this time?"

"I suppose," he said, reaching for the glass knob.

I placed a hand on his back in an effort to slow him down. "It feels wrong to be wandering through someone's place without permission."

"Evan's not going to mind," he said. "He's not the kind of guy who —"

His next words were lost when the door swung open. I don't know if Gav stopped talking, I stopped listening, or both. I sucked in a hard breath of surprise, then wished I hadn't. My hand flew to my face, covering my mouth and nose from the room's hot, acrid stench.

Gav stiffened then shuddered. We were so close — touching — I felt the reaction run through him as though it had run through me. Maybe it had. His training took over in an instant. He swept an arm sideways, stopping me from taking another step into the room. His words were icy sharp. "Get back, Ollie."

Too late.

Three, no, four. No, wait. Five men lay on the floor, bound and gagged. In a breathless second, I knew they were dead. My instincts kicked in. I had to check. I desperately wanted to be wrong.

"Ollie, no," Gav said.

I'd started past his outstretched hand, but he was faster than I was. He grabbed my upper arm and hauled me close with an urgency I didn't understand. "Back in the other room," he said. "Now."

Holding me tight, he spun and started back the way we'd come.

"But what if they're still alive?"

"They're not."

I chanced a look up at his grim expression. I knew better than to fight. "What's going on?"

He walked fast, the corners of his mouth revealing the pain I knew must be shooting through him with each step. If he hadn't been holding, half dragging me along, I wouldn't have been able to keep up.

"Slow down, Gav. You'll rip your stitches," I said.

We'd almost made it to the door when it swung in toward us. Five men, one woman. All wearing suits and bright-white gas masks over their faces. The leader's body language suggested he was as surprised to see us as we were to see him.

Gav stepped in front of me protectively, a human shield. "Who are you?" he asked.

The first guy pointed to the man directly behind him. Wordlessly, he then pointed to us and gave the unmistakable hand signal to get us out. The second man complied immediately. He grabbed Gav and indicated to a third man to grab me. The man held tight, but not enough to hurt. It all happened so fast, I didn't even have time to scream.

A blurred second later we were outside and the man's grip on me loosened. A little.

The two men pushed us toward a dark cargo van that was double-parked at the curb. My guard said, "Get in." The other one similarly urged us to hurry. Their white masks and mechanized voices made me feel as though I was a member of the *Star Wars* rebel alliance being shuttled into custody by the Imperial guard. Except they weren't restraining us, exactly; it was more like we were being shepherded.

"What's going on?" I asked.

Gav's hand found mine. He gripped tight as he sized up the van idling quietly in the dark. I'd been dragged into a cargo van much like this one before. It was not an experience I cared to repeat. I pulled back, my instincts telling me to get away now. Just then, the van's side door slid open to reveal equipment inside and a man at the controls.

"Gav?" I asked in a small voice.

He didn't look as alarmed as I would have expected, given the circumstances. I'd say his expression was puzzled rather than panicked. Leaning close to my ear, he whispered for me to follow his lead.

At that he stopped short, causing the Imperial guard behind us to bump into his back. "Who's in charge here?" Gav asked. He didn't let go of me. His voice was strong and brave, but I felt him tense.

The guy in front of us turned around. He lifted the mask, allowing me to see his red, sweaty, furious face. "Agent Gavin, we are here on assignment. If you and your friend don't want to suffer ill effects of a toxic substance, I suggest you cooperate."

Gav looked as though he'd been slapped. "Nick."

"Get in," Nick said.

The words *toxic substance* bounced around in my brain. Five dead men, no blood. That harsh smell. Had they been killed by an airborne pathogen? Like anthrax? Had we breathed in some of that as well?

Night had settled while we'd been inside and there were no pedestrians on the street. None that I could see, anyway. That meant that no one noticed as we clambered into the side of the van. Not good. Not good at all. Nick and the other man who'd escorted us out tugged their masks back into place and rushed to return to Evan's building. The others in their group had now been on their own in that death cell for at least a minute or two. What was going on?

The lone agent in the van sized us up. His job, apparently, was to keep an eye on all the expensive equipment and to watch the proceedings remotely. Slightly built with colorless hair, he wore thick glasses but no protective gear. There were several monitors behind him. Three were live feeds, sending footage of those poor, slain men as the masked team checked them for life signs. From the monitors' perspectives, I had to guess that cameras were mounted atop three of the gas masks.

The man inside the van waved us into the tight space that looked like a prop from a big-budget Hollywood spy movie. "Agent Gavin," he said by way of greeting. "I thought you were still on medical leave, sir. Didn't know you were in on this one."

"I'm not," Gav said. "What's going on?"

The guy turned to me, holding an instrument that he waved around my head and hands. He then wiped a damp pad under my nose and another across my fingertips. I fought the urge to pull away. "You're probably safe out here, but it doesn't hurt to be sure." He examined the small pads and said,

"You're clean."

"Hydrogen sulfide?" Gav asked.

The man gave a somber nod. "That's our best guess." He waved the instrument over Gav, swabbed him, and gave him the all clear, too.

"Agent Taglia," Gav said. "You want to tell me what happened in there? Evan's dead. Along with four other people."

Taglia closed his eyes for the briefest moment. When he opened them again, he gave a quick nod, as though deciding he would set that fact aside to think about later. I knew that sentiment. I'd done the same thing myself any number of times.

"Anyone else you recognized?" he asked.

"We weren't in there long enough. When I saw them lying there and put that together with the scent —"

"Good thing you got out quickly. Chances are the chemical dissipated by the time you got there, but it never hurts to be safe. What are you doing here anyway?"

Gav squared his jaw. "Evan asked me to come by."

"Why?"

"He wouldn't say. You know how he is. He just said it was important."

Taglia sent a perplexed glance my direction. "Who are you?"

"My name is Olivia Paras —"

"The chef?" He sent a disconcerted look at Gav. "Tell me it isn't true."

Taglia's reaction stopped me cold.

"What isn't true?" I asked, my head twisting back and forth between the two men. "What's wrong?"

Taglia ignored me. "I heard rumors but didn't believe them. You're the man. You've always been the man. How can you do this to us?"

Gav's voice was a warning. "Taglia . . ."

"Do what?" I turned to Gav. "What's he talking about?"

Taglia gave me a withering stare. "I'm sure you're a lovely person, but Agent Gavin is one of the most respected individuals in our ranks. It does him no good to be seen carousing with someone of your reputation. No offense."

"Carousing?" I repeated. "My reputation? Gav, is this true? Am I causing you more trouble than I realize?"

"Taglia doesn't know what he's talking about. He would be best served by keeping quiet," Gav said through clenched teeth. "Is that understood?"

Taglia didn't look pleased but he answered, "Yes, sir."

Gav worked his jaw and addressed the

other agent again. "You want to tell me what's going on here?"

Taglia pulled his lips in. Shook his head. "Classified."

"That's my friend who's dead in there. Your friend, too, Taglia. I understand if you can't say much in front of Ollie. I get that. But I plan to find out what's going on here and I need to know who to talk to. You owe me that."

Taglia jutted his chin toward the front of the building where the others still remained. "We're the only ones on this detail. That's it. Super-tight controls. Nobody knows what's going on this time." He wagged sparse eyebrows. "And I mean nobody. Bad news for you that you stumbled on this by accident."

"Bad news, why?" I asked.

He ignored me. "Tyree is in charge."

"That's who led them in?" Gav asked, but it was clear he didn't need Taglia to confirm it. "I didn't see his face."

"What's wrong with Tyree?" I asked.

Gav put a hand on my shoulder. "We've had issues in the past. If he thinks I've stepped into his investigation, whether I intended to or not, it's not going to be pretty." Gav cast a look over his shoulder, staring back at the front of the desolate, black-painted building. "Who am I kidding? It already isn't."

CHAPTER 4

"What happens now?" I asked.

Gav turned to Taglia. "Let me take Ms. Paras home, and I'll check back with Tyree when I'm finished."

"I'm not sure that's a good idea, sir. It would be best if you waited here until he returns. I'm certain Agent Tyree would want you to remain on-site for debriefing."

Gav kept an eye on the storefront as though he hoped the gas mask team would emerge at any moment. I think we both knew that wasn't going to happen. The look in his eyes told me he was debating his next move. He turned to Taglia. "You're certain we're not a hazard to the public, correct?"

"Yes, sir."

"I want to know what happened to my friend Evan," he said without inflection. "You tell Tyree that I will be in touch. Very soon."

"But, sir —"

"He knows where to find me."

Gav pulled the sliding door open, wincing as he got out. I could tell it hurt for him to straighten even though he did his best to hide his infirmity from the other agent.

"Come on," he said.

His tone was gentle, but I could tell he wasn't seeing me. He'd slipped into agent mode, the personality he'd been locked into when we'd first met. I hadn't cared for Gav much those first few days, but I'd come to know the man behind the duty. In this instance, I knew to follow where he led.

As I started back toward the car, Gav spoke quietly. "Keep a leisurely pace, Ollie. No reason to call attention to ourselves."

I glanced around. There was no one behind us on the dark, deserted street except for the van parked in front of Evan's place. Of course that didn't mean some Gladys Kravitz wasn't peeking out her window right now and dialing the police to report suspicious activity.

"What's going to happen now?" I asked again.

Gav opened my car door, but his eyes never stopped scanning the area around us. "It's too much of a coincidence that Evan asked me to stop by and now he's dead." Emotion worked its way across Gav's features so briefly that if I hadn't been looking for it I would have missed it. "Agent Tyree has some explaining to do."

The drive was short and silent. Gav dropped me off at the front door, grabbing my left hand as I reached for the handle. "I'm sorry you had to see that."

"When you find out more, you'll let me know, won't you?"

"If I can," he said. "I don't have any idea what's going on. How about I come by your place tomorrow after work and I'll tell you what I can. Is that okay?"

"Perfect," I said, wanting to do whatever I could to make it better. Knowing there was no help for that. "I'll make dinner. And we'll talk." Before I left him, I had to know. "Are you all right?"

"I will be." Gav squeezed my hand. "You put up with a lot having me in your life."

I shook my head. "I'd say it's the other way around."

"People close to me are always dying," he said. "You shouldn't have to deal with that."

I thought about those five bound, gagged men, their vacant eyes, and the swift efficiency of the agents who'd swarmed in. I didn't know any of the victims, yet my heart was heavy with loss. Could it really have been only yesterday that Gav had asked me

53

to marry him? I'd been so happy. Just yesterday? It felt more like two years ago.

There was a storm brewing in the White House kitchen the next morning. I arrived to find Virgil leaning deep into Peter Sargeant's personal space, scowling. He had both hands fisted into his hips. His voice was rising and thin.

Sargeant stood as erect as I'd ever seen him, his diminutive body so rigid that if I touched him, I thought he might give off a high-pitched *pluck.*

So deep were they in their argument, neither Sargeant nor Virgil took notice of me.

"And what about Doug's feelings in all of this?"

Wait a minute. I'd never known Virgil to care about anyone's feelings but his own. Something was amiss here. Big-time.

Virgil was still talking. "He worked hard to get the chief usher's office back into shape."

Uh-oh. Although it hadn't been announced to the press yet, I knew that Sargeant, our sensitivity director, was to be named chief usher very soon. His promotion to the lofty position meant that henceforth, I would report to him. Virgil technically reported to me, but that didn't mean he didn't have a personal interest in this reporting structure change. Virgil's friend Doug Lambert, who had recently been dismissed from serving in the chief usher role in an interim arrangement, had expected to be named to the position permanently. I thanked my lucky stars that he hadn't been.

"Back into shape?" Sargeant huffed. "Paul left everything in order. Precise order. If Doug had been half the man Paul was, the office wouldn't be in the shambles it is now."

With a glance at my watch, I realized that Bucky and Cyan were due to arrive at any minute. I also realized that it was precariously close to the Hyden family's regular breakfast time. I noticed a savory dish in progress on the stovetop and another course in the oven, but it didn't look as though Virgil had remembered that it was time to serve. Butlers would arrive soon, intent on taking a finished meal up to the Commander in Chief and his family. Virgil should know better. Even Sargeant should be aware. Yet these two combatants showed no sign of slowing.

"Doug deserved that position. I can't believe you were able to convince the Hydens that you had any right to it. You're hardly qualified. And that chef friend of yours, she had a hand in this. Doug said so. This isn't fair. Not fair at all."

"I serve at the president's pleasure," Sargeant said. "I'm sure I don't need to remind you that you do the same."

Virgil's face, already blotched with emotion, darkened. "And you'll be only too happy to weave your insidious little lies about me in reports to them, won't you? Just like Paras does." My ears perked up at the mention of my name. "The two of you are out to get me. With your high-and-mighty airs and with your obvious agenda to undermine me. Make no mistake: I'm onto you, Sargeant."

"Enough," I shouted.

The two men started, turning to me with unvarnished surprise. They really *hadn't* seen me come in.

Glaring, I pointed to the clock. "Forgetting the First Family's breakfast because you're fighting with the chief usher is not good form, Virgil." I stepped closer, lowering my voice. Even though I was shorter than both men, this was my kitchen and they both needed to remember that here, at least, I was the boss. "And for the record, Peter and I never need to make up insidious lies about you. You've proved more than capable of botching things up on your own."

At the word *breakfast,* Virgil dropped his hands. His jaw went slack and the shift in his brain was evident from the expression on his face. With one glance at the clock, distress replaced his anger. He blew off the rest of what I'd had to say as he rushed to open the oven door. In his haste, he didn't bother with protective mitts, instead dragging a dishtowel from his shoulder to examine the sizzling casserole.

Behind him, Sargeant tugged at the hem of his suit coat, stretched his neck, and pulled in a deep breath through his nose. To me, he said, "The news of my impending promotion has not gone over well in all corners."

Part of me wished I'd kept my mouth shut and let Virgil fall on his face. Although he added a measure of value by handling family meals, thereby freeing up the rest of us to create lavish state dinners and food for official events, he was a toxic personality. His presence in the kitchen caused more harm than good, in my opinion. Bucky, Cyan, and I had covered for him in the past, hoping he'd eventually become an ally, or at least stop bickering with us. So far, no luck.

I sighed. Maybe I should have let Virgil and Sargeant continue to argue. Let breakfast burn. Allowed Virgil to suffer the consequences.

But that wasn't my personality. Above all, my job here as executive chef was to ensure that the president, his family, and his guests were served the very best meals every single day. On time. Even though it might have served my own selfish purposes, I couldn't shut off that sense of duty.

I turned to Sargeant. "I'm sorry to hear that. Have you found out when the official announcement will be made?"

"Tomorrow morning," he said. "They've called the press in. Can you believe that?"

Despite Sargeant's downturned mouth and furrowed brow, I could tell he was pleased.

"Just don't let the fame go to your head, like some people do." I pointed to Virgil, who was practically dancing the casserole to the central counter, complaining the entire way about how he'd been interrupted, and how if breakfast was ruined it wouldn't be his fault.

"Your confidence in me is underwhelming, Ms. Paras."

I debated my next move, took a breath, and touched his arm. "A moment, Peter?" I asked, urging him to follow me across the small kitchen to the hallway that ran along its perimeter.

At the elevator, I stopped to take a look around. We were alone. "Seeing as how you'll be my boss tomorrow," I began, keeping as quiet as I could, "I believe there is a matter I need to bring to your attention."

His eyes were bright, alert. "Go on."

"Last night, I . . . that is, Gav and I . . . that is, Special Agent in Charge Gavin . . ."

"For heaven's sakes, Ms. Paras, when have you ever been at a loss for words around me? I know who Gav is. Get on with it."

Sargeant's pique and his dependably annoying tone were reassuring to me, normal. Oddly, they provided the comfort I needed. His familiar irritation made me strong. "Gav and I happened upon a crime scene last night."

Sargeant leaned back ever so slightly, but said nothing.

"It's probably best if I don't share details with you," I said. "Not yet, at least. Not until I know more or am given clearance to tell you. I wanted to put you on alert, though. In case I get pulled away. In case things get strange around here all of a sudden."

"With you here, Ms. Paras, things are always peculiar."

He made that pronouncement without any trace of humor. Given the circumstances, I wasn't surprised. "I can't say why, exactly, but I don't believe we'll be seeing this crime on the news tonight."

He gestured west with his eyes. "Have you alerted anyone else about this 'situation'?"

"No."

Sargeant's eyebrows lurched upward.

"Without divulging too much," I continued, "the Secret Service already knows. They'll know what to do. Until I'm advised otherwise, I won't breathe a word of this to anyone. Except this much, to you."

"Noted."

Behind us, in the kitchen, I could hear Virgil banging. "Breakfast ought to be ready by now," I said.

As if to corroborate my statement, two butlers pushed their way into the small pantry area on their way to the kitchen. Right on time.

They disappeared in where the banging sounds escalated. We could hear Virgil muttering to himself, issuing orders to the butlers, his frustration building to a cringe-worthy crescendo. I patted Sargeant on the shoulder, which was about as friendly as the two of us would ever get. "I should probably get in there and help him," I said.

He stopped me. "You know that Virgil believed that if Doug had been named chief

usher, he had a chance at taking your job."
With a sigh, he added, "What a fool."

"Then we're especially lucky the Hydens
were wise enough to appoint you. Congratulations again, by the way."

"Ms. Paras?"

I turned.

"Tomorrow, at the press announcement?"

"Yes?"

"Your presence there would give the illu-
sion of support," he said. "I would appreciate it if you could attend. If you aren't
otherwise engaged, that is."

I smiled. "I wouldn't miss it, Peter. See
you then."

CHAPTER 5

At nine that night I put dinner away. I'd made a vegetarian lasagna, one of Gav's favorites, along with a few side dishes. For dessert, I'd picked up lemon sorbet. Even though I'd sampled the entrée and accompaniments as I'd cooked, I'd held off eating because I'd been waiting for Gav.

As I cleared the table settings and put away the lasagna, I tried not to worry. I tried not to think about what might be keeping him from being here. He'd planned to come for dinner tonight and it wasn't like Gav to leave me hanging without a word.

Every sound in my apartment kitchen seemed to echo the emptiness I felt. I hadn't spoken with him since he'd dropped me off after our gruesome discovery on Ainsley Street. I needed to know more about what had happened there. But mostly I needed to know that he was safe.

He hadn't called. His phone had gone

straight to voice mail every time I'd tried calling him. Much as I wanted to, I realized there was no point in leaving multiple messages. So far, I'd left only one asking him to call me when he had the chance. If he had received it, he would have called. I knew him well enough to know that with certainty.

The only scenario that made sense was that he *couldn't* call. The big unknown was why.

As I moved green beans from the stove to a glass storage bowl and covered it, I glanced up at my kitchen clock. The minute hand hadn't moved. Not in the last fifteen times I'd checked, at least. I needed to get a grip. Gav knew me well enough to know I'd be worried out of my head. He would get in touch with me the moment he could. What was keeping him?

So distracted by his absence, I didn't notice how close I was to the table with the green beans. I clipped the corner, sending the bowl tumbling out of my hands and crashing to the floor in an explosion of glass and skinny, slippery vegetables.

"Of course," I said louder than I should have, frustration gripping me. "What else can go wrong?"

Muttering to myself about how these particular bowls were supposed to be shatterproof, I pulled my wastebasket out from under the sink and crouched, setting myself to the tedious task of cleaning up the big pieces without cutting myself. I would have to finish up with the broom, then the mop.

Less than ten seconds later, a knock at my door.

Smiling, I leaped to my feet, dumping the glass from my hands, and rushing to answer. This wouldn't be the first time Gav made it to my apartment without James noticing. The elderly man had a tendency to snooze at the front desk.

I grasped the knob and threw the door wide.

When I saw them standing there, I fought to keep my face from falling. "Mrs. Wentworth." I forced cheer into my voice. "Stan. How are you?"

"Is anything wrong, Ollie?" my nosy elderly neighbor asked. She didn't try to hide the fact that she was trying to see behind me. "We heard a crash. Are you all right?"

"Fine." Disappointment collapsed over me like a giant wave, threatening to pull me under. "I dropped a bowl," I said. "Green beans."

Though I wasn't lying about the noise, I wasn't fine. Shrewd woman that she was,

Mrs. Wentworth seized on that fact. I could see it in her narrowing eyes. "Where's your young man?" she asked.

Stan tugged her arm. "Ollie's got her hands full. Let's let her be. Come on, honey."

"Gav is . . ." I didn't have an answer and there seemed no reason to fake a chipper mood any longer. I held up my hands. "Don't know. Out on some assignment, I suppose."

She nodded sagely, then switched subjects. "You're coming to the wedding, aren't you? You haven't returned your RSVP."

That made me laugh, if only for a second. "You sent them last week. They aren't due for another two." At her frown, I added, "Yes, I'll be there. I wouldn't miss it."

"Are you bringing the young man?"

"If . . ." Another wave of disappointment washed over me. "If he's available, yes, of course."

"Good." Eyeing me, she backhanded Stan's forearm. "Something's wrong with our girl here," she said. "Look at her."

Ever polite, ever unassuming, Stan put an arm around his betrothed's shoulders. "We should let Ollie get back to whatever she was doing."

Mrs. Wentworth wasn't finished. "When

are the two of *you* going to get hitched?" she asked. "I want to come to your wedding and I'm getting up there, you know. Don't make me wait too long."

My heart ached, thinking about our trip to the marriage license bureau. All our plans. Since that blissful moment that Gav had asked me to marry him, nothing had gone right. I felt bereft. Emotion threatened to overtake me. I worked hard at maintaining my composure, always, but the dam had a crack in it today and I couldn't stop myself from letting it all out in sharp, staccato sentences. "We're engaged. Applied for the license. But we have to wait. There's a backlog."

Mrs. Wentworth's mouth dropped open. Stan's, too.

"When did this all happen?"

"Two days ago."

"Then why aren't you happy?" Mrs. Wentworth asked. All of a sudden, her concern for me was less nosy and intrusive. She took both my shoulders in her bony hands and waited for me to make eye contact. "What's wrong?"

"I am happy," I said. "That's the truth. It's just that we have a problem."

She cocked an eyebrow.

"Not a relationship problem. A . . . situation."

"Oh, my dear." She shook her head. "Again?"

I sighed, thinking about the ridiculousness of it all. "It'll be all right."

When she smiled, I was moved by the kindness I saw in her face. "What did your mother say when you told her?"

"My mom!"

From the moment we'd found the bodies lying on the floor at Evan's place, I hadn't given another thought to sharing the good news with my family.

"You haven't told her?"

I covered my mouth with my hand. "It slipped my mind."

"Slipped your mind?" Mrs. Wentworth gave me a very motherly stare. "That had to be some situation you encountered." She tapped Stan on the arm again. "Let's go. Ollie, call your mother. Right now, you understand?"

"I want to be there," Mom said. She'd burst into snuffling tears of joy when I'd told her the news, then had rushed downstairs to bring Nana up so they could both talk to me at the same time. "Chicago is less than two hours by plane from D.C. As soon as

67

you have a date, you let us know."

Nana piped in. "I'll get my 'go' bag ready right away. That's what they call them on that criminal profiling show I watch. You never know when you need to grab it and run, and I plan to be ready when you holler."

"We may not have a date for a while." What had first seemed a mere inconvenience because the judges were booked up for weeks was now so much more than that. I wondered how these mysterious deaths and the investigation into who had committed them would affect Gav — and our plans. What if today was only the beginning of a long time apart? "Gav and I will talk more about it when I see him next."

"When will that be?" Mom asked.

I gave my best theatric sigh, masking sadness with exaggeration. "You know how it is," I said. "Sometimes I don't hear from him for a week." *Please,* I thought. *Don't let it be that long. Not this time.*

We talked for a while, both Mom and Nana expressing their happiness so many times that I couldn't wait to get off the phone. They were the world's most supportive people and I knew that if we talked much longer, I'd break down and tell them how worried I was for Gav tonight. As there

68

was no way to do that without mentioning, or at least alluding to the massacre, I chatted as long as I could, then begged off.

"Early morning for me tomorrow," I said, making myself smile so they'd hear happiness in my voice. "I'll talk with you both soon."

We hung up finally, and I returned to staring at the kitchen clock.

Where was he?

Bucky and Cyan beat me to work the next morning, which surprised me. They both seemed to be in high spirits about this upcoming Durasi dinner and for that I was grateful. Their enthusiasm was contagious, and though I tried, it was difficult to put Gav's absence out of my mind.

I reminded myself that it wasn't like this sort of thing hadn't happened before. He'd often been pulled away for long periods of time. And during those absences he hadn't been able to communicate. The only difference was that in prior instances, he'd known ahead of time that he'd be gone and I'd known not to expect him.

Plus, none of his prior absences had resulted from his stumbling onto a crime scene the way we had — with five murder victims, one of whom was a friend who'd asked him for help. The fact that Gav didn't care for the agent in charge didn't bode well, either.

Yeah, this time everything was different. I didn't like it.

In between dinner plans and menu decisions, Bucky and Cyan asked me for specifics about my personal plans, and wanted to know details about how and when Gav and I began seeing one another. We laughed a bit. It felt good to talk.

Bucky grinned and wagged a finger. "I'm telling you, from the first day he showed up here and you started sassing him, I knew the man was smitten."

"You mean when he came here to teach the bomb courses?"

"Yep. He was crazy about you."

"He was not," I insisted. "He couldn't stand me."

"Uh-huh. Try to convince us. You got under his skin all right." Bucky gave me a pointed look. "Just not the way you led us all to believe."

"No, you have to understand," I said, trying again. "He drove *me* crazy. I thought he was full of himself. Arrogant. Annoying."

"And that's why you're marrying the guy, right? Because you can't stand him and you're hoping for a lifetime of aggravation?"

Bucky laughed. "I'm telling you, I saw this one coming."

I sighed, knowing it was useless to argue.

"I called my mom last night," I said, wrapping up, "and she and Nana want to be here, too."

"You sound surprised," Cyan said. "Of course they want to be here for you." She got a thoughtful expression on her face. "You know, since you're stuck having to wait for so many weeks, why not make some plans?"

"Plans?" I repeated. "Like . . . what?"

"Come on, Ollie, you can't be that dense. You ought to start looking for a place to hold a reception."

She must have reacted to the look on my face because she quickly added, "A small one, I mean."

"You don't understand," I said. "This isn't about the wedding, this is about the marriage. I don't need a reception or . . . or . . . any hoopla for that matter."

Cyan wore an expression of exasperation, one that would be more at home on a woman my mom's age than on my young assistant chef. Her eyes fairly glimmered with glee behind bright-blue contacts as she adopted a patient tone. She put her hands up, like a movie director framing a shot.

"Really? Picture this. You and Gav get in front of the judge exactly the way you plan. Great. Keep in mind that your mom and grandmother are there in the courtroom with you. They're sitting and smiling and incredibly happy for you."

"Okay," I said.

She continued gesturing animatedly. "What exactly do you think happens once you've said your vows? Do you leave your family there to chat with the deputies when the ceremony is over? Of course not. You'll want to take your mom and nana out somewhere nice to celebrate, won't you?"

I truly hadn't thought that far ahead. Too much on my mind. "I suppose . . ."

"Yeah," she said, with emphasis. "And what do you plan to wear?"

"Wear?" My head started to hurt. When Gav and I had set out for the courthouse, we'd been under the impression that we could be married within three days. With that short of a time span, there would be far less to fret about. Then our lead time turned into three *business* days, which turned into eight weeks, which could have been one week if Evan had . . .

Evan.

How could I worry about what to wear when there were five murdered men at the

Ainsley Street Ministry and Gav had gone AWOL immediately afterward? "I don't care what I wear," I said to Cyan. "Really I don't. Gav will marry me even if I show up in splattered chef's whites."

She gave me a look that was half amused, half sympathetic. "I'll back off for now. Keep in mind, though, if you need any help, I'm here."

Cyan meant well. And from the grin on Bucky's face, I could tell he did, too. "I'll remember," I said. "Thanks."

My cell phone timer went off a few minutes before ten A.M. I dug the device out of my pocket and shut off the chimes. "Thank goodness I set that," I said aloud. I'd been concentrating so hard on the guest list in front of me and working to keep my mind from worrying about Gav, that I'd lost all track of time.

Bucky watched me. "What's the alarm for?"

"Sargeant's promotion. He asked me to be there when the First Lady makes the announcement to the press."

Across the kitchen, Virgil tossed vegetables into a sizzling skillet. He spoke over his shoulder. "What's up with that? You and Sargeant have sure gotten lovey-dovey over

73

the past few months." He laughed. "You'd make a perfect couple."

I ignored him. "Cyan," I said as I untied my apron, "can you take over here? I was about to cross-check this preliminary guest list with the dietary restrictions we have on file. I've gotten about one-third of the way through." I pointed to where I'd left off. "Looks like we have a lot of work ahead of us. We have dietary dossiers on only about half the people I've checked."

"No problem," she said.

"When Sargeant's free, we'll need his help to determine the final guest list. We've got four preliminary lists we're working from and we need to cross-check those to ensure no one's been missed."

"Go," Bucky said. "The dinner isn't for another week. You know we'll have fourteen more 'absolute final' lists to wade through between now and then."

I smoothed my hands down the sides of my smock and inspected it to ensure I hadn't spilled on it yet. I pulled on a toque and straightened it. "Do I look okay?"

Cyan laughed. "I swear, Ollie. You're more worried about how you look for Sargeant than you are for your own wedding." Coming close enough to whisper, she added, "Maybe Virgil isn't so far off."

"Bite your tongue," I said.

A wave of worry slammed as the words escaped my lips. I'd often said that very thing to Gav — whenever he made casual mention of dying or getting hurt. We both knew that being involved in potentially life-threatening scenarios was part of his job description. I'd learned to accept that he faced danger on a regular basis, but that didn't mean I liked to talk about it. "Bite your tongue" — I'd said that so often. And right now I worried, a lot, that he was in even deeper trouble than usual.

CHAPTER 6

As I made my way upstairs via the pantry staircase, I decided that the thousand worries dancing in my head had to go if I had any hopes of making it through the day with my sanity intact. I'd start now. This was Sargeant's moment and I needed to be there for him. Even though he'd caused me grief in the past — lots of grief, if I were being totally honest — we were facing a new beginning here today. Sargeant and I had reached a détente of sorts. If my appearance and support here at his appointment helped continue that truce, I was happy to comply.

Because the White House was open for tours at this time of the day, I could hear the gentle murmurs and happy exclamations coming from the adjacent State Dining Room. Tourists were still making their way from that room across the Entrance Hall to exit out the home's front doors. Visitors weren't, however, allowed into the Family Dining Room, which is where the press conference was being held.

As news went, Sargeant's appointment didn't rank as high as, say, the president's message announcing peace talks with Durasi. That one had been held in the East Room, just across the hall. Good thing, too. The number of reporters, cameras, and dignitaries in attendance for that earth-shattering news wouldn't have been able to squeeze into any other room in the White House. I'd snuck upstairs to listen and watch, myself.

President Hyden had been passionate and vocal about how the time had come for compromise. Surrounded by members of his cabinet, he'd talked about plans, about how these meetings with the president of Durasi might herald new hopes for global harmony, and he very eloquently called upon all citizens to pray in their own way that this unexpected opportunity with the Durasi would prove beneficial not only to both countries, but to the entire world.

Today's press conference was nowhere in the same league as that had been, but personnel changes at the White House always made good news copy. This promotion and its ancillary attention meant the world to Sargeant, and I truly wished him the best.

Like every room on the residence's first floor, the Family Dining Room had high ceilings and classic lines. Painted a buttery yellow, there were two north-facing windows draped in mustard-colored silk with coordinating tassels. A lectern had been brought in and set up between the two windows. Sargeant fidgeted behind it, shuffling a small stack of index cards. Although he looked as put together as always — starched shirt, careful tie, sharp-edged handkerchief in his suit's breast pocket — his eyes darted about the room, seeing nothing. I could tell because he'd glazed over me twice as I approached. My presence hadn't yet registered.

There were about eight reporters in attendance. A couple of them had cameras, but all in all the mood was calm rather than rapacious, the way it had been in the East Room for the president. Sargeant's appointment would make a decent article in tomorrow's papers and, of course, online. If Sargeant was lucky, his news might even garner a Twitter hashtag.

Secret Service agents were stationed throughout the room, doing their best to look ominous and imposing. I recognized all but two as members of the Presidential Protective Division, the PPD. A second later, I reassessed. The two unfamiliar men standing together at the back of the room were definitely not part of the PPD. I'd bet a week's worth of onion chopping on that. I wasn't close enough to see if they wore Secret Service lapel pins, but it didn't matter. The pair studied the room differently. They both wore gray suits with jackets open, but their manner was off enough to make them stand out — at least to me. The reporters probably paid them no mind, and because the Secret Service agents in attendance weren't alarmed, I wasn't, either.

The taller of the two men caught me watching. He glanced away, though not before chilling me with an icy stare. What was up with that? I concentrated on Sargeant again, but a random thought flashed and I chanced another look at the two men. There was something familiar about the way the taller one — the one who'd caught me looking at him — moved. His manner and build teased at my memory, but I knew I'd never seen his face before. I tried shrugging it off. Their presence here was none of my business, but I still wanted to know who they were. Couldn't help it. It was my nature.

For his part, Sargeant looked like a prisoner about to be executed. He stood apart from the others: the First Lady, the White House press secretary, and the myriad assistants who were there to ensure a quick and smooth event. With consternation on his face, and index cards in hand, his lips moved, as though practicing his speech in silence. He was so fidgety, I realized that if a person could pace in place, he was doing it.

It wasn't until I was almost to the lectern, saying, "Good luck, Peter," that he blinked. His eyes were bloodshot, like those of a man who'd been abruptly roused from sleep by an air horn.

"Do you suppose they'll ask me questions?" he asked. Without waiting for me to reply, he went on. "I've been trying to come up with answers for whatever they might ask. I've been up all night imagining they might try to get me to comment on some of our foreign guests. Especially with the Durasi president due here soon. I don't want to cause an international situation. You don't think they will, do you?" He waved the white cards between us. "I wrote a few notes, in case they do."

He held them in both hands now, staring down. I could only read what was written on the top one. Even upside down it was easy to make out the words he'd jotted so precisely: "No comment."

In my opinion, rather than corner him for his views on foreign affairs, it was far more likely they'd ask about his background and want to know what he thought he might bring to the position that was new and different. Reporters would be eager to discover what Sargeant's unique stamp on the position might be.

Our new chief usher's fastidious nature was well-known within the residence — his meticulousness was legendary. If I could hazard a guess, those attributes were probably what had helped seal his appointment to this position. The local newshounds didn't know these facets of Sargeant yet. They would no doubt. Soon.

"I'm sure they'll ask a few things about your career thus far," I said, "but their goal, mostly, is to get to know you. Don't worry about them pressing you for anything you aren't comfortable sharing. You're surrounded by the First Lady and her assistants, don't forget. The White House press secretary is here, too. He's good at putting out fires."

"So you *are* expecting them to press me on specifics?"

At that moment, the press secretary stepped away from the First Lady and approached Sargeant. "We need you over here," he said, indicating a spot near the far window. "The First Lady and I will say a few words, then introduce you." To me, he said, "It's nice to have you here, Chef. Why not take a spot over there." He pointed to the northeastern corner of the room. "When Mr. Sargeant's promotion is announced and he steps forward, I'd like you to move in behind him, next to me and the First Lady. It will make a perfect publicity shot."

I whispered, "Good luck," to Sargeant and headed for the far corner.

Within moments, the press secretary had silenced the already tranquil crowd and talked briefly about Paul Vasquez's tenure as chief usher. I missed Paul. I'd heard from him a couple of times since his departure. His wife remained seriously ill, but at least there was hope on the horizon. I knew he missed working here and all of us, but he was where he was needed most.

The press secretary skimmed over Doug's on-the-job performance, stressing the fact that he'd been appointed as an interim chief usher, suggesting that Sargeant's permanent appointment had been the ultimate plan all along.

Two days ago, as soon as it had become clear that the rumor of Sargeant assuming the position was, indeed, fact, Doug had demanded an explanation as to why he'd been passed over. While no one considered him to be a security threat, his loud grumbling and out-of-control deportment brought Secret Service agents running. He was allowed to gather his things before being escorted out.

We all would have preferred a smooth transition, but Doug's knee-jerk angry response put a quick end to that plan. Doug would have a hard time getting references after that stunt.

The First Lady spoke next, also briefly. She talked about how she'd gotten to know Peter Everett Sargeant, and how he'd impressed her from the start with his devotion to duty and attention to detail.

By the time it was Sargeant's moment in the sun, little beads of perspiration had formed above his brow. Though the lighting in the room was by no means hot or glaring, the brightness above sparkled, making the man's glistening discomposure obvious to all. As he cleared his throat, I did as instructed and eased in to stand slightly behind him, to his left.

He began with the requisite thanks for being given the opportunity to serve. I held my breath, concerned by the faint tremble in his voice. As he went on, however, his words shook a little less, became a little stronger. He spoke for about two minutes and as his cadence shifted I could tell he was moving to close. Nice. Brief. All good. I felt myself relax.

A twenty-something male reporter raised his hand. He didn't wait to be called upon to speak. The guy had a scruffy, who-cares air about him. Skinny, with a Mick Jagger haircut, he wore a dingy, white button-down shirt that was at least two sizes too small. "Daniel Davies from *The People's Journal*," he said, introducing himself to Sargeant as well as to the rest of the small audience.

I'd never heard of him, though his publication was well known.

He tilted his head, squinting. "My readers will want to know how you plan to handle the chef's antics and maintain control over her tendency to interfere with the workings of government. She *has* been in the news frequently." At that, he gave an insouciant nod in my direction.

Blood rushed, squeezing hot behind my eyes as Davies went on, "I'm sure I don't have to remind you — or my esteemed colleagues — of her many extracurricular activities. If I understand correctly, Mr. Sargeant, you were involved in one of these exploits recently, yourself. Will your obvious friendship with Ms. Paras impact your ability to manage her?"

My cheeks warmed, and I fought to keep my expression neutral. *Obvious friendship?* If this reporter only knew the rocky and treacherous journey Sargeant and I had traveled just to get to where we were today. We'd finally gotten to the point of mutual respect, more or less. Friends? Not yet. Maybe not ever. How dare this un-put-together pipsqueak take that tone?

My brain roared with anger. *Exploits?* If this guy knew the truth . . . I took an involuntary step forward, barely stopping myself from stepping in front of the lectern to lash out.

Sargeant cleared his throat. His nostrils flared. As his hands clasped together below his chest, I recognized his familiar gesture as an attempt to calm himself. I hoped he could hold on. He needed to, for both our sakes.

The First Lady and press secretary wore twin, tight smiles and body language that told me they were ready to pounce. But Sargeant was a big boy now. He would have to learn to handle himself in all kinds of situations. Some might prove to be even tougher than this one, though at the moment I couldn't imagine how. I'd have been willing to bet that no one in the room had expected this turn in the questioning.

All eyes were on me all of a sudden. I could barely breathe.

"Ms. Paras runs her kitchen to the best of her abilities," Sargeant began, speaking slowly. While not exactly a rousing endorsement on his part, it was a good start. "As for the other activities you brought up, I don't see where any of that matters in the fulfillment of my role as chief usher. Ms. Paras has proved to be an exemplary employee, and beyond that I have no comment. Thank you for your question." Ever proper, Sargeant paused before shifting his attention to the other members of the press.

The young reporter ignored Sargeant's attempt to deflect, interrupting again. "You have to admit that the chef has been embroiled in an uncanny number of national-security-sensitive situations since she's been here. How do you intend to squelch her amateur sleuthing tendencies?" Before Sargeant could gather himself to answer, the reporter continued, "Or don't you?"

The other reporters took notes, a few of them murmuring among themselves. The

First Lady and the press secretary exchanged a glance, but Sargeant straightened and answered in the sort of commanding, belittling tone that I'd so despised in the past. "Mr. Davies," he said. "Are you utterly ignorant of protocol? I will remind you that I was promoted to the position of chief usher after successfully discharging the duties of the White House sensitivity director for several years. One doesn't make a name for himself by casting aspersions on others without proof."

This time, Sargeant didn't take a breath or give Davies the barest of openings. He continued in his familiar, high-handed, fussy way. "If you have questions about security, I suggest you direct them to the Secret Service. If you have questions about the running of the White House kitchen, I suggest you contact Ms. Paras directly. Today, however, we are here to discuss the running of the household and my appointment to this prestigious position. Period. I will thank you to stay on topic." With a glance over the younger man's head, Sargeant lifted his chin. "Next question?"

CHAPTER 7

The two mysterious men in the back of the room had begun leaning forward as Davies challenged Sargeant. Now, as another reporter lobbed a softball question at our newly appointed chief usher, the two men put their heads together. From their body language, it seemed that their interest had been piqued. By the reporter or by Sargeant, I couldn't tell. When the taller one caught me staring again, I squirmed.

Minutes later, the press conference over, two of the PPD agents escorted Mrs. Hyden from the room, another pair herded the reporters out, and the mysterious strangers moved to talk with the agents who remained. We staff members were left to disperse on our own.

The First Lady's assistants and the press secretary were gone in a flash. "Masterful job, Peter," I said as I removed my toque and fell into step alongside him. We made our way east, toward his new office. "You handled that wild set of questions very well. What was that all about, anyway?"

"I wish I knew. Did you see how sloppily that young man was dressed? He had no business here."

"My presence may not have been such a good idea after all."

"I suspect he would have attacked me whether you were present or not. It's clear from his manner of questioning, however, that you will continue to be the proverbial thorn in my paw." Sargeant's voice dropped, almost as though he was talking to himself. "I can't say I anticipated such venom." Blinking, he returned his attention to me. "I fear he's out to make trouble for me. For you. With that in mind, Olivia, you must take care not to overstep again," he said. "Is that clear? I will not tolerate shenanigans in this house. I can't afford to."

"Shenanigans," I repeated, deadpan. "You know better."

He didn't meet my eyes. "I knew that media attention would be on me, but I'm facing far more scrutiny than I had expected. That was made abundantly clear moments ago. I knew you had a high profile and had established a reputation. What I hadn't realized was how adversely your actions could affect my position."

I tried my best to see things from his perspective. He'd just been promoted and within seconds of the official announcement, had been taken to task by a smart-aleck reporter clearly bent on stirring up trouble. "I will do what I did with Paul," I said, striving to be accommodating. "I will keep you apprised of any unusual activity. Like I did yesterday."

"See to it that you do," he said. "I am not a man who enjoys surprises. Especially the sort of surprises you tend to deliver."

We took a half flight of stairs to the chief usher's office. I hadn't been here since Sargeant had moved in, and the change in the room took me by surprise. Where Doug had allowed paperwork to pile up, leaving the area looking haphazard and messy at all times, Sargeant had restored order and class to the small space. The administrative assistant's desk was clean, too.

"The office looks wonderful," I said as he took his seat behind the desk. I took one across from him, pulling my toque onto my lap. "How did you get it in shape so fast?"

He ignored the question. "We need to discuss the running of your kitchen." Opening his calendar, he pulled up a pen and stared at me. "I'd like to make an appointment for such a meeting next week. What is your schedule?"

We were interrupted before I could answer. The two mysterious men from the back of the Family Dining Room walked in, accompanied by two members of the PPD. With almost-perfect precision, they lasered their gazes on me. Sargeant could have been invisible for all they seemed to care.

"Ms. Paras," one of the agents said, "a moment?"

I assessed them. Not one of the four wore a pleasant expression. "Of course," I said. Getting up, I shot a confused look to Sargeant.

The chief usher's brows came together over alert eyes. "We will continue our discussion later," he said. "You can bring me up to date."

The agent who'd addressed me took my elbow and spoke to Sargeant. "Don't count on it."

I squirmed out of the agent's grasp as the four tall men walked me across the entrance hall to the Green Room. I knew I was short, but next to these enormous fellows, I felt like a toddler. The area was quiet. Empty. Tour time had ended during the press conference and the floor had been cleared of visitors. One of our maintenance people, buffing the already shiny marble floor, didn't even look up as we passed.

We arrived to find a uniformed Secret Service agent giving the room a final check to ensure there were no stragglers. When we entered, he looked up in alarm. Without waiting for any of my escorts to say a word, he nodded and ducked out of the room.

When I heard the door shut behind him, I knew I was in trouble.

I fingered my toque, still tight in my hands. "What's going on?" I asked.

The two PPD agents I knew closed the doors that led to the adjoining rooms, then took positions in front of them. To prevent anyone from walking in, or to prevent me from getting out? The two agents I didn't know edged me toward a small upholstered wooden chair. The taller of the two men spoke. "Sit down, Ms. Paras."

He was built like a football running back, muscular and lithe. Dark skinned with black hair clipped close to his scalp, he had a slightly misshapen mouth that told me he'd been born with a cleft lip. His surgeon must have been skilled because the narrow, pale scar that ran vertically to his left nostril barely marred his chiseled good looks. His eyes were so dark I couldn't tell where the pupils ended and the irises began.

I'd been in enough of these situations over my White House career to know how disconcerting it was to be seated when a person in authority loomed above. "I'd prefer to stand, thank you." I gave a quick, perfunctory smile as if to say that I wasn't afraid.

"Sit down," he repeated. "That is not a request."

All of a sudden it hit me. "It's Gav, isn't it? Did something happen to him? Where is he? Is he all right?" I sank onto the hard cushion of the antique chair, my legs no longer sturdy enough to hold me up.

The agent stood directly in front of me, hands clasped by his waist. At my question he blinked, but otherwise his expression didn't change. His associate had taken one step back. Neither of them seemed particularly willing to answer.

The room was quiet, save for the sounds of the gardeners buzzing across the expansive south lawn outside the window. The air was still as a placid pond, making me believe I'd cause a ripple if I moved even a little bit. I sat frozen in place, afraid that one of those ripples could result in bad news for Gav.

With my hands clasped tightly in my lap, I asked again. "Please." Surely if I was polite they'd see I meant no harm. That all I needed to know was that Gav was safe. I kept my voice low to keep from sounding harsh. "Where is he?"

The agent before me didn't unclasp his hands, but he did raise the fingers of one, silencing me. "You will answer my questions," he said. "If you are forthright and truthful, you'll be free to go."

Tension sharpened my words. "And if I'm *not* forthright and truthful?"

So much for politeness.

"Ms. Paras, I don't believe you know the gravity of your situation."

"Wait." I turned to one of the PPD agents, then the other, but both studiously avoided me. Collecting myself as best I could, I tipped my head up to make direct eye contact. "Who are you?" I asked. "Before I answer a single one of your questions, I deserve to know who's asking them."

He sniffed in deeply. "You can call me Agent Tyree." He unclasped his hands long enough to gesture to the side. "This is my associate, Agent Larsen. We —"

"Tyree?" My exclamation came out reedy and high. "You were the agent at . . ." His sharp glare and a sudden realization on my part allowed me to catch myself before finishing the thought. Tyree had been the

94

man in the gas mask who'd accosted us at the murder scene. The leader. I shot a glance to the two PPD agents, still standing sentry at the doors. I was about to ask if I was free to speak in front of them, but Tyree was way ahead of me.

He lifted his chin toward the PPD agents. "Thank you, gentlemen. We have the situation covered here."

The two men left. Doors closed behind them with mournful, solid clicks.

My stomach churned. When I'd last seen Gav, he'd been intent on returning to talk to Tyree. I was sure this man knew where Gav was, but it was clear he wasn't willing to share that information. Or even let me know that Gav was all right. Determined to find out, I attempted to get to my feet, but Tyree was standing too close for me to be able to make it all the way up.

"Last night, Ms. Paras," he said very quietly, "you saw something that you were not supposed to see." When he spoke this time, his voice was different. Cold, clinical. Between Gav's response to this man and his suddenly icy demeanor, I began to realize how much trouble we might be in.

I turned to Tyree's colleague. Larsen was thinner, with a shaved head that appeared to be carved from ivory. His skeletal look was exacerbated by his sucked-in cheeks. He stared down at me with pale, angry eyes. No help there.

Tyree seemed to be expecting an answer, so I obliged him. "Yes."

He shifted his weight but still remained too close, too tight for me to stand up. Mostly, when people invaded my personal space, they did so to be friendly. Tyree here was using it to intimidate. I stared up at him, hoping to communicate that he'd better not expect it to work.

"Who have you told?" he asked.

It hurt my neck to keep my face upturned enough to maintain eye contact with Tyree, but his manner brought my stubbornness into full strength.

"You obviously don't know me," I said.

Tyree's nose twitched. "I asked you a question."

"And I'm telling you that if you knew me, you wouldn't need to ask. I let the chief usher, Peter Everett Sargeant, know that Gav and I stumbled upon a 'situation' and that I may get pulled away" — I fluttered my hands as though to encompass the room — "and I anticipated a debriefing very much like this one. But I shared no details with him. I know better than that."

Tyree made a sound deep in his throat.

Beside him, Larsen coughed.

"What happened at the Ainsley Street Ministry?" I asked, twisting my head back and forth to try to detect humanity in one of their faces. I came up empty. "Who did that to those men?"

"How do you know Evan Bonder?"

I folded my arms, to keep my bubbling anger from allowing me to tremble. "Until you tell me where Gav is and if he's all right, I have nothing to say to you."

Tyree's scar brightened and I swore I saw it pulse. He barely moved his lips as he spoke. "I suggest you cooperate. We can make your life difficult. I trust you understand that."

Sitting while these two men towered over me was not my idea of a position of strength. I couldn't help but believe, however, that there was a good reason why they remained civil and I hadn't been hauled away yet: They wanted to keep my involvement quiet. I had no idea why, and right now, I didn't care. All I cared about was Gav.

"I'll make you a deal," I said. "I'll answer every question you throw at me as long as you tell me about Gav."

Larsen turned toward the windows, his disgust obvious.

Tyree shook his head.

I tried again. "In case Gav hasn't mentioned it to you himself, he's injured. He's on medical leave."

"I am well aware of his status. Now, how did you know Evan Bonder?"

Fine, I thought. I'll answer that much. Maybe then they'll answer me. "I don't," I said. "That is, I didn't. Gav wanted me to meet Evan. Said he was an old friend."

"He took you to meet him Thursday," Tyree said, deadpan. "Special Agent Gavin chose *Thursday* for an impromptu visit."

"He did."

"Why?" Tyree's black-hole eyes narrowed. "What was so special about Thursday?"

"You make it sound like Gav should have known Evan and his group were in danger."

"Did he?"

"No." I pulled in a breath. "If you must know, Gav and I plan to be married."

For the first time since I'd met him, Tyree reacted. From his expression I could tell this wasn't news, but the revulsion on his face was impossible to miss. "Go on."

"We want to — we hoped to — get married quickly. When we discovered that the courthouse was backed up for eight weeks, Gav thought of his friend Evan." I spoke quickly, keeping as succinct as I could. "Apparently Evan was a minister and Gav

98

thought that we might ask him to perform the ceremony for us." I left out the part about Evan having called Gav, asking for help. Gav could share that if he wanted to. It would be hearsay coming from me, anyway. At least that's how I rationalized keeping mum with that information. "Unfortunately . . . as you are well aware, Evan and several others had been murdered by the time we got there."

Tyree's eyes tightened. "Who said anything about murder?"

Flabbergasted, I shook my head. "You saw the bodies. They were bound and gagged. What would you call it?"

"Were any of the victims still alive when you got there?"

That took me aback. We hadn't had time to check. I'd wanted to, but as soon as Gav had detected the scent, he'd rushed me back out the way we'd come. I hadn't been able to check any of the victims for a pulse. "I don't think so," I said.

"Think harder, Ms. Paras."

I jerked backward at the malevolence in his tone.

"Did any of them speak to you?" he asked.

"Are you joking?" Irritation made my voice rise. "They were dead. Or don't you remember what happened there?"

"You did not state unequivocally that all the victims were deceased when you arrived. You said you didn't 'think' any were still alive. I'm asking you if you're withholding information from me. Who spoke to you and what did he say?"

Invasion of my personal space or no, I pushed to my feet, going chin to chest with Tyree. He took an instinctive step back. Good.

I shook my toque in the man's face. "Don't you get it? We were there less than a minute before you arrived. No one spoke. They couldn't." I repeated myself, this time more slowly. "They were bound and gagged. And oh, yeah, dead."

"A minute is a long time," he said. "A dying man could have a lot to say in that amount of time." His nostrils flared, and he opened his mouth to continue.

I couldn't help myself, I cut him off even though I knew my next words would cause trouble. "Exactly what were *you* doing there, Agent Tyree?" I turned to the other man, Larsen. "I assume that was you under one of the other gas masks. How did you know to protect yourselves, hmm?"

The moment I'd gotten to my feet, Larsen had shot back to stand by his partner's side. An oddly protective move. Like there was

100

any chance I could hurt either one of these toughies.

Tyree's voice was a growl. "You be careful, Ms. Paras," he said. And in a very ominous, un-Secret Service–like gesture, he pointed two fingers toward his eyes, then turned them toward me. "We will be watching you."

CHAPTER 8

"What's wrong?" Cyan asked when I returned to the kitchen. "Was Sargeant's first order of business in his new job to toss you overboard?" Her tone was light, but as she drew closer, her voice lowered. "Seriously, what happened at the press conference? You look furious. And you were gone a long time."

"I am furious, but it has nothing to do with the press conference." Flexing my fingers, I rested a hip against the stainless steel island at the center of the room. Virgil had his back to me, working at the stove. "Where's Bucky?"

She flipped a hand toward the refrigeration area. "Taking inventory. Where have you been? I mean, really? Sargeant's been back for a while. He called down here to leave a message for you."

I couldn't answer her question about where I'd been, so I deflected. "What did he want?"

"To set up a meeting with you. One-on-one, he said." Her eyes clouded. "Uh-oh. What's going on?"

I needed to blow off steam. Usually, the best way to do that was to throw myself into work, but right now that option wasn't going to cut it. "What time is Josh due down here?"

"You're not answering my questions."

I pointed at her. "Astute observation." It was a lame attempt to keep the moment light. Failed.

She fisted one hip and studied me. "Josh is supposed to join us in about an hour. You know how he's intent on helping with the state dinner? Well, he wants to be in on the planning as well as the execution. Why do you ask?"

"I'll be back," I said, still not answering her directly. Slamming my toque onto the workspace, I left the kitchen, taking a right into the refrigeration area, a left into the basement hall, and a final left through the double doors that led into the ground-level outdoor courtyard that wrapped around the northwest corner of the kitchen.

Once freed from the constraints of having to watch my every word, I drew in a deep breath of the hot, sunny air and expelled it, hard. "What is going on, Gav?" I asked aloud. "Why can't I reach you?"

Fortunately for me, the president was off the premises at the moment, which meant that a good portion of the Secret Service detail was away, too. Sure, there were plenty of agents guarding the First Family, and we had our ever-present snipers on the roof, but I didn't feel swarmed and claustrophobic out here the way I sometimes did in the White House.

Being out in the fresh air by myself didn't do much to abate my anxiety level where Gav was concerned. Tyree's presence had upped the stakes. All I could imagine was that something — some unknown thing — was very wrong. I couldn't put my finger on it because I didn't know what was going on behind the scenes. Not knowing was often worse than the truth. I desperately wanted to know what was happening.

All I knew for certain was that Gav would have contacted me if he could have. In frustration, I clasped my hands behind my head and stared at the sky. *Get a grip, Ollie,* I told myself. *You've been through worse.*

I needed to focus on something other than Gav. Worrying about him — though it came naturally, and far too easily — was counterproductive and a worthless endeavor. Logically, I knew that my worrying wouldn't keep him safe. Emotionally, I needed to make myself believe it.

My team depended on me to stay strong. The president depended on me to feed his important guests. The president's son, Josh, who also happened to be my number one student, depended on me for guidance. I didn't have time to waste here. I couldn't give in to the luxury of worry.

And yet, as the sun warmed my bare arms, I allowed myself this moment to let it all out.

"What now?" I asked, knowing that the answer needed to come from within.

And it did. Simply put, I couldn't let my team down. I couldn't let Josh down. I most definitely couldn't deliver anything less than my best effort where this upcoming state dinner was concerned. The president of Durasi visiting the White House could make all the difference to peace between our nations. I had to do all I could to make sure my portion of it went well.

That meant I needed to focus.

I paced and circled the courtyard three times. The air, the sun, and the ability to move did me good, exactly in the way I'd hoped. A nun I'd had in high school once advised us that if we were taxed mentally, we should get out and do something physical to reclaim our energy. Similarly, she told us that if we were taxed physically, we should resort to mental exercises to restore ourselves. That advice had always served me well.

Thus refreshed, I headed back inside, ready to take charge again, to keep my kitchen moving forward. This was my job. This was what I did best. In trying times like these, I needed to remind myself of that as well.

I found Sargeant at his desk. What surprised me more than the sight of his head bent over papers he was studying, was the fact that this scene seemed perfectly natural to me. Paul had been the chief usher for years and I'd grown to love the man. Doug Lambert — despite his protestations to the contrary — had never been able to handle the demands of the job and I'd been uncomfortable seeing him in the role.

I was too savvy to fool myself into believing that Sargeant and I would never experience any turbulence in the future, but having him in charge of the entire residence filled me more with relief than dread.

I knocked at the jamb. "Peter?"

His head came up and he peeled frameless spectacles from his face.

"Are you in trouble again?" he asked.

I didn't wait for him to invite me to sit. I simply took the chair across from him. "Maybe. At this point, however . . ."

He waved his reading glasses in the air, wearily brushing away my words. "I know. You can't tell me. I trust that when you're able to, you will bring me up to speed?"

He phrased it as a question, but his gaze was sharp, his mouth downturned like a marionette's.

I gave a quick nod. "That's about the size of it." Focusing on my reason for seeking him out, I switched subjects. "You wanted to talk about the kitchen's reporting structure?"

Folding his arms across the desk, he leaned forward. "I won't beat around the bush. We need to discuss whether Bucky or Virgil is to be considered the acting executive chef in your absence."

"Fine. Let's get this done once and for all."

"Not so fast," he said with an indignant sniff. "You may prefer to leap into decisions, but I take a more measured approach. One step at a time, please."

Bristling at his chastisement, I swallowed my impatience and said, "Go on."

He resettled himself. "For the record,

there's no doubt in my mind where your preferences lie on this issue."

"What about your preferences?" I asked.

One side of his face crinkled up. He pursed his lips. "Let's clear the air, shall we?"

I leaned forward, mimicking his posture, perching my elbows on my end of his desk. "I didn't realize anything needed to be cleared between us, Peter," I said. "As far as I'm concerned, you and I have never held back. By all means, continue."

He brought his head lower, speaking barely above a whisper. "If you don't already know, I'm certain you at least suspect that I, too, cannot abide Virgil. If it were up to me, he would have been dismissed when Doug left. Perhaps sooner."

I didn't react, even though I longed to release a giant breath of relief. Sargeant and I were on the same page for once.

"The problem," he went on, "is that Virgil has an incredibly high public profile. One that rivals even yours. The difference is that his reputation is built on cooking talent, whereas you are better known for . . ."

He let the thought hang, but I sat up straighter, my back stiffening in reaction to the obvious conclusion. From the very start, since slightly before I'd taken over as executive chef, my face had regularly appeared in news reports. Unfortunately for me, and for the residents of the White House, the focus of these articles tended to deal more with murders than marsala.

Sargeant went on, either oblivious to my sharp attention, or simply choosing not to acknowledge it. "This morning's press conference aside, I believe your goal as executive chef is to continue to produce high-quality events and to maintain the relationship you have with the boy."

"Josh," I said.

"My role," he continued with a quick nod, "is to oversee the running of this household in such a way as to make the First Family's life here as effortless and trouble-free as possible."

"Again, we are in agreement."

"I am aware that Virgil handles the family's meals, allowing you to focus on the state events." He held up both index fingers, parallel — like vertical railroad tracks, preventing me from interrupting. "I do, however, have a very clear view of how disruptive Virgil can be to the day-to-day running of the kitchen. I intend to discuss his future with Mrs. Hyden. If she's agreeable to recommending he seek other employment, then we will proceed accordingly.

I must get an answer from you first, how-ever: Are you willing to take on the family meals again, if Virgil's dismissal is the ultimate outcome?"

I hadn't expected Sargeant to offer such a tied-up-with-a-bow solution. "Absolutely," I said, not even trying to hide the excitement in my voice. "My team has always enjoyed preparing the family's meals. We miss it."

Sargeant gave a quick nod. "In the mean-time, I suggest you continue to do your best to work with Virgil. Play the hand you've been dealt, as it were." He scribbled a note as he spoke. "I will let you know the result of my discussion with Mrs. Hyden. She and I are due for our first consultation tomor-row. She suggested that I take the whole day today to get acclimated." He sighed. "As though it would take me that long."

Sensing that we were done, I stood. Sargeant didn't stop me, but he regarded me with curiosity.

"Is there something else?" I asked.

He pursed his lips again. This time when he spoke, I got the impression he was less sure of himself. "Do I understand correctly that you and your special agent beau are intending to wed soon?"

That took me aback. "You understand correctly."

Another quick nod. "I have heard a rumor that you've run into a problem because the judges are backlogged."

"Word travels fast around here." I placed both hands on the back of the chair I'd vacated. "We'd planned to be married just as soon as the license was issued." I shrugged as though it was nothing, but the discussion reminded me that I still hadn't heard from Gav. Like a sharp bite from within, my stomach clenched. "We were disappointed to discover that it may take us a bit longer than we'd first thought. Unless, of course, we find a minister on our own who's willing to perform the ceremony."

"Do you know any ministers or members of the clergy?"

The image of Evan Bonder and his four colleagues slid into my brain. I sucked in a quick, hard breath. "Not personally, no."

Sargeant tilted his head, doing his curious-squirrel imitation. This time the personal quirk didn't annoy me so much. "I expect you to provide notice if you intend to take any days off."

"Of course."

"You will not allow this disappointment of yours to adversely impact your job performance." He didn't phrase it as a question.

Bristling irritation danced its way up the

back of my neck. "Certainly not."

"Thank you, Ms. Paras. That will be all."

I bit the insides of my cheeks to keep myself quiet. Sargeant was fully within his rights to question me. I would have liked to believe, however, that he knew I wouldn't allow personal problems to affect anything I did at the White House. If he only knew how much was on my mind right now.

I made my way back down to the kitchen, reminding myself that he was new in the job and probably wanted to establish his authority. Made sense. I'd probably do the exact same thing. By the time I made it back to the kitchen, I'd almost convinced myself of it, too.

A half hour later, I had my back to the pantry doorway and my wrists deep in a gooey flour mixture, when a lightning bolt of an idea hit. I opened my mouth, and almost blurted "Yablonski," when good sense halted me before the name tumbled out.

At the other end of the center countertop, Cyan reacted to the look on my face. "What?" she asked.

Suddenly cheerier than I'd been in hours, I pulled my hands out of the bowl and grinned. "I remembered something important." I hurried over to the sink to wash up. Bucky and Virgil weren't paying us any attention, but I could tell Cyan was curious. "A friend of Gav's," I said by way of explanation, knowing it was no help to her at all, "I need to call him."

Cyan narrowed her eyes but didn't question me. She returned to experimenting with a molasses and orange juice mixture that we hoped would become our sweet potato side dish.

Joe Yablonski had, at one time, been Gav's commanding officer. Now he was a good friend, one who had helped us in the very recent past. We trusted him completely and I knew that even Gav would believe it safe to tell him about the five dead men on Ainsley Street. More important, I could tell Yablonski that I hadn't been able to reach Gav since he'd dropped me at home Thursday night.

Once he had that information, I had no doubt that Yablonski would move heaven and earth to find out what was going on. My only problem was being able to get in touch with him without leaving a trail that led back to me. I didn't have direct contact information for the man, nor would I, ever. He'd made it clear that any association with me — and my reputation — could be hazardous to his.

I did, however, know Quinn, an agent who worked with Yablonski and who had acted as one of the man's spies when I was under surveillance a couple of weeks ago. "I'll be right back," I said.

"Where are you going?" Cyan asked.

I hurried out the door, pretending not to hear, turning the corner and nearly hurtling into two Secret Service agents escorting the president's son.

"Josh!" I exclaimed. That's right. He was due here, right about now. I was so distracted by my mission, I'd temporarily blanked on that detail. Thinking fast, I said, "Go on in, I'll be back in a few minutes. I forgot something I needed to do." It wasn't a lie, exactly. Unfortunately, the thing I'd forgotten was Josh's visit to the kitchen. Internally, I cringed.

The little boy grinned, unaware of my lapse. "Sure, Ollie. I'll wait for you."

I faced him as I walked backward. "Cyan can get you started," I said. The two agents accompanying Josh followed him into the kitchen as I made my way to the corridor that opened to the center hall. Guilt made me raise my voice enough to call out, "I won't be long."

There was a small Secret Service office on

the ground floor, a few steps east. As I made my way to it, I went over my hastily arranged plan, trying to come up with the right words to voice my request. The door to the inner office was closed and the female agent at the desk in front of it gave me a quizzical look when I walked in.

"Chef?" she said. "May I help you?"

It took all my self-control to keep my request conversational, casual. At this point I was beyond worried for Gav. I was fighting a gnawing frustration on his behalf. The man was on medical leave, for heaven's sake. He needed time to recover. Whatever he was enduring right now couldn't be doing his injuries any good.

"A few weeks ago," I began, in an attempt not to appear overly eager, "we had Agent Quinn here. He worked with a few of us in the kitchen."

She nodded, but her expression was blank. Quinn's name obviously didn't ring a bell.

"He's since been reassigned," I said. "I don't know where he is, but I need to get in touch with him. Would you be able to help me do that?"

She was prevented from answering when the door behind her opened and Agent Rosenow, another female agent, emerged. She was talking with a man I didn't recognize. He was half turned away from me and the two chatted amiably in a way that made it obvious they'd recently come to some agreement. I was delighted to see that Rosenow was on duty today. She knew Quinn and would, most likely, be of more help to me than the woman at the desk could.

The gentleman talking with Rosenow turned. His expression shifted from one of pleasant camaraderie to pure surprise. He blinked twice and turned to Rosenow, who was clearly startled to see me standing there, too.

"Ms. Paras." She ran a hand through her close-cropped blond hair. "We were just talking about you. Allow me to introduce Alec Baran."

I studied the man as he offered me his hand. He was taller than Gav by half a head, which put this guy at a muscular six foot five at least. His square-cut jaw and large forehead combined to give him an intimidating appearance, but his eyes softened that impression. Crystal blue, they were framed by lashes so long and dark that it almost looked as though he'd applied mascara. Put together, he was an extraordinarily handsome man.

His large hand engulfed mine as we shook. "I'm pleased to make your acquaintance,

Ms. Paras."

I shot an inquisitive look to Rosenow. "Talking about *me*?"

She hastened to explain. "Alec Baran will be working closely with the Secret Service over the next few weeks."

I addressed him. "Are you some type of consultant?"

A corner of his mouth curled up. "I suppose you could call me that."

He held a hand out to Rosenow, allowing her to explain. "You may have heard of Mr. Baran's company, Kalto?" She phrased it as a question.

"Of course," I said, feeling idiotic the moment my brain made the connection and the name clicked. Who *hadn't* heard of Alec Baran? He was a wealthy philanthropist who'd risen through the ranks of the military and had started Kalto because he felt strongly about protecting America. "It's a pleasure to meet you."

Although I wasn't clear on specifics, I had a basic understanding of the nature of his firm. Kalto was, in essence, a civilian security team made up of both former soldiers and new recruits. From what I understood, the pay was better than what the U.S. government offered, and training was top-notch. There were other such businesses out there, but Kalto was considered the elite, the best. Kalto's team members were credited with saving many American lives in enemy countries and occasionally here on home soil as well.

"Please, call me Alec," he said. "If we're to work together, I'd like to maintain an air of informality. May I call you Olivia?"

"Ollie," I said, using manners to cover for my momentary confusion. "Why will we be working together?"

"I'd intended to come talk with you later," Rosenow said. "But now is as good a time as any. We know that sudden personnel changes might give you cause for concern."

"Personnel changes?" I felt very parrot-like, repeating their words. "What sort of changes?" I tried to make sense of these statements, but came up empty. "Is Kalto taking over PPD responsibilities?" That would be unheard of. PPD agents were handpicked to protect the president and his family. I couldn't believe that any outside company, even one with Kalto's reputation, would be hired to take over those duties.

"Not exactly," she said quickly. "The PPD will continue to guard the president and First Family. That will not change. What *will* change is that we will be augmenting the PPD's other assignments with personnel from Kalto. Their responsibilities will be to protect the White House staff, its visitors, guests, and grounds."

"Protect the staff?" I caught myself repeating her words, yet again. "You mean we'll have guards shadowing us?" I'd had to deal with bodyguards in the past and I didn't care to repeat the experience.

"No," Rosenow said, and I think she almost laughed. "That's not quite the idea. Kalto personnel will assist here at the White House. They'll simply be an additional presence here. They'll take their direction from the Secret Service and will help fill in any gaps in security."

I didn't think our Secret Service allowed any gaps, but I didn't say that aloud. It sounded to me as though the Kalto team members were to be given busywork while the Secret Service saw to its own duties. But why? "Are we facing some sort of threat?" I asked.

They exchanged a look.

Baran's face was grim. "We aren't at liberty to discuss security with you at this point."

I understood. Too well. Even though he'd as much as told me to butt out, I couldn't help asking. "This has to do with the Durasi state dinner, doesn't it?"

Again, the exchanged glance.

"The president will cover more details tonight when he addresses the American people about the upcoming Durasi visit. For now, all you need to know is that Mr. Baran's team will be available to assist with whatever we need," Rosenow said. "You can go to them with any problems you may encounter, or any unusual situations that may come up." She took a hesitant breath, and I knew what was coming even before she spoke again. "We recognize that you have a certain knack for stumbling into trouble."

I kept my face expressionless, although that description pretty much summed up many of my adventures, most recently the encounter at the Ainsley Street Ministry.

"I can assure you, Ollie, that we're being proactive with regard to the upcoming dinner," she continued. "Our hope is that such efforts prove extraneous and unnecessary. Mr. Baran will be installing his team members here over the next few days. We'll keep you updated."

I took her tone to mean I was dismissed. "Before I leave, I have a question for you," I said. "I stopped by to find out if you had contact information for Agent Quinn." I waited a beat. "You remember him? From our visit to the Food Expo?"

"Of course." The look on her face told me that she wanted to ask what I needed Quinn for but that she thought better of it with others around. "I'll see what I can come up with."

"Thank you. It's a matter of some urgency, so I'd appreciate whatever help you can offer."

I took my leave and hurried back to the kitchen, where Josh was waiting for me.

CHAPTER 9

For the first time since I'd begun mentoring Josh, I struggled to stay in the moment. The president's son's love for cooking and creating delicious foods was real, and I always looked forward to working with him. The more I'd gotten to know him, the more of myself I saw in this enthusiastic young boy. I recognized his excitement as each new experience opened his eyes to possibility. Watching as he discovered new tastes, new methods, and new combinations was a true joy.

Today, however, my mind was scattered. From Sargeant's press conference, which felt as though it had occurred last week rather than this morning, to my debriefing with Tyree and Larsen, to the news that the White House would require additional security measures for our upcoming event, I found it hard to concentrate on the tasks at hand.

"Is this how to do it, Ollie?" Josh asked.

I leaned over his shoulder. The carrots in his orange-stained fingers weren't coming out quite like the matchsticks we'd hoped for. More like angular, impressionistic worms. "I know it's tough to keep the veggies from slipping," I said. "Here, try this."

Picking up an extra knife, I demonstrated, slowly, how to maintain pressure while slicing. "Holding a knife the right way is key. The trick is to achieve balance, yet grip tight, while keeping your fingers out of harm's way."

"I tried that," he said.

I knew he had. I also knew that these sorts of necessary skills — mundane and boring though they were — required hours of practice before they could be mastered. "Do you remember that scene in the movie where Julia Child chopped up a pile of onions this high?" I gestured to a level above his head.

His eyes went wide. "We don't have that many carrots." Then, with an uneasy glance in the direction of the refrigeration room, he asked, "Do we?"

I smiled. "We do, but don't worry. I think you've had enough chopping for one afternoon."

Josh seemed relieved, but less cheery than

123

normal. Could he be picking up on my mood? The last thing I wanted to do was to quash his spirits with the heaviness of my own. Not knowing Gav's whereabouts gave me insight into what mothers all over the world must feel when they can't get in touch with their kids. I couldn't help my constant, furtive glances at the clock.

"Tell you what," I said to Josh, drawing on every bit of strength to keep from ruining his experience here today, "let's make a stuffing instead."

"A real recipe?" he asked. "Instead of just chopping stuff for practice that nobody's going to use?"

I pointed to the uneven pile of carrots. "We'll use every one of those. Nothing goes to waste around here."

Virgil puttered around us, doing his best to pretend that he didn't notice that the president's son was working in our midst. Across from him, Bucky and Cyan collaborated on menu items for the upcoming dinner. I could afford spending a little extra time with Josh.

"Here you go," I said, pulling out a recipe I'd printed for rice stuffing that I'd been hoping to experiment with. I handed it to him.

"Ms. Paras?"

I had my back to the door when I heard my name called. The voice wasn't familiar, but when I turned, I recognized one of the PPD agents who'd accompanied Josh down to the kitchen. On days when it was the basic cooking staff: me, Bucky, Cyan, and Virgil present, Josh was allowed to join us while the PPD agents remained outside the working area. If we ever had guest chefs, or Service by Agreement (SBA) chefs in the kitchen, the PPD agents stayed close by his side.

"You have a phone call," the agent said.

I gave him a quizzical look. Phone calls were usually routed straight to the kitchen. I pointed. "Can I take it here?"

He shook his head. "Secret Service office."

Josh frowned. "Are you in trouble again?"

Sigh. Even *he* was aware of my reputation. "Hope not," I said, wiping my hands on my apron. "I'll be right back."

I returned to the Secret Service office, and the agent at the desk showed me into Agent Rosenow's immediately. Rosenow stood. "For you." She lifted the phone's receiver and handed it to me as she punched a button.

"Hello?" I said.

"This is Quinn."

A quick glance at Rosenow, who watched

with interest. "That was quick," I said into the phone.

"You needed to speak with me?" His words were clipped.

Not only had I not expected him to call me, I hadn't planned to conduct my conversation with him in front of an audience. Thinking fast, I stammered, "I did. I needed to find out if you could put me in touch with someone else."

"What's going on?" he asked.

Rosenow remained standing, with no indication she intended to leave me to my conversation. I knew better than to say Yablonski's name aloud in front of anyone.

"We have a mutual friend. Do you remember?"

A moment's pause. "Why do you need him?"

I opened my mouth. Unable to speak freely, I hesitated. "It's important."

"I'm sure."

I could tell he was waiting for me to explain further. My pulse echoed in my ears as I stared back at Rosenow, trying to communicate that I would prefer a little privacy, please. Unperturbed, she continued to study me. The Secret Service could be so intrusive sometimes. I was on the phone with another agent, for crying out loud. Didn't that warrant a little leeway?

"Listen, I just need five minutes with him," I said. "Not even. Two minutes. Is there a way you can put me in touch?"

"No can do." I got the impression Quinn was smiling as he said that. "Our 'friend' is out of the country. On assignment. I couldn't get in touch with him even if I wanted to."

I brought my hand up to massage the bridge of my nose. "Oh."

"Sorry I couldn't be of any help," he said.

For a split second, I considered asking Quinn to do what *he* could to find out Gav's whereabouts, but Rosenow's piercing glare and the other agents' visit this morning, warning me not to speak of yesterday's encounter with anyone, kept me mum. "I don't really believe you're sorry," I said, regaining a bit of my spirit. "But I thank you for taking the time to get in touch."

He hung up without saying another word.

"Anything we can help you with?" Rosenow asked.

I trusted this woman; I had from the very start. She was as solid an agent as I'd ever encountered, and she was a nice person to boot. Until I got the all clear from Gav, however, I'd keep it all to myself. The only exception I would have made was with

Yablonski. Unfortunately for me, he was out of reach.

"Thanks," I said. "This time it's a personal matter."

"Personal?" Her brows arched as she regarded me. "If you need something, or you encounter trouble, don't hesitate," she said. "I hope you know that."

"I do."

My disappointment at not being able to reach Yablonski slowed my pace as I crossed the corridor. I'd held out hope that the man would work magic behind the scenes to find out what was up with Gav. Now that the avenue was closed, I felt hopeless and antsy, as though I had an itch beneath my skin — over my entire body — that I couldn't reach, let alone scratch.

"Hey, Josh." I injected cheer into my voice as I returned to the kitchen. This kid deserved my best effort and that meant I needed to be fully involved in teaching him. As hard as it was for me to let go of my anxiety, I again willed myself to compartmentalize. I couldn't help Gav and knew that sitting and staring at the clock until he called or got word to me was out of the question. I had a young, capable boy here, eager to learn all he could about mastering kitchen basics. Waiting was probably my least favorite thing, but in this case, I needed to buck up and embrace whatever patience I could muster.

As though he sensed my newfound resolve, Josh grinned at me. "I think it's going okay, Ollie. Want to check?"

I tousled his head. "Looks great."

I'd checked my cell phone a hundred times throughout the day and I checked it again as I made my way down the escalator at the McPherson Square Metro station. It felt apt, somehow, that as I descended into the depths below street level, my mood plummeted, too. I'd worked later than usual, hoping to keep my mind occupied, my worries at bay, but nothing had helped. Not completely.

I boarded the train that would take me to Crystal City, and grabbed a window seat that would permit me to stare out at the darkness, at the nothingness of tunnel for at least part of my journey. As the train whooshed me home, its motion served to lull my brain, coaxing me to blank out. Too often I'd encountered trouble on the Metro and I knew better than to allow myself to lose alertness, but today it couldn't be helped. I'd been wired for too long.

I alighted at my stop, and as I made my

way to street level for the short walk to my apartment, I noticed for the first time that a storm was brewing. Sharp winds blew my hair across my face, and chilled my bare skin. The temperatures had been in the upper eighties all day, but now gunmetal clouds rolled in overhead, like giant, gray waves in the sky. The slate-colored patch behind them didn't offer much hope. Thunder shook the sidewalk, and an electric zigzag lit the sky, as though some angels had just taken my picture. I rubbed the bumps forming on my upper arms and hurried across the street, ducking against the first fat raindrops that plopped atop my head.

I made it to my building's front door two seconds too late. A rush of icy water caught me straight in my back as I yanked open the door. Shaking off as much rain as I could, I waved hello to James at the front desk.

"You're lucky," he said by way of greeting. "Supposed to pour all night. Looks like you missed the worst of it."

I shivered. "Looks like."

"I hope you're not planning to go back out again. Supposed to be a doozy. Time to batten down the hatches." He laughed. I didn't know why.

I turned to stare out the door as rain sluiced across the glass, making the world look both gloomy and blurry-beautiful at once. Returning my attention to James, I reminded him that if Gav came by there was no need to make him wait, or even call upstairs for my authorization. "Let him come straight up, okay?"

"I haven't seen your young man here for a few days. Everything okay?"

"Fine," I lied. "He's working tonight. I don't know what time he'll be free."

James winked.

When I got to my floor, Mrs. Wentworth was waiting for me outside her apartment door, which she'd left slightly ajar. "Did you call your mother?"

"I did. She's very happy for us."

Beaming, Mrs. Wentworth spoke loudly into her apartment. "Stan, Ollie did call home. Her mother and grandmother are thrilled."

Despite myself, I smiled at Mrs. Wentworth's announcement. She watched out for me, and regarded me fondly, like she might a daughter. Or maybe even granddaughter. I often felt like an only child in this apartment building, among dozens of parents. The average age here was probably near sixty. I liked it quiet, and for the most part, the other tenants were gently friendly, though most kept to themselves. Except for the fact that they all seemed excessively interested in my work at the White House, I had no real complaints.

My elderly neighbor inched closer, lowering her voice. "What's wrong, Olivia? You should be floating on clouds right now."

"Everything is fine," I said. Not my first lie of the day, though I hoped it might be my last. "There's a lot going on that I can't talk about."

She winked. "Classified, you mean?"

"Exactly." I pointed to my door, hoping she'd take the hint. "I should probably get in. Lots to do tonight and I'm wiped."

She pulled up a freckled wrist to check her watch, but her bones were so small she had to spin the jeweled band to see the time. "It's Saturday night and it's early. Don't start getting all housewifely already."

"Not a chance of that," I said. By this point, tension had me ready to run screaming into my apartment, where I could bolt my door against the rest of the world. I liked my elderly neighbor very much but I needed to put an end to this grueling day. The sooner I made it safely into my personal enclave, the happier I'd be. "Have a good evening, Mrs. Wentworth. Please give Stan my best, too."

She regarded me suspiciously, as always. Mrs. Wentworth saw conspiracies in everything. As I scooted past her, I realized that over the years I'd given her plenty of reason to be leery. I couldn't blame her for her nosiness. Just as I couldn't blame myself for mine.

Once inside my apartment, I peeled off my damp shirt and threw it into the bathtub. I grabbed a fresh top and pulled it over my head when I heard a knock at my door. Tugging the shirt's hem down, I hurried to answer, knowing that it was Mrs. Wentworth who must have forgotten to mention "one last thing."

Pasting on my politest smile, I unlatched the bolt and opened the door barely wide enough to peer out. Maybe she'd get the hint.

It wasn't Mrs. Wentworth.

"Hey."

With one hand gripping his cane so tightly I thought his bones might break through the skin, Gav stared down at me, trying to smile. His hair was wet from the rain, dripping onto his shoulders. "Can I come in?"

CHAPTER 10

I'd already swung the door open, grabbing his free arm as emotion crashed over me in hot, happy waves. "Get in here and let's get you dried off. Where were you? What happened?" My voice rose with each frantic word.

"Are you angry?" Gav took longer to make his way in than he should have. He winced with every step.

I heard Mrs. Wentworth's door shut one second before I closed mine. "What happened?" I asked again, trying hard to modulate my tone. "I'm not angry with you. I'm . . ."

I struggled to sort myself out. I'd always been fully in charge of my emotions and able to remain objective. Since Gav had entered my life, however, I found myself suddenly more vulnerable, so much more at risk.

"I'm furious at whoever kept you from

calling me," I finally said as I got him a towel. "Who was it? What did they want?" A second later I noticed the deep creases around his bloodshot eyes. I noticed his clothes. "You haven't changed since I saw you last."

He waved away my concerns. "I'm fine."

Finally softening my reaction, I said, "Sit down. What can I get you?"

He made his way in, lowering himself slowly onto the sofa in my living room. Although he looked as though he'd prefer to sprawl out backward and stare at the ceiling, he sat at the far end, looping his cane over the couch's rolled arm. "I'm too tired to eat." Patting the cushion next to him, he said, "Sit with me, Ollie."

I sat down, one leg crossed underneath me, facing him. "You're hurt."

He reached an arm around me, causing me to shift so that we sat side by side. Pulling me in tight, he asked, "Have you told anyone what we saw at Evan's? Anyone at all?"

"Sargeant knows that you and I encountered a problem, but I didn't give him any specifics."

Gav took a deep breath and let it out. "Good."

"But two agents came to see me."

Gav's grip on my shoulder tightened. "Who?" he asked. "Did they give you their names?"

"It was two of the men in the gas masks," I said. "Tyree and Larsen."

Gav let his head drop back against the top of the couch cushion. "I told them to leave you alone. I told them."

"What's going on?"

He didn't answer. "Let me guess: They wanted to know if any of the victims spoke, right?"

"Exactly. I take it they asked you that, too."

He grunted the affirmative. "I told them to leave you alone," he said again.

"What's happening?"

Head still back, he rolled it side to side. "Whatever it is, it's big."

"Are we involved? Or now that they've debriefed us both, are we in the clear?"

"I think they'll leave us alone. For now."

"What do you mean, 'for now'?"

"Did you read the newspaper?" He started to get up, but I pushed him back.

"I'll get it." I hurried to the kitchen and grabbed my copy. "Here," I said, handing it to him.

He opened to page five. Down low, a one-column, three-paragraph story sat next to an ad for discount mattresses. "Take a look."

The article was attributed to Daniel Davies of *The People's Journal.* "That's the guy who was giving Sargeant such a hard time," I said, and explained about the press conference.

"He clearly didn't get his facts right," I said, pointing. The article reported the accidental deaths of Evan Bonder and four others, all named. The story went on to explain that the five men were apparently the victims of carbon monoxide poisoning. "This was clearly a murder. The victims were bound and gagged."

Gav nodded.

"And he says they died of carbon monoxide. It's summertime. Doesn't that usually happen when furnaces back up?"

Gav took a deep breath. The stitches probably still hurt him, but he masked the pain. For my sake, I'm sure.

"No question that it's a cover-up. Pure and simple. There's much more at stake here, but it's clear they want to keep the truth out of the public eye. Whether this reporter is in on it, or he's been fed erroneous information, I can't tell." He tapped the paper. "Tyree warned me to walk away. Leave this alone. This article seals it. It's clear they've got the power to keep this quiet."

"But you aren't going to walk away, are you?"

"Evan was my friend," Gav said. "He asked me for help. How can I walk away? There's no chance that this is a simple co-incidence. He called me for help with a problem that he thought was too big for him to handle. Next thing I know, he's dead."

"How long were they like that before we arrived?"

"They're not going to share pathology with me," he said, "but from what I could tell, it didn't look as though they'd been dead for very long."

We were silent for a while, then Gav said, "I owe it to Evan to look into this on my own. I don't trust that Tyree and his cohorts will keep me informed."

"Can I help?"

He shook his head. "Not with investigating," he said. "I know these people and you don't. They're liable to resort to drastic measures if they think security is at stake."

"Is it?"

"There's too much to take in right now for me to know what's going on. I have to dig. Quietly, though." He must have seen the look on my face because he added, "You know I'll tell you whatever I learn. We'll talk. You have good instincts, Ollie. I've always said that. Don't worry, you'll be involved. I just can't have you out on the front lines."

I considered that. And understood. "What do you make of their fixation on one of the victims having talked? Do you think they were hoping that one of them might have told us who did this to them?"

"I'm convinced of it," he said. "They thought I knew more than I did, that's for sure. Did they try to intimidate you?"

I liked the way he phrased that — "Did they *try,*" as though he knew they wouldn't succeed. Gav's faith in me made my heart swell.

"A little," I said. A second later I realized that their attempts to intimidate Gav wouldn't have been nearly as polite as mine had been. "They didn't hurt you, did they?"

He gave me a sideways glance. He seemed amused by the question. "Tyree's not that foolish. They questioned me hard, but they did everything by the book. I had no reason not to comply."

"Who are *they,* anyway?"

"Friends. At least, they used to be."

"Not Tyree, though."

"No, not him." Gav straightened. "Tyree's smart. Top of his class at Glynco. Kicked everyone's butt in training. He's good. Really good."

"You usually hold people like that in high regard. What's different about this guy?"

"Tyree is out to make a name for himself. Always has been," Gav began slowly. "Most of the time that wouldn't bug me. I get it. We all strive to go above and beyond, and if we're recognized for our efforts, all the better."

I waited.

"Tyree and I were friends at first. Not the kind of friends who hang out together on our days off, you understand, but we liked each other. Respected one another."

"Until?"

"Until the first time we had to work together. It was one of those team-building exercises. You know, the kind of setup that isn't life or death, but trains you for that kind of situation. Tyree and I were the senior members of a five-person group. The three others were recent recruits. All men. The idea was for the two of us to work with the new guys and assess them. Submit reports." He waved a finger in the air, emphasizing. "You need to understand that this was a first run for the younger group. We allow mistakes. At that point in training, we *want* them to make mistakes. Sometimes that's where you learn the most."

Gav took a deep breath, tensing again. I knew he was exhausted, but he was determined to finish his story.

"These kids were good. Really good. Instead of Tyree being supportive, however, he knocked them down at every opportunity." Gav stared up at the ceiling as though watching it all happen again. "Could be he thought that by being tough he'd get more out of them, I suppose, but I got the impression Tyree felt intimidated."

"By newbies?"

"That's the thing," Gav said, turning to face me. "It was like he saw these kids as a threat. Anybody who was in the service before him, or who came in alongside him — me, for instance — was considered worthy in his eyes. Not so the rookies. Worse, one of the three kids came across like a comedian. I'm pretty sure he was using humor to keep his head straight. We all have coping mechanisms to keep fear at bay. This was his."

Gav shrugged. "Tyree hated that most of all. The guy has no sense of humor." He held up his free hand in a helpless gesture. "I find that to be true with anyone who can't laugh at himself or herself. They resent those who can. Anyway, I could practically see fireworks shooting out the top of Tyree's head whenever this kid had a good idea, or suggested a method or tactic we hadn't tried before."

"Why would that bother him? I'd think that if your subordinates succeeded, that would reflect well on both of you."

"That's how I saw it." Gav shook his head. "Tyree told me he was going to wash the kid out. Write up a report that would have him tossed from the program. I told him I thought he was nuts. The kid was smart, quick, and exactly the sort of guy we needed on the job. Tried to explain the young guy's humor, but Tyree wouldn't listen. He filed his report. I filed mine."

"And the kid?"

"He got to stay. They took my word over Tyree's. I made the case to my superior that Tyree might have anger management issues. They took it under advisement and sent him for a psychiatric evaluation."

"You have to do that before you join the Secret Service, don't you?"

"That doesn't mean they can't order follow-ups." Gav's shoulders relaxed as he continued. "Tyree passed, but his career stalled."

"All of this from a report he filed?"

Gav fixed me with a look. "The last thing

you want in the field is an out-of-control agent. This episode with Tyree, due in part to my involvement, sent up warning flags. He must have realized how close he came to blowing it because he toed the line from that point on. Since then, he's become the model agent. Never steps out of bounds anymore. Never shows emotion." With a sigh of resignation, he added, "I had a feeling it was all simmering beneath the surface. Got my proof today. Loud and clear."

"Can't you do something? Report him?"

"If I thought he was a threat to national security, I wouldn't hesitate to do everything in my power to see him pitched. But that's not the case here. Anyway, he managed to beat the anger management issue. Maybe he deserved to."

"He sounds like a jerk."

"Arrogance isn't a deal breaker." Gav's arm snugged tighter. "Good thing, otherwise I'd have been bounced a long time ago."

"You're not arrogant."

"Oh yeah? Think back to when we first met. Remember that guy?"

I did. Tucking myself in closer, though careful not to press hard against Gav's stitches, I mumbled a nearly incoherent, "Uh-huh."

He pressed his lips against the top of my head. "At that point, did you ever envision this?"

I laughed. "Not a chance."

As we talked, Gav's limbs loosened and his words started to come more slowly. "Get some rest," I said.

He didn't argue. As I disengaged myself from under his arm, he peeled open one eye. "President is talking tonight. Don't forget."

I glanced at the clock. President Hyden would be on in about ten minutes. While it was still unusual for the president to schedule an address on weekends, we were getting used to the practice. Recently, President Hyden had begun taking advantage of the all-news-all-the-time culture that had evolved over the years. He'd said he hoped the move toward more transparency would benefit us all. "Wouldn't you rather sleep?"

"Let's watch," he said, stifling a yawn.

I grabbed the remote and tuned to a local network; a reality show was just winding down. I switched to an all-news channel where political pundits were doing their best to predict what the president might have to say tonight.

Making my way to the kitchen, I said, "I'll get you something to eat." Even if he didn't touch it until after he'd slept for a while, Gav needed strength to heal. He'd been coming along well since his emergency surgery, but the last few days' events weren't exactly what the doctor meant when he'd ordered time off.

I put together a very basic ham and cheese sandwich, grilling it just long enough to melt the cheese and toast the rye bread. With about thirty seconds to spare before the presidential address, I scooped some leftover pasta salad onto Gav's plate, and rinsed off a few fresh strawberries for dessert. By the time I made it back into the living room, President Hyden was greeting the American people and Gav was fast asleep.

I placed the plate on the coffee table and turned down the TV's volume so that Gav wouldn't be wakened by spontaneous applause from the audience. The presentation was being held in the Brady Press Briefing Room. How appropriate, I thought. That was one of the places where Gav and I had first gotten to know one another.

The president talked about our country's relationship with Durasi and then segued into the reasons for the upcoming state dinner. I'd have thought that any discussions of peace would be welcomed throughout the land, but it wasn't so. Outside the White

House, across Pennsylvania Avenue in La-
fayette Square, a group had arranged an
anti-Durasi rally. I wasn't entirely sure what
they hoped to gain by protesting the Durasi
president's visit, but they'd been a loud and
vocal presence lately, nonetheless.

Although most people spoke highly of
peace, some, like those chanting in La-
fayette Square tonight, balked when it came
to inviting sworn enemies to the table. Others voiced their disapproval in much less
civilized ways. When news of the upcoming
peace accords and state dinner had become
known, protests against Durasi grew violent
in some cities around the country.

President Hyden's talk tonight sought to
quell such displays and bring the American
people together in compromise.

Everything he said was more or less a
rehash of what he'd said before, the only
difference being that this time it was a
formal address. I turned away from the TV
to look at Gav. With his head back and his
mouth gone slack, he was finally finding his
own version of peace. I was about to move
his legs, so that he could lie on his side
versus remain sitting, when President Hyden's next remark caught my attention.

"And as we move forward with more
diplomatic methods, one of the most impor-

tant and groundbreaking changes we plan to adopt will be reducing our reliance on mercenary forces in Durasi."

Mercenary forces were exactly what Rosenow had been talking about today, Kalto in particular.

I sat forward and increased the volume ever so slightly.

"What's going on?" Gav asked.

"I'm sorry. I didn't mean to wake you."

He rubbed his face and straightened, leaning elbows on his knees. "How much did I miss?"

I pointed, not wanting to talk over the president and miss what came next. When he called on a reporter in the audience for a follow-up question, I said, "Mercenary forces."

Gav nodded.

The president went on, repeating himself. His goal, he said, was to eliminate the United States' need for any mercenary teams anywhere. He went on to explain that we had contracts with several such companies and that we would be availing ourselves of their teams' services to the extent of our contractual obligations, but that in the future, if all went as planned, those contracts would not be renewed.

"That's weird," I said.

"President Hyden has been against mercenary forces from the very start," Gav said. "Why do you think this is weird?"

I told him about talking with Agent Rosenow earlier and how she explained that Kalto would be working with us at the White House.

Gav frowned. "At one point not long ago, mercenary forces — hired troops — seemed like a great idea. Little by little, however, we started to find that a few of the companies have been working to undermine the efforts of our armed forces, in an attempt to bolster their own worth. They claim to have the United States' security as their top priority, but we've found that many of these companies operate under their own agenda."

"That's not good."

"Not good for the country, definitely not good for morale. Kalto and others are businesses. They exist to make a profit. Nothing wrong with that, unless you play dirty."

"Kalto is dirty?"

Gav shook his head. "I've heard complaints against a few other protective companies, but never Kalto. You met Baran, huh?" Gav looked impressed. "He tried to hire me away from the Secret Service a few years ago. Made a nice offer. Gotta admit, I was tempted."

"What stopped you?"

Gav's gaze was fierce, though not with anger. More with passion. "I'm already where I want to be," he said. "The Secret Service. Working for the protection of the country, of the president."

"A sense of duty?"

He heard the compliment in my question and waved it off. "Call it what you will, but I knew that a fatter paycheck wouldn't provide the same satisfaction. It was an easy decision, actually. Still, because I wanted a second opinion on the matter, to reassure myself I wasn't making the mistake of a lifetime, I talked it over with Joe Yablonski before I gave Baran a final answer."

"And?"

"Joe supported me. Not only is he not a fan of mercenary forces on principle, he told me that he believed that the job prospects were not nearly as good as everyone believed them to be. Turns out, his predictions were right." Gav nodded at the TV. "President Hyden isn't a fan. Neither is the secretary of defense. I'd hazard a guess that, including Joe, they're the triple threat behind this decision."

"The secretary of defense?" I repeated. "Cobault?" A retired four-star general, Theodore Cobault was one of the most respected and revered members of the president's cabinet. And an incredibly nice man, whom I'd had the pleasure to meet a couple of times.

Gav pointed at the screen. "You can bet that Cobault's hand is guiding this decision in a big way."

"How do you know that? Cobault is notoriously mute when it comes to talking to the press. Do you remember that altercation when he was being pressed for an answer to explain his position on a diplomatic crisis *before* the press conference announcing the president's decision? I know I'm paraphrasing, but Cobault said something like, 'If I wanted my views known to the public, I'd take out an ad. Now get out of my way and let me do my job.' "

"I remember." A corner of Gav's mouth curled up. "Joe and I had lunch with him not long ago."

"You had lunch with the secretary of defense?" I asked. "And you didn't tell me?"

"You didn't need to know," he said with a grin. "You see why I wouldn't want to give all this up? If I'd taken Baran up on his offer, I'd miss out on being part of the real decisions. Part of what shapes our country for future generations. I'd have been off in a faraway land for the past half-dozen years."

He leaned sideways so that our shoulders touched. "And if I'd gone that route, I would never have met you."

"Well then," I said, "you definitely made the right decision."

CHAPTER 11

The night gremlins — the nasty, nefarious little buggers that find their glee in being able to explode molehills into a range of Everests — kept me from sleeping well. Gav had gone back to his own apartment after the president's news conference. He hadn't changed clothes in more than forty-eight hours and, once he'd shaken off the fogginess from his catnap, had woken up sufficiently to make his way home safely. I saw him off, advising him to try to sleep, never realizing that I would be unable to do so myself.

I'd always found that the way to thwart the night gremlins was to give up any hope of sleep, to abandon the demons and their insidious ways, and start the day despite their trickery. Somehow, the act of getting out of bed, of showering and turning lights on, made the little fiends less intimidating. Starting the day was the only way I knew to fight back.

Thus, I found myself on the earliest Metro to the White House in the morning. Ever since Virgil had taken over the First Family's meals and I was no longer responsible for breakfast, I'd taken to coming in a little later. Today, however, once I'd decided to get out of my apartment, I thought I'd be nice and see if Virgil could use a little help.

His presence in my kitchen caused me significant angst, and the conundrum of how to better our situation was never far from my mind. If Sargeant couldn't negotiate Virgil's release — and I had serious doubts that he could — I needed to turn the testy chef around, to convince him that I wasn't his enemy.

The Metro train was quiet this morning. Lonely. I ignored the jostling melancholy that could easily overwhelm me. Being up and out and ready for work gave me strength to shake off the gremlins' hold. Once I was on my way, I couldn't be touched. Or so I told myself.

By the time I reached the McPherson Square Station, I'd come up with a radical solution for handling Virgil. I'd asked myself: What, more than anything else, drove the man to his best efforts? Fame. No question about it. Virgil adored being in the limelight and no matter how much media love was showered upon him, he craved more. A natural performer, he knew precisely how to craft a sound bite that would resonate and repeat. One that would always be attributed to him. Clever Virgil. Talented Virgil. He wanted to be the first person everyone thought of when the title "White House Chef" came to mind.

To his everlasting dismay, he wasn't. I was.

As far as I was concerned, celebrity was overrated. He could have it. I would be happy to run my kitchen without ever encountering the media again. The thing was, as gladly as I'd give up my reputation with the press, I would not relinquish power over the workings of the White House kitchen. Not without a fight. Not to anyone, and especially not to Virgil.

The trick was in finding middle ground.

These days — due to some fabulous dinners we'd produced, as well as a few adventures that had taken place behind the scenes and resolved successfully — I felt about as secure as I'd ever felt in my role as executive chef.

But that didn't make working with Virgil any easier.

This state dinner with Durasi dignitaries promised to be an extraordinary event at the White House. Newspapers, magazines, websites, blogs, Facebook, and Twitter would cover every moment in loving detail from the time the Durasi dignitaries left their country until they departed U.S. soil. Every nuance would be analyzed. Minutiae would make headlines.

With the way our kitchen was structured now, Virgil had nothing to do with state dinners. Bucky, Cyan, and I handled the process of food preparation from start to finish, overseeing temporary staffers where necessary. Virgil, if he helped at all, did so only under duress.

What if, I thought. What if I *included* Virgil in the plans? If he felt as though his contributions were valued, if he thought that he could be credited with some of the evening's success, then maybe he'd begin to feel more like a team player. I knew that if I attempted this, I couldn't simply give him a task or two and hope he'd fall in line. I'd have to truly include him fully, every step of the way. My attempt would have to be a genuine one.

I wasn't wholly certain that Virgil would go for it. Nor was I convinced that it would work. This would be a heck of a leap of faith for me, but if it resulted in better relationships between team members, then we'd all succeed.

Virgil was busy with breakfast preparations when I walked in. Except for the sound of his bustling and the few ingredients he hadn't yet cleaned up around his workspace, the place was quiet and clean. I took a deep breath of the warm, eggy smells that rolled out of the oven when he opened the door, and smiled. My plan for the new day was working. Nighttime's gremlins — even those that hung around after waking — were beginning to lose their hold on me. "Hi, Virgil," I said.

He jumped, then glared at me.

"Sorry," I said. "Didn't mean to startle you. Whatever you're making smells fabulous."

His face was pink from the oven's heat as he lifted the casserole dish to the countertop. "What's that supposed to mean?" he asked.

I snapped on a smock and grabbed an apron. Deep breath. "Exactly what I said. Whatever you've made smells heavenly. What is it?"

"A breakfast casserole."

Well, wasn't that helpful? I decided to ignore the snub. "I'm sure the First Family will enjoy it. It looks great."

He eyed me suspiciously despite the fact

156

that I routinely made sure to compliment him whenever he deserved it. I was willing to do almost anything — short of compromising my own core values, of course — if doing so might calm the rough waters between us. It hadn't helped thus far, but being nice to another person couldn't hurt, so I never stopped trying. That old definition of what constitutes a fool flashed through my mind.

Still giving me the evil eye, he asked, "Why are you in so early?"

I told him the truth. "Couldn't sleep."

He'd used a pair of dishtowels to get the casserole dish out of the oven. He tossed one atop the counter and slapped the other over his shoulder. "I thought you and Sargeant were buddies. I heard he threw you under the bus at his press conference."

Was that glee I detected in Virgil's glittering eyes? "Not at all," I said. "The press conference wasn't about me."

"It's always about you."

"Virgil." I strove to keep a pleasant expression on my face. "This is no way to start out our morning. Is there something on your mind?"

He dragged the towel from his shoulder and held it tight in his fist. Glancing around as though worried that others might hear, he took a step closer. "It's the same thing that's been on my mind from the very start," he said quietly. "Except now it's all fresh again, with Sargeant in charge and Doug let go. Why do you even have to ask? We both know I deserve to be the executive chef here, but because you're the first woman in the role nobody wants to touch you. You're golden."

I bit my lip tight to keep from retorting. I sensed that we were going to have it out now and I hoped this would prove to be our "once and for all." If so, I needed to let him vent until he believed he'd had his say. Harder still, I needed to listen if I had any hope of having a working relationship with this man in the future. I reminded myself to take the high road.

"Not only am I *not* the executive chef," he went on, "which, I'm sure you recall, was the agreement I had before I started working here . . ."

That wasn't true, but arguing the point wouldn't change his perspective. I kept quiet, focusing on what was driving him — what he was truly trying to communicate — as his voice rose.

"Not only do I suffer that particular indignity — Do you have any idea how many magazines had me pegged to take over for you? No, of course you don't. You don't care about magazine features. You prefer to make headlines with your reckless adventures." He'd gotten louder and seemed to catch himself. Muttering now, he added, "Like that requires any real talent at all for cooking."

None of this was new, but the fact that I wasn't responding to his diatribe was. I could tell that my silence unnerved him. He crossed his arms and stared down at me with insolent impatience. "The worst of it is that I'm not even next in command. Whether I'm named, or that fool Bucky is, hasn't been decided yet. You can't run a kitchen like that."

"That's a point we can agree on."

He blinked, startled.

I held up my hands. "And with that in mind, I'd like to try a new approach."

He lowered his eyelids, as though feigning boredom. "Yeah? Like what?"

"It's true that I would favor Bucky as my next in command."

Shifting his weight, he gave a dramatic sigh. "News flash there. Not."

I let his comment roll off of me, reminding myself to keep my eyes on the prize. Getting into a battle with Virgil at this point, even if I emerged the victor, wouldn't be a win at all if our relationship remained as strained as it was. Baby steps. I needed to take this slowly.

"Bucky and I have worked together for a long time. You and I are still getting to know one another." When he looked about to make another disparaging remark, I added, "It's been a rocky road. I think we can both admit that."

"What are you proposing?" he asked. "If you're trying to get me to back off, I won't. I deserve to be treated better than I have been."

"I'm not asking you to back off." We were getting to the crux of it now. "I'm hoping for the opposite, in fact. I want to suggest a blurring of the lines."

"Come again?"

"You do have a lot to offer, Virgil. Whatever else you might believe, you have to know that I respect your talent."

His mouth twisted. "What are you up to?"

"A truce," I said. "The question is, are you up to it, too?" I broached my idea, suggesting he play a bigger role in our event planning. That he help us with state dinners, guest banquets, and events.

"What's the catch?"

"No catch. Everyone knows that you provide wonderful meals for the First Family every day. There's no question. What the public *doesn't* see is you taking part in the state-level events. Like this one we have coming up with the president of Durasi. You know this will be a mammoth undertaking. The press will want to sniff out every detail. Being part of it will be like being part of history."

"I'm supposed to believe that you'd open yourself up to criticism?"

"Criticism? How do you figure?"

"Allowing me to work my magic for this event would mean that you'd risk being overshadowed by my brilliance."

Did this man actually hear the words that were coming out of his mouth? I began to second-guess my decision, though it was a little late for that now. He was the sort of person who didn't understand the basic concept that sharing the responsibility meant sharing accolades. I was willing to include him in this experience only because I knew that when people came together, everyone rose a little higher.

Though I had no words to be able to explain this, I held out the fervent hope that once he saw it happen, once he felt that camaraderie and experienced it for himself, he would finally understand.

"Keep in mind," I said, "this isn't a

competition. It isn't you versus me. Nor you versus Bucky. We work as a team. Team," I repeated. "All of us. Cyan, the SBA chefs, the butlers, too. Can you do that?"

"I've run kitchens far larger than this one," he said, as though that was an answer.

"Our physical kitchen may be small, but our impact is huge. I'll ask you again, Virgil. Can you be a team player?"

He regarded me with suspicion. "Of course I can. And I accept your challenge. Without doubt, I will be the best team player this kitchen has ever encountered."

Not quite the sentiment I was looking for. Still, it was a start.

CHAPTER 12

Bucky wasn't thrilled with the new arrangement.

"Here's the thing," I said. We were in the refrigeration room, a short walk to the kitchen, but fairly safe for a private conversation. "Life here in the kitchen can't continue the way it's been going. Virgil's behavior has become intolerable."

"So you decided to reward him?" Bucky asked. "Don't you see that by giving him more responsibility instead of less, you're sending the message that he's your go-to guy?"

"That's not the message, and you know it."

Bucky ran a hand along his bald head, back and forth as though trying to massage away tension. "Maybe I know better, but does he? What about Sargeant and Mrs. Hyden? If Virgil gets to be the diva with the family's meals *and* special events, there will be no stopping him. He'll be your go-to guy by default, at least in everyone else's mind. Before you know it, he'll be coming after my job." Bucky faced the ceiling, frowning. "What am I saying? He already is."

"He will never have your job. Not if I have anything to say about it."

"Mark my words: Once he has my spot, he'll come after yours, too."

"Bucky." I laid a hand on his arm.

He shook me off, turning away. "Maybe you know what you're doing." He scratched his head again, harder this time, frustration leaving white lines that turned red as his fingernails pressed back and forth. "You've turned this department upside down since Henry left." Facing me, he quickly added, "That came out wrong. I didn't mean it as a slam."

"How *did* you mean it?"

He put his hands out as he explained. "Henry was great. A big personality, a big heart. One of the best bosses I've ever had. When he picked you to succeed him, I wasn't too happy about it."

"I remember."

"And yet . . ." Bucky wrinkled his nose and shook his head. "You were exactly the right choice for the job. I gave you grief at first."

I remembered that, too, but kept quiet.

"You turned me around," he said. "You even turned Sargeant around, and to this day I have no idea how you managed that." He pointed toward the kitchen. "Your decision to include Virgil more instead of less goes against every fiber of my being. I can't stand that guy. I want him gone, not up in my business every minute. And you know he will be."

"There may be some bumps in the road," I agreed. "With a personality like Virgil's, I'd expect quite a few."

"Yeah," Bucky answered me absentmindedly. He clearly had more to say. "What I'm getting to is this, Ollie. I don't agree with you, but I trust you." He shrugged. "You've earned that."

My heart warmed so much that I almost pulled Bucky into a hug. The only thing that stopped me was knowing how much that would embarrass him. "Thank you," I said. "That means a lot to me."

He pointed at me. "Don't think I'm going to go extra easy on him or anything."

"Virgil has had a chip on his shoulder from the start. Maybe if we work hard to treat him as a friend instead of an interloper, he'll come around."

Bucky gave a wry frown. "I wouldn't

165

count on it, Ollie. In fact, I think this may be your toughest challenge yet."

Cyan tapped a pen against the side of her head as she studied the chart on the counter before her. "There is so much information here. What did you call this file again, Ollie?"

"It's our spreadsheet of fun," I said.

She looked up. Her contacts today were such a dark chocolate brown that their depth took me aback. "You've got a warped sense of amusement," she said. "Did you see all the new people who've been added to the guest list? I don't have dietary information on any of them."

I came around to look over her shoulder. Bucky was at the computer, pulling up new entrée options for us to consider for the Durasi state dinner. Virgil was busy preparing lunch for the First Lady and her staff. Butlers lined up as Virgil ladled savory tomato-basil soup into a large tureen to be served tableside. As soon as that was done and sent along, he plated the meal: wedge salads sprinkled with crumbled blue cheese. Not bad, I thought. Virgil often served odd combinations, but today's choices were some I might very well select myself.

Both Josh and Abigail were out for the day

with their grandmother. The president had chosen to take lunch in the West Wing's Navy Mess, so Virgil's responsibilities were a little lighter than usual. A perfect opportunity to bring him into our discussion.

Cyan hadn't reacted well either when I'd forewarned her about Virgil's new involvement. Arms crossed, she'd pressed her lips and pronounced that this plan was a bad one. Unequivocally bad. Where Bucky had been willing to cut me some slack, Cyan told me flat out that she thought this was a terrible idea. "I'm a team player and a good worker," she'd said, "so I'll cooperate. But nothing will help with that guy, Ollie. I don't know how you can't see that."

Such rousing support. Buoyed by my belief that there was good in almost everyone — even someone as difficult as Virgil — I waited until the last butler had taken off for the First Lady's luncheon in her East Wing offices before rallying the troops.

I gathered them all together to talk. Bucky, Cyan, and I leaned forward, elbows on the chilly countertop, huddled around the information we'd assembled thus far. Virgil stood to Cyan's right, drying a handful of forks, watching us with disdain.

I started our impromptu meeting with an overview. "We all know that this upcoming state dinner may very well turn out to be the most important one President Hyden has ever hosted in his presidency."

"Assuming it goes smoothly," Virgil said.

"We will make sure it does," I said. "Moving on and maintaining a positive attitude, let's work with what we know so far. In addition to most of the regular guests, for which we've prepared dietary dossiers, we'll be required to prepare for the entire Durasi contingent. Do we have information on their individual needs yet?"

Cyan pulled a sheet out from beneath several others. "Sargeant told me to count on at least forty Durasi dignitaries. At this point we have updates for three of them." She made a face. "That's the bad news. The good news is that none of them have any dietary restrictions."

"Three down, thirty-seven to go. You'll stay on top of this?" I asked her.

"I never thought I'd say this," she said, "but Sargeant is a lot easier to work with than I'd have expected. He's been in the job, what, a couple of days? Already he's got lists and charts . . ."

"Spreadsheets of fun?" I teased.

She gave me a sardonic smile. "He's on top of everything. What a relief, after the Doug fiasco."

Across from me, Virgil reacted with a frown. He was still drying the same set of forks, and doing so with such fidgety energy that I was afraid he'd wear them away to shiny toothpicks. "Doug had a lot of ideas for change around here," Virgil said. "Too bad he never got the chance to prove himself."

"We have Sargeant in charge now, and that's all that really matters," I said. "Now, getting back to the topic at hand, I'm glad to hear that things are working well for you, Cyan. I've found that Sargeant always strives to do his best. Mind you, I've had occasion where I've disagreed with his methods, but we're getting along better now." I waited for her to make eye contact with me. "And who'd have ever predicted that?"

Cyan got my message. She bit the insides of her cheeks as she slid a glance toward Virgil. He remained oblivious.

I turned to Bucky next. "Any changes to the menu we need to discuss?"

"There's news of another listeria situation coming from some farms down south. We're going to need to reconsider some of our fruit options. I'm working on that today."

"That's not good news, but I'm glad you're on top of it." Still leaning forward, I turned my attention to the final member of our group. How many times did he need to wipe down those forks? Was our arrogant chef nervous? "I was thinking that you might want to participate with the tasting, Virgil. Bucky is running it. We're facing a quicker time frame than we're used to, but Mrs. Hyden agreed to hold it tomorrow" — I shuffled through the papers to see the note I'd scribbled — "at three o'clock. That's cutting it close with a Thursday dinner, but everything about this one has been last-minute."

Virgil took a few steps across the kitchen, placed the hyper-dried forks in an upright container on the far side, then rejoined our circle. He gave Bucky a quick glance before asking me, "I've done many, many tastings with Mrs. Hyden before she became First Lady. They weren't these über-structured events like those you run here. They were more casual and, if I may be so bold, more enlightening. There's absolutely no doubt in my mind that I could handle this on my own with no problem." He glanced at Bucky. "No offense."

Bucky pushed off from the countertop, rolling his eyes at me as if to say, "You see?"

Slow and steady, I reminded myself. "We're all sure you could handle the tast-

170

ing, too, Virgil," I said, doing my best to ignore Cyan's huff of indignance. "The thing is, Bucky has already done most of the work —"

"No," Bucky interrupted. "It's okay. Yeah. Sure." His words came out in sharp staccato as though he'd had a sudden brainstorm. "I think it would be great if you handled the tasting on your own." Virgil missed the conspiratorial look that passed between Bucky and Cyan, but I didn't. "How better to leave your mark on the event, right?"

I leaned back far enough to be able to watch both Bucky and Cyan at once. She'd caught Bucky's eye for a confused moment, but then I practically saw the lightbulb flash on over her head. Her words were a half step behind her brain. "Oh . . . yeah. Yeah. Good idea. I mean, great idea." She turned to Virgil with what was obviously a fake nod of approval. "Can't wait to hear how it goes."

What was going on? I narrowed my eyes at her, but she looked away, clearly avoiding me. We would revisit this later.

"Well then, Virgil. It's yours if you want it," I said. "You're sure?"

"I could do it in my sleep."

"Moving on," I said, "let's look at whose

171

information we still need from the American guests who will be attending." I picked up the list. "Is this the most recent version?"

Cyan studied it. "No. Sargeant sent additions in an e-mail about an hour ago. I didn't print it because he said there were likely to be more. Let me go check." She hurried to the computer. While she was gone, Bucky, Virgil, and I continued talking.

"Since you're not doing the tasting tomorrow, Bucky, maybe you and I can sit down and figure out staffing. Have you thought about how many SBA chefs we might need to bring on for this?"

"I . . . uh . . ." It was not like Bucky to stammer at such an easy question. "I have given it thought. We'll need at least eight. Twelve would be better."

"It'll be crowded in here." Wouldn't be the first time, wouldn't be the last. "Let's schedule an hour or so to go over specifics," I said. Dragging out a printout of our combined schedules, I pointed. "Now that you and Cyan don't have to worry about the First Lady's tasting, you're both free for a couple of hours between noon and two, right?"

Cyan hurried back with a freshly printed list. "No, I think we're busy then, aren't we?"

"Doing what?" I pointed to the schedule again. "You haven't listed anything here."

She scratched her nose. "Here, take a look at the updates."

I was about to question her further about the schedule when a name caught my eye. "Tyree?" I said aloud.

"Do you know him?" Cyan asked.

How to answer? "We've met. Briefly." I scanned the remaining names. Tyree's friend Larsen had made the cut, too. "Baran," I said.

"Who is that?"

"Alec Baran. Owner of Kalto."

"The mercenary soldier company?" Bucky asked. "He's coming to the dinner? I don't get it."

"Haven't you read the updated dinner agenda?" I said. "Baran is scheduled to give a speech emphasizing how conditions in Durasi have so greatly improved that his company is no longer needed out there. As a matter of fact, I think at least one other Kalto official has been tagged for a speech that night."

"Plus probably about fifty other people," Cyan said.

I laughed. "Maybe not fifty, but I'll bet at least a dozen. In fact, when I talked with Baran —"

"You talked with Baran? What's he like?" Bucky asked.

It dawned on me that I'd forgotten to mention that I'd met him, too. "Charming. Handsome." I shrugged, careful not to voice my suspicions about the need for additional security during the Durasi dinner. "The important thing is that Kalto is leaving Durasi. That's what they'll want to emphasize during the speeches. One of the fallouts of that decision, however, is that because the president has these contracted hours, he's putting Kalto's people to work here."

"That makes no sense."

"I don't make the decisions," I said. Turning to Cyan, I continued, "But none of this answers my question about the schedule. What's going on? Why can't I meet with you and Bucky?"

She held both hands up. "I forgot. Until just now. Bucky and I promised Sargeant that we'd confer with him."

"About what?" I asked.

Bucky glared at her as he answered me. "He's insisting that every staff member in every department meet with him for a one-on-one."

I couldn't help stating the obvious. "Except that you're going together. That would be two-on-one."

174

Cyan laughed. At this point there was no question about it. They were keeping something from me. I hoped it didn't have to do with Virgil, or my decision to bring him deeper into the fold. It would be a hard enough slog to get him to behave without having to deal with any mischief these two might dream up. The sooner I found out what was going on, the better.

One thing I'd bet my job on: There was no way Sargeant would have called them both in for a meeting, together. I'd talk with him first, then corral these two another time, preferably when Virgil wasn't around.

CHAPTER 13

I decided to talk with Sargeant on the Q.T. The question I had for him wasn't one I cared to put in an e-mail, and calling him on the phone meant I risked being over-heard. I didn't want Bucky or Cyan to know I was checking up on them. I decided to drop in and see if he had a spare moment. When I arrived at the anteroom just outside the chief usher's office, however, a woman I'd never seen before looked up at me.

"May I help you?" she asked.

"I'm looking for Peter Sargeant," I said, starting for his door.

At that, she stood, blocking my way. "I'm sorry. He isn't in right now." A slim, fashion-forward forty-something, she had short, dark hair and a pert expression on her face as she gave me an efficient once-over. Tiny in stature, she wore oversized tortoiseshell glasses and she fingered the side of them as she resumed her seat. "My name is Margaret. I'm Mr. Sargeant's assistant."

"Olivia Paras," I said, leaning to shake her bony hand. "The executive chef."

Her lips formed a circle and if she'd made a sound, it would have been "Oooh . . ." Instead, she said, "Of course. I'm happy to make your acquaintance. May I have Mr. Sargeant call you when he returns?"

Inwardly I grumbled. So much for keeping this on the down-low. "Sure," I said. "But please let him know that this is a conversation I'd prefer to have in private."

Her perfectly trimmed dark eyebrows reacted with a tiny twitch. "Of course," she said smoothly.

"I have time now, Ms. Paras." Sargeant appeared behind me, his voice deeper and more authoritative than I'd ever heard it. "Thank you, Margaret," he said to his assistant. He strode to the door between the two offices, opened it, and ushered me in.

Once he closed the door behind us, I pointed the way we'd come. "She seems very nice."

Sargeant took his seat behind the desk and I sat across from him. "Paul's assistants were out of the office most of the time, running errands, performing tasks." He waved the air. "It got to the point where anyone could pop in and talk to Paul anytime. And

177

when Doug took over, things got worse."
Sargeant shuddered. "My plan is to run a
much tighter organization. Paul was a good
man and a good organizer."

"He was," I agreed.

Sargeant's lips pulled together. Almost a
smile. "I intend to be better." Placing his
hands atop his desk, he regarded me. "Now,
what's on your mind?"

"I understand you're meeting with all staff
members one-on-one," I began.

He nodded. "I think it's wise to start off
by getting to know the people working for
me. I've met nearly everyone, but I want to
give each person a chance to tell me about
his job and about what he brings to the
organization."

"That's a great idea," I said. "I know
Bucky and Cyan are looking forward to
their appointment with you."

He blinked. Then blinked again. "Yes."

"Are you talking with them . . . together?"
I asked.

He puckered his lips, blinking yet again.
"Why do you ask?"

"They said they were meeting you tomorrow. Together."

"And?"

"That seemed a little odd to me."

"Did it?"

"For one-on-one meetings, yeah, I'd say so."

He did a little wiggle with his shoulders. "Nothing at all the matter with that. We have many things to discuss."

I digested that, taking in the fact that the good news was that Bucky and Cyan weren't lying about their alleged meeting with the chief usher. The bad news is that none of this made sense. Unless . . . I lowered my voice despite the fact that I knew Margaret wouldn't be able to hear through the door. "Does this have anything to do with Virgil?"

He fidgeted. "Why do you ask?"

"I've invited Virgil to work on the upcoming Durasi dinner with us. Even though you and I both believe the kitchen is better served with him gone, the fact is that he's here until further notice. Rather than keep fighting, I thought I'd try enticing him to join us. Maybe turn him around."

As I spoke, I watched Sargeant relax. "Good plan, Ms. Paras. I most definitely approve."

"That said," I went on, "there is still the matter of your meeting with Bucky and Cyan. Would you like me to attend, as well?"

He pressed his lips together as though considering it, but I could tell it was for show. Clearly, he didn't want me involved this time. "Thank you, but no. I need to establish a relationship with both staff members, and having you here could slow that process down."

I found all of this very odd. Still, Sargeant could often *be* odd and perhaps this was nothing more than he claimed: an attempt to get to know Bucky and Cyan better. If that was the case, I had to admit that my presence could serve to hinder communication. We had guidelines in place instructing employees how to air grievances. If my staff ever had complaints about me and I wasn't able to resolve them, they'd be required to take their concerns to Sargeant. The idea of a problem of that magnitude was distasteful, but I had to admit that it could happen.

"Fair enough," I said. "If you need anything or change your mind, you know where to find me."

"I do indeed."

I paced the McPherson Square Metro platform that evening, staring at my feet as I walked back and forth, thinking about what Gav had said. I'd missed the prior train by mere seconds and as I paced, more commuters joined me, making me look up from time to time to avoid bumping into them. Within minutes, the area became too crowded for me to keep up my mindless treks up and down the long walkway. I heaved a sigh and stopped moving, choosing instead to stare at the endless sea of concrete rectangles that made up the underground Metro's walls and ceilings. Dull and dim, they presented an ideal, bland surface on which to project my ruminations.

I chanced a look around. Much too crowded to move now. Instead, I bounced on the balls of my feet. Eager, anxious, and wary. I couldn't wait to talk with Gav tonight to find out if he'd discovered anything of interest. Last we'd talked, he'd voiced his intent to discover more about the other victims killed alongside Evan Bonder.

A homeless woman carrying two large shopping bags mumbled what might have been an apology as she bumped my backside.

"It's okay," I said, but she didn't react. I was delayed from returning to my reverie by a prickle teasing its way up the back of my neck. A memory tug. For some reason, the homeless woman seemed to have triggered it. But that made no sense. Shrugging it off, I went back to staring at the lifeless walls, replaying the scene at the Ainsley Street Ministry.

It had been quiet there, too quiet. The

entire neighborhood had appeared desolate. I still wondered if anyone — a neighbor, perhaps? — had seen something and was too afraid to report it. Then again, maybe someone had. Maybe that was the reason for the misguided newspaper piece about a carbon monoxide accident. As Gav had pointed out, there were powerful forces at work here. Clearly, they'd spun the story. But to what end?

Again I thought about how the neighborhood had looked that night, what it had sounded and smelled like. The moment I did, I felt a pinch in my brain. I glanced at the homeless woman again. Her presence seemed to be reminding me that it *hadn't* been completely quiet that day. Rubbing my hands up against my eyes, I recreated the scene . . . walking in . . .

Wait. Back up.

The homeless guy.

Before we'd walked in, we'd parked down the street.

My hands dropped to my sides as a vision of the half-naked man with the walking stick shot to my brain. "He tried to warn us," I said aloud. Embarrassed, I glanced side to side to see if anyone had heard me. The other commuters paid me no attention whatsoever.

I got a better look at the homeless woman. Overflowing with her belongings, her parcels were wide, bulky, and encased within plastic grocery bags that were wedged inside giant paper ones. I couldn't hazard a guess at her age because she kept her head down and wore a purple, patterned scarf over her hair. The day was too warm for so many layers, but maybe it was easier for her to wear as much as she could rather than add it to the bundles she carried. The bags themselves seemed to weigh her down, and I watched people give her a wide berth as she made her way through the crowd, heading back to this end once again.

Her clothes were nondescript, but not dirty. Not ragged, either. She walked hunched over, like an elderly woman might, but she didn't move like an old person. I knew I should ignore her, but curiosity nibbled at me once again. She didn't fit the mold of a homeless person — not exactly. I wondered what her story was.

I wanted to get a better look at her face, but she didn't raise her head. From this distance, about ten feet away, all I could see was a slightly bulbous nose and the bottom of her chin. She bumped into a few other commuters who hadn't seen her coming, but she didn't seem to care. She stopped to stare upward at the arrival time sign, giving me a better look at her face. Definitely not elderly; she was slim with high cheekbones and sucked-in features. Her nose was a smidge too large for her narrow face, and her mouth looked to be permanently down-turned.

I followed her gaze, relieved to see that my train would be arriving in two minutes. Finally. Giving up on my perusal of the homeless woman, I smiled as the distant sound of the oncoming engine poured from the tunnel. The sooner I was home, the better.

As the sounds grew louder, I shuffled closer to the edge, along with the rest of the crowd. I heard a man on my right make a noise that sounded like "Oof," then complain loudly, "Hey." With a dramatic gesture, waving both hands in the air, he stepped away from the homeless woman. "Watch where you're going, lady."

On the move again, probably to snag a prime position to board, she ignored him. Commuters knew that there was no real precision at guessing where the train's doors would land, but we all tried to predict it anyway. I stood with a smaller group, hoping to avoid the crush of boarding that usually happened when a train finally arrived.

The homeless woman wound up next to me, still keeping her head down, her back hunched. The guy she'd bumped gave me a pointed eye roll before inching farther away from her.

In the past whenever I'd encountered a homeless person, they didn't smell so great. Stale body odor usually coupled with weathered mustiness to deliver an unpleasant aroma. This woman, however, had no such scent about her. In fact, I could have sworn she smelled like lavender.

Less than a minute to go before the train was to arrive, I started to look down the tunnel again when I felt firm pressure against my back. In the breathless half-second it took for me to process what was going on, I felt my body weight forced forward. I stutter-stepped at the edge instinctively reaching out to grab something . . . anything . . . to regain my balance.

My fingers grazed another person's bare arm. He or she, reacting just as instinctively, yanked away.

Helpless, I pitched forward. Fear gurgled in my throat and I saw nothing but the dark tracks below me, heard nothing but the approach of the rumbling train. I think I screamed. I know I turned. In an instant, like I was taking a picture, I saw that everyone on the platform had their attention on me. They were alarmed, eyes wide, mouths gaping. One or two reached out to grab me as the homeless woman gave me a final, vicious shove.

I fell sideways, landing hard on the tracks below with a bounce. I scrambled to my feet, aching and bruised. I'd avoided hitting the electrical rail — how? But didn't have time to wonder. My mind screamed at me to climb back up the embankment. Even as adrenaline shot fireworks up the back of my spine, even as I lunged for the reaching hands, I knew it was too late.

The train's light grew larger, its grinding approach louder. I felt the vibration beneath my feet and heard the screams of those above me, urging me to jump. Everything melded at once into a dull roar of terror.

Our brains are amazing instruments. Capable of processing information faster and more efficiently than any computer ever made, they leap into action at the first sign of trouble. In less time than it took to take a breath, I knew that there was no way I'd make it to safety above. No way at all. My brain had vaulted into high gear and had made all the necessary calculations, informing me dispassionately that there was not a chance of outrunning the train, and extremely unlikely I could reach the safety of the platform in time. It also reminded me, unnecessarily, that this engine was too powerful for me to stop with my bare hands.

My brain searched for another way out, assessing, calculating, reporting. Nope. Uh-uh. No. Not going to work. I could feel it surrender to the inevitable.

This was it.

CHAPTER 14

I was dead, or would be in seconds. I knew it deep in my soul, the same way I knew that Gav would take the blame, somehow. He would never forgive himself.

Giving up and going along with a perceived inevitable, however, had never been my style. The helping hands above me, even if they managed to haul me up, wouldn't be enough. There wasn't time to get myself entirely clear of the train's path. My brain's calculations assured me that, even if I were lifted in time, enough of my body would remain hanging over the platform, smack in the train's path. My brain's best guess was that I'd miss my escape opportunity by about one second.

There was no footing for me to use to boost myself up. It was an open, gaping space at my feet. My heart pounded. There was a small, open space beneath the platform lights.

New information. Could I fit?

The only thing my brain knew for certain was that I didn't have time to weigh options. I had to go with my gut or do nothing at all.

I dropped to my hands and knees and scrambled into the dank opening, turning sideways and rolling as deeply into the space — as far away from the tracks — as I could. My elbows hit the side of the wall, my knees scraped the filthy ground and my hand landed on a warm, furry body that squeaked and scurried away. Stifling a scream, I tucked my head, making myself as small as I could.

I pulled myself into a ball, my left foot catching on the rail for a breathless extra moment as the ground vibration grew.

I shut my eyes and covered my head, screaming to be heard above the clacking metallic racket. All at once there was nothing but roar — my own and that of the train — as I was surrounded with squealing, rushing, head-banging noise. The train shot bursts of hot, acrid air under my clothes, and sucked at me like a vacuum. In defiance, I yelled again, louder this time. I refused to die quietly.

When I lowered my arms from the sides of my head, I realized that the noises were exactly right.

The sound the train made as it arrived at my station was the sound it had always made, though quite a bit louder because my head was a mere inches away. I detected no collision, no interruption. It was certainly not silent, which I would have expected if I were dead. The squeaks, the shrill metal sounds, and the whoosh as doors opened above were no different than they'd ever been.

Was I safe? I opened my eyes.

The train blocked my view of the dull concrete wall I'd been studying only moments earlier. The giant, metal monster had stopped next to me. Huffing and idle, but tamed. Quiet.

As heated air continued to buffet my face and arms, I felt a nibble at my ankle. I shook my leg, new panic rising like bile in my throat.

But I was *feeling* it. Really feeling it. Not gazing down after death, via an out-of-body experience.

I came aware of screaming, shouting. People above me, calling for help.

Another nip at my ankle. Hoarsely I yelled, "Get away." Instinctively, I twisted to look over my shoulder then wished I hadn't. Beady eyes caught the scant light and glowed back at me. Two rats, maybe three. There was barely room for me to move. I clenched my eyes, shaking and wiggling as much as I was able. "Get out of here!"

I heard the skittering sounds of little claws over candy wrappers. Heard the hollow *bump* of an empty water bottle. The eager critters were gone for now. I hoped they were gone for good.

"Help!" I called. I braced my hands on the sticky concrete beneath me. Papers and goop. It smelled like sour milk. Or week-old meat left to simmer in the sun. But I didn't care. I was alive.

What probably took no more than twenty minutes for them to get the train to move out of the way felt like an excruciating eternity. I fended off my rodent roomies' advances, trying without success to conjure up pity for them. I thought if I could do that, I might have a better chance of staying calm.

My knees were weak, my whole body sagged. I had little energy left, but if I didn't clamp down on my rising panic, I knew I could lose it here, quickly and badly.

Little squeaks and munching sounds behind me didn't help.

I tried to convince myself this was the critters' turf and I was the unwelcome giant thrown into their midst. If I were worried, imagine how frightened they had to be, right? I kept trying to feel sorry for them, because if I could manage that, maybe I wouldn't be quite so terrified. As a coping mechanism, it fell flat.

In the past, I'd faced killers straight on and still managed to keep my head. I'd managed to outmaneuver, or outwit. But I'd never encountered rats. There was no reasoning with rats. I shouted again, "Get me out!" There was more than a little "I'm freaking out here" tremble in my voice. I couldn't help it.

On the edge of delirious fear, I worked harder to keep my revulsion at bay. In one of my favorite childhood books, *A Little Princess,* Sara Crewe named and tamed her roommate rat Melchisidec. If she could do it, why couldn't I?

I was sweating, feverishly. What nonsense to think at a time like this. My nerves were raw, my skin tingling, and every inch of me was frazzled. No, I thought, nonsense was what I needed right now. And Melchisidec was a lovely name.

A shriek of metal against metal made me wince and clench my eyes. Slowly, the metallic monster that held me captive began to ease away. There wasn't enough room in this confined, damp space for me to move and I remained as still as I possibly could, waiting for an escape route to open.

Every brush against my leg, every draft of wind through my hair built screams in my chest. My breathing ragged, I wiggled my feet and waved my head back and forth, hoping to keep Melchie and his buddies from coming too close.

With a *whoosh,* the last car cleared, engulfing me in a rush of fresher air. I nearly burst out of the small space, calling for help.

I was aware of the crowd's collective gasp — they'd clearly been convinced I'd been smashed — but I ignored their cheers, shouts, and expressions of surprise.

I wanted out and I wanted out now.

The hands that reached down to help me this time knew what they were doing. I looked up into the face of a uniformed cop crouching at the platform's edge, reaching for me. The beefy, middle-aged man had me by the wrists before I could say a word. Another cop hoisted me by the back of my shirt, their muscled teamwork bringing me flying up to the platform like parents playing "whee" with their toddler.

When my feet landed on solid ground, I sat straight down again.

The crowd formed a circle around us, the cops urging them to stay back. In my peripheral vision, I noticed paramedics making their way over. I scanned as many faces as I could but I knew deep in my soul that the homeless woman was long gone. At least four people were taking my photo with their phones. I hoped to heaven they weren't recording this, too.

The beefy cop identified himself as Lawrence. Dragging me up had taken a toll on him; his face was red with exertion and sweat beaded his almost-bald head. He wiped himself down with a wrinkly handkerchief. "What were you thinking?" Patently furious, whether at me or at the situation, I couldn't tell, his voice was raspy. "Did you jump?"

"If I was suicidal, that would be one heck of a way to start the conversation, don't you think?" I snapped. Then, realizing that these guys were probably reacting to their adrenaline rush the same way I was, and hearing how sharply my words came out, I softened my tone. "I was pushed," I said before I remembered all the cell phones snapping around me. I put a hand up to cover my face and stared at my feet.

The other cop was only a few years younger than Lawrence. Trim and dark-skinned, he squatted next to me. "My name is Durson," he said. "Paramedics are here. They'll get you to the hospital."

Keeping my head down, I said, "I'm fine." *Please don't let anyone recognize me.* "I really am." I fumbled for my purse, which — probably because I wore a cross-body version — was still tight at my side. It had been upended in the fall, however, and I could tell some of its contents were gone. I inched over the side of the platform to look for my cell phone.

"Where do you think you're going?" Lawrence asked. Like he thought I was going to take another leap.

"My phone," I said. "I have to call someone."

He pointed down to the tracks. "That it?" he asked.

I followed his gaze and my shoulders dropped. Enough of the casing had jumped between the tracks for me to recognize it, but the device had been smashed to bits. "Yeah," I said. "Looks like it is."

The other cop was still by my side. "I know you," he said quietly. His eyes were kind and I trusted him. To Lawrence, Durson said, "Get all the gawkers out of here. The young lady's going to be okay. Give us some room." He waved the paramedics forward. "Listen," he said to me, "there are going to be a lot of questions. The sooner we get you out of here, the better."

He stood up and took charge. The crowd dispersed, many of them complaining about the delay I'd caused by my tumble onto the tracks. I grabbed Durson's sleeve when he crouched to speak with me again. "There was a homeless woman," I said. "She's the one who pushed me. It was intentional. No question about it."

"We'll need a description," he said. "Let's get you out of here first."

"Whatever you say."

Durson accompanied me and sat with me inside the parked ambulance as two young techs hooked me up to devices that checked my pulse, my breathing, and my blood pressure, and then sped that information to the nearest hospital.

"You're the chef at the White House, aren't you?" Durson asked.

Safe within the closed vehicle, I leaned back against the cushion and nodded. At least they'd allowed me to remain upright. "I need to call someone," I said. "It's important."

Durson dug out his cell phone and started to hand it to me. "Use mine."

196

"Just a moment, please," one of the paramedics said. "I need to ask you a few questions, first."

"Let me make one phone call," I said.

The paramedic pushed Durson's phone out of my reach without comment. "Did you hit your head when you fell? Were you ever unconscious?"

Durson shrugged an apology. "Want me to wait outside?"

His was the only friendly face I'd encountered since I'd left the White House. Plus he was willing to let me use his phone. I wasn't about to let him out of my sight. "No, please stay," I said.

It took a while, but after I'd been poked, prodded, and assessed, the paramedics determined that I'd managed to escape unharmed. My pulse was a little fast, my blood pressure a little high, but both were normal after the sort of trauma I'd been through.

"I don't need to go to the hospital," I said, for probably the fifteenth time in as many minutes. "Please," I begged. "The media will find out and show up there. You know they will. I need to get home as quickly as possible."

Durson stared out the vehicle's back windows. "The media is here now."

I groaned.

He turned to the paramedic. "You're sure she's okay?"

"Yeah," the young man said. "I sent in all her telemetry. There's no problem. As long as she didn't hit her head. As long as she's not suicidal."

"I was pushed."

"Tell you what," Durson said to the paramedic. "I'll tell the news trucks to meet you at the hospital. As soon as they pull away, Lawrence and I will get her safely home."

"I don't know." The paramedic turned to me. Something in my expression must have helped him make up his mind. He asked, "That okay with you?"

"The best idea I've heard all day." To Durson, I said, "Thank you."

Durson wanted to bring me in to the police station first, but I begged him to let me go home.

He conferred with Lawrence, and although they debated it for a moment, the two men finally decided that my position at the White House granted me a little latitude. They also made me promise to make myself available soon to complete paperwork. I couldn't agree fast enough.

When I was finally ensconced in the passenger seat of a squad car that, despite its stale-body-odor aroma, was still fresher smelling than the cavern under the platform had been, Durson let me use his cell phone. I called Gav.

"Where are you?" he asked as soon as he realized it was me on the other end of the unfamiliar number. "What happened? Your face is all over the Internet. They said that you're en route to the hospital. I'll meet you there." He took a breath, but not enough of one to allow me to jump in. "Thank God, you're all right. You are all right, aren't you? Thank God you called."

"Don't go to the hospital," I said, then explained about trying to avoid further encounters with the network news. "Officer Durson is bringing me home."

"Shouldn't you get checked —"

"I'm fine." I wasn't about to argue this point any more than I already had. "Please. Trust me. I'll be there soon."

"I'll meet you there." He took a deep breath and let it out slowly. "If anything had happened to you —"

"Nothing did," I said. "I'll be there really soon." I knew I was repeating myself but I was too shaken right now to think straight. I didn't have it in me to be quick or clever.

"I'll tell you all about it then. Let me give this phone back to Officer Durson and take a minute to catch my breath. Honest, I'm fine, Gav. I really am."

When I hung up and handed the phone back to the officer, he smiled. "Husband?"

I stared out the window. "Almost."

CHAPTER 15

Gav hadn't been the only one waiting for me when I got home. He'd been joined by Mrs. Wentworth, Stan, and James, all demanding that I tell them what happened, and asking me repeatedly if I was really okay. I did my best to assure them that I was fine, really. My legs were shaking and all I wanted was to disappear, but I put on a brave face and made them believe me.

It took far too long to break away, but when we finally did, Gav put his arm around me. "You really are a trouper, you know that? You've got nerves of steel."

"You didn't see me when all those rats came over to say hello." I shuddered. "Hardly nerves of steel. I was more like a quivering bowl of jelly."

"Why don't you lie on the couch while I make dinner. Can I get you anything?"

"What I really want is a shower," I said, holding up my hands to inspect their filth.

"This grime feels bone deep."

"Go ahead," he said. "I'll keep busy. You shout if you need anything."

"I'll be fine." I started to turn away but he was looking at me in an odd way. "What?" I asked.

"Ollie." He raised his chin, worked his lips several times as though struggling with which words to say next. I'd seen Gav's emotions laid bare only a couple of times. He stared at me now with his jaw so tightly clenched, I was afraid his teeth might begin to crumble. Every inch of his hard body vibrated — not with fear, but fury. I wanted to touch him, to dissipate the electrical charge of anger that was so obviously shooting through him right now. I held back, though. Waited. He had more to say.

The room, the walls, the furniture between us fell away and it was just he and I and that unwavering gaze of his. Brightness shimmered his eyes.

"Ollie," he said again. His voice cracked. "We will find out who did this to you."

"I know we will."

He looked like a man ready to take on the world, beat it up, and ask, "Who's next?" Instead, he said, "And when we do, they will answer to me."

I closed the distance between us and laid

a hand on his arm. "No," I said softly, "they'll answer to *us.*"

He pulled me into him, wrapping both arms around me, holding tight. With my head against his chest, I heard him take several deep swallows, fighting for composure.

He held me for a long moment, kissing the top of my head. "They will. They'll answer to us."

When I emerged from my shower, skin pink from being scrubbed clean, I sniffed the kitchen air. "Smells good."

"Toasted sandwiches. Lots of fresh veggies and plenty of cheese. Hope that's okay by you."

"I'm starving," I said. He'd set the kitchen table and I sat down. "I guess ducking a Metro train will do that to you."

He pointed to the landline phone. "I turned that off. It's been ringing like crazy. Seems the newshounds weren't thrown off your scent for very long."

I ran my fingers through my wet hair. "This isn't going to go over well with the Secret Service, is it?"

He half turned and gave me a "Seriously?" look.

"I guess I'd better get the first part over

with," I said. I turned the ringer to the landline phone back on. Sure enough, it started
jingling. My caller ID provided a number I
didn't recognize. When the caller gave up
without leaving a message, I lifted the
receiver and dialed the White House Secret
Service office. They immediately patched
me through to Tom.

"You're home?" he asked. "Are you all
right?"

"I guess you heard, huh?"

Gav gave me a look that said, "What did
you expect?"

"Every news outlet is reporting your alleged jump in front of a moving Metro train.
You even have your own Twitter hashtag."

I closed my eyes. "Please tell me you're
joking." When I looked up, Gav was watching. I mouthed, "Twitter." He shook his
head. "My phone is gone," I said. "I would
have called you sooner, but . . ."

"I'll get a replacement out to you immediately. Hang on." I heard him direct
someone in his office to deliver a new
White-House-issue phone, on the double. A
second later he returned to the conversation. "You're staying home the rest of the
night, I assume."

"Yeah."

"It'll be there in less than an hour."

204

I wasn't surprised. This wasn't the first time I'd lost a cell phone while fighting for my life. Last time that had happened, I'd been given a new one almost immediately, too. "Thanks, Tom."

"I know you didn't jump, Ollie. What happened?"

"I was pushed."

I heard his sharp intake of breath. "Who?"

"A woman. I only got a brief look at her face. All I can tell you is that she was trying to pass herself off as homeless — a bag lady — but there was something odd about her."

"Why would she push you?"

Almost as if Gav had heard the question, he turned. I shrugged. "No idea."

"Are you okay?" Tom asked.

"I'm a little shaken up, I suppose."

"Taking a few days off?"

I barked a laugh. The thought hadn't even occurred to me. "With the big Durasi dinner coming up in less than a week? Are you kidding?"

It sounded as though Tom chuckled. "Now I know you're all right. Do me a favor, give me a heads-up when you're in tomorrow and I'll make time to meet with you. I want to ask you more about this. For now, however" — he sighed — "we're scrambling to get a press release out that says you suffered an unfortunate accident but that you're healthy and unharmed. We're trying to stop the media spin that you're so overwhelmed with responsibility that you've become suicidal."

"Give me a break," I said, anger stirring. "There were witnesses who saw me being pushed."

"Yeah, well, that's not an optimal headline, either."

"Please, whatever, try to make it stop."

"We'll see how it goes," he said. "See you tomorrow."

After dinner, with my new phone safely arrived and charging on the kitchen countertop — thank goodness they'd allowed me to keep my cell phone number — Gav and I sat on the sofa together. He started to put his arm around me, but I scooted sideways to face him.

"I really need to hold you tonight, Ollie," he said. "When I think —"

I couldn't let him go down that path. "We need to talk first."

He almost seemed to have been expecting that. "Go ahead."

"There's no doubt in my mind that this supposed homeless woman targeted me. Not just any commuter — me. Why? That's

206

the question I've been asking myself."

Gav's eyes narrowed. "Go on."

"Do you think this could have anything to do with what we saw" — I took a deep breath — "at your friend Evan's place? You and I were pulled in for some very odd questioning. They asked us both if any of the victims had spoken before they died."

Gav remained silent.

"There's something not right about that situation. Why did the murders of five men make it to the news as a carbon monoxide poisoning? How did Tyree and Larsen know to be there mere moments after the men were dead? I mean, it was so precise, it was almost choreographed."

"I thought the same thing."

"Could whoever have killed Evan and his colleagues be out to get us now, too?"

"Tyree and Larsen didn't know what they were going to find at Evan's," he said. "At least that's what they tell me."

"That doesn't make sense, based on what we saw."

"We're not getting the whole story, that's for sure." Gav leaned forward, elbows on his knees, hands clasped between them. "Tyree and Larsen had been warned about a toxin. I got that much from Agent Taglia."

"You've talked with him?"

"I managed to corner him today while you were at work. He wasn't exactly happy to hear from me but he's a decent guy. Always tries to do what's right. He told me what he could."

"That's a bit of a turnaround."

Gav gave me a sideways glance. "After my interrogation, Taglia seemed more willing to help. He thought that the way Tyree and Larson handled my questioning was over the top. The fact that they came for you sealed it. There's more at play here than either of us realize. The thing is, I don't believe Taglia knows the whole story, either."

"Did you find out more about the other men who were killed?"

Gav nodded. "The other names didn't mean anything to me, so I did a little investigating on my own. I was able to come up with information on three of them. Pretty much the kind of people you might expect to visit Evan. They all had rap sheets, mostly drug-related. Two of them were working hard at getting clean. The other one was just starting a detox program. From their addresses and what I could discover, it seems they happened to be in the wrong place at the wrong time. Very sad."

"What about the fourth guy?"

"Jason Chaff." Gav spread his hands.

"There are individuals with that name living in the United States, but none of them around here. It's as though he's the invisible man. I've got nothing on this guy, and believe me, I've done some serious digging."

"So what are you saying? That he was using an alias?"

"That's the only thing that makes sense right now."

I knew Gav would continue to follow this lead, even though right now it looked like a dead end. In the meantime, I needed clarification. "Tomorrow, when I talk with Tom about the incident on the Metro . . ."

"Don't forget to make time to talk with the police, too."

I shook my head. "That woman is long gone. I'd bet on it."

"You never know."

"Tomorrow, when I talk with Tom," I began again, "how much can I tell him about Evan and the others?"

Gav leaned back, thinking. "At this point, I'd rather you not offer anything."

"You don't trust him?"

Gav fingered my hair, looking sad for the briefest moment. "I do trust him. But he's in a position where he needs to delegate, and I don't know everyone he might choose to work with. Not well enough to trust *them.*

After I check a few more things, I'll talk with Tom myself. I suspect this update is better coming from me, anyway. If he has questions or asks you for specifics, have him call me. Until then, I'd like to keep the Ainsley Street business to ourselves as much as possible."

CHAPTER 16

"And you have no idea who the woman was who pushed you?" Tom asked in his office the next morning.

"I saw who did it, if that's what you're asking. I told you. A woman trying to look like a bag lady. She wasn't, though, I'm convinced of that."

Tom sat forward, clasping his hands. There was no one else in the room with us, but he kept his voice low. "Why you, Ollie? Why always you?"

I matched him, leaning toward the desk. "Don't you think I ask myself that question all the time?"

He sat back. "Why now, then?"

Again I answered with a question of my own. "Don't you think I'd like to know that?"

He studied me for a moment. "Tell me what's going on."

"A lot, I think," I finally answered. "But

for more than that you'll need to talk to Gav."

Tom's mouth twisted. "I'll do that. Today." He blew out a breath. "Speaking of Gav, I hear congratulations are in order."

That surprised me. I knew word traveled fast in the White House, but I didn't realize this update had made its way to the West Wing. "Ah . . . thank you," I said.

"Agent Gavin is a lucky man."

Despite the fact that Tom and I were not suited to each other, we'd had some good times together. It was taking a lot for him to offer his good wishes, just as it had been hard for me to offer mine when he'd moved on. "Thank you, again."

He nodded acknowledgment. "Next on the agenda: a bodyguard."

"For me?" I felt my shoulders slump. "Not again."

He shot me a warning look. "No argument. It's a done deal."

"Who's my lucky bodyguard this time?" I asked.

"Don't know yet. One of us will get back to you. Let me know if you have any problems, okay?"

I stood up. "Thanks, Tom."

He gave me a lopsided smile. "Do me a favor, Ollie. Try to be more careful."

■ ■ ■ ■

I returned to the kitchen to find Bucky clenching a wooden spoon in his raised, trembling fist. His bald head was red as a tomato, his teeth bared behind angry lips. I half expected blood to come bursting out his ears as he enunciated his words, one bite at a time. "That. Is. Not. How. We. Do. It."

Across from him, with his back to me, Virgil leaned forward, both hands propped on the gleaming countertop, fingers curled white around its edge. "Maybe it's time you opened your mind, then."

"Being in charge of the First Lady's tasting this *one time* doesn't put you in charge of this kitchen permanently." Bucky didn't make eye contact with me, but I could tell that he'd seen me walk in.

"You're afraid. I know you are," Virgil said. "All I need is this one foot in the door, and before you know it" — he pointed to Bucky's chest — "you're history." Lowering his voice, he continued, "And before you know it, she will be, too."

I took that as my opportunity. "She, who?" I asked, smiling as fake-pleasantly as I could. "You aren't talking about Cyan, because I guarantee you, she's not going anywhere."

The look on his face was a combination of panic and anger when he turned. He glanced back at Bucky as though blaming him for not alerting him that I'd entered the room.

I wasn't finished. "I don't have any intention of letting Cyan go. She's an incredibly valuable member of this team." Feigning surprise, I clasped a hand to my chest. "You couldn't possibly mean me, could you?" I walked around Virgil to stand next to Bucky, a symbolic show of solidarity. "I hope you aren't plotting behind my back" — I waited a beat — "again." To Bucky, I said, "What's the problem?"

He'd lowered the spoon to the countertop, but his fingers were so jittery, the wooden utensil beat a ringing rhythm against the stainless steel. "Virgil intends to host the tasting here. In the kitchen."

"You're joking."

The spoon shot back up and Bucky gave me a look that said, "Would I kid you about this?"

"No," I said to Virgil. "Use the Family Dining Room. Mrs. Hyden prefers that."

"How do you know she wouldn't prefer to taste our samples down here?"

"In case you've forgotten," I said, "Mrs.

Hyden is the First Lady of the United States of America. I will not have her scrounging for food as she makes her way around this countertop. I will not have her standing as she eats. Not only that, she invites several guests to join her. Staff, mostly. Did you forget that? This is a small space. It's a busy work area. That's not the experience you're striving for."

"If you would give the idea a chance . . ."

"Virgil," I said slowly, "we talked about this. Team player. Remember?"

He didn't answer. Folding his arms across his chest, he said, "Have it your way," and stormed out of the room.

Bucky waited until he was gone. "If I were a lesser man, I might be tempted to say I told you so."

"Good thing you're better than that," I said, but I couldn't help wondering if maybe Bucky was right.

I glanced around at the samples Virgil had prepared. He had several items warming in one oven and two trays in another. He stood at the stovetop, stirring a pot that sent aromatic steam twisting into the air above it. When he caught me watching, he clanked the lid back down and moved to my end of the room. "Excuse me," he said before opening the oven. He blocked my view of the interior with his body, which I thought was odd.

"Where are the butlers?" I asked. "Shouldn't they be here by now?" When we'd first arranged for the tasting, I'd taken it upon myself to contact the head butler, Jackson, to ensure that adequate staff was assigned to assist us.

"I'm fine. You can leave now."

"I have no reason to leave."

Bucky, Cyan, and I had worked hard on creating an ambitious menu, and I hoped to heaven that this tasting would go off without a hitch. Once the First Lady approved of our choices — which we expected her to do — we could get busy amassing ingredients. The sooner, the better. I skirted the narrow area behind Virgil and grabbed a hot pad, intending to lift the lid of a simmering sauté pan to see how preparations were going.

"Don't touch that."

I turned. "Why not?"

"That needs to remain covered until it's time to serve."

I'd memorized the menu and every step of every process. I knew these were the vegetables for the lobster tail sauce. "No, it doesn't."

"I know what I'm doing."

I took a deep breath and tried to quell my annoyance. I couldn't believe we were having this conversation. I pointed to a nearby saucepan, which, if I was correct about what it held, should have been simmering uncovered. "I hope you intend to combine these soon. The sauce takes a while to thicken."

"I don't need your help," he said, slamming the oven door. Before I could say another word, he was next to me, his hot pad pressing against mine, preventing me from opening the lid of the sauté pan.

"What's going on here?" I asked. "What don't you want me to see?"

"You put me in charge. I'm in charge. Why don't you leave me alone and allow me to do things my way?"

I was about to respond when Mrs. Hyden walked in, accompanied by Josh, seven assistants, and a collection of Secret Service agents. "Good afternoon," she said.

Virgil wiped his hands on his apron to greet the First Lady. "Denise!"

I nearly choked. *Denise?*

"Come in," he said, taking her by the hand and leading her into the room. Her entourage followed, single file. "Wonderful, I'm so happy you all could make it."

The grumbling, frowning Virgil had abruptly transformed into a cheery man I didn't recognize. As he urged everyone to come around the center countertop, Josh broke away from the group and sidled up to me. "Hi, Ollie," he said, beaming. "Did Virgil tell you that I made breakfast this morning for my family all by myself?"

I snaked another look at my colleague. Smiling and chatting, he practically bounced with enthusiasm as he worked to space everyone out evenly. "There," he said, "plenty of room for all."

"Did you?" I asked Josh. "He didn't mention that."

From across the kitchen, I glared at my diva staff member. Clearly, there were other things he hadn't mentioned, either.

An hour later the tasting was complete and Mrs. Hyden thanked us on her way out. "With the few exceptions we discussed," she said to Virgil, "the menu is approved."

I stood outside the doorway as her assistants paraded past. The Secret Service agents were waiting for Mrs. Hyden to escort her and Josh to the family's quarters upstairs.

"I didn't really like the beets with green beans today," Josh said in a conspiratorial whisper. "Didn't we have that once before? I liked it last time. Did Virgil change the recipe?"

"Good catch, Josh," I said, working as hard as I could to maintain my composure. "We *have* served that dish before but today's version had a twist."

"Yeah. What was that?"

I wish I knew. I winked and pointed to Virgil. "He kept that a secret, but I'll find out."

"Whatever it was" — Josh widened his eyes and shook his head — "don't let him add that ingredient again."

"Oh, I'm going to make sure Virgil doesn't do *anything* like that again," I said.

Mrs. Hyden came around the corner and touched my arm. She lowered her head and spoke quietly. "This was . . . unconventional."

Behind us, in the kitchen, I could hear Virgil clearing away the dirty plates. He wasn't waiting for the cleaning staff this time. Probably because the First Lady was here to notice. All for show. That was Virgil.

When faced with situations like this one I usually preferred to take the high road, but this time I couldn't let it go. "The setting was Virgil's idea," I said, "but ultimately my mistake for putting him in charge. I thought a little extra responsibility might do him good."

Two light lines formed between her brows.

219

"And the items we nixed from the menu?"

I'd gone this far, might as well be fully honest. "He made unauthorized changes to some of them."

The look on her face was one I didn't fully understand. She was annoyed, clearly, but seemed resigned to the fact. We could hear Virgil humming as he worked. Mrs. Hyden heaved a sigh. "If you would like us to sample those items again, made the way you intended them to be served, we'll be happy to do so. There isn't a great deal of time left before the dinner, but your choices are usually spot on. With the misfires this time, I had a feeling Virgil was involved."

I didn't get the impression she was lying to me, but if she understood that Virgil's presence was more a hindrance than a help, why was he kept on staff at all? Especially in the prestigious role as family chef?

I was about to be thoroughly impertinent and ask her, when she continued, "You and your staff always come through, Ollie. Your choices have always been impeccable. No need for a formal tasting. I'll sample whatever you send up, when you can. I'm certain we will wind up with the original menu, exactly as you proposed."

"Thank you," I said. "I appreciate your faith in us."

Josh piped up, "And you'll make those beans the old way, right?"

I smiled down at him. "You know it."

As they left with their escorts, I steeled myself. It was time for a showdown with Virgil.

CHAPTER 17

Virgil had pulled in a few extra hands to help with the dishes while I'd been talking with Mrs. Hyden. Surprise, surprise. As much as I wanted to take the man to task, it would be wrong of me to do so in front of others. "Virgil," I said, calling him into the hallway. "A moment of your time?"

He turned to me looking as free of guile as a man could, given that he'd single-handedly bungled things so badly. Giving the dishwashing helpers a few extra instructions, he made his way over. "That went perfectly, I must say," he began.

He didn't get any further.

"Ms. Paras?" Alec Baran stood in the opposite doorway, taking up most of it. Gosh, that man was tall. "I believe you were expecting me?"

I searched my memory. "Did we have a meeting scheduled? If so, I'm sorry that it slipped my mind."

Baran eyed Virgil, who still watched me eagerly, as though he expected a pat on the shoulder and a happy "Attaboy!"

"This shouldn't take very long," Baran said. He gestured toward the corridor that surrounded the kitchen.

"I'll be right back," I told Virgil, and followed Baran across the hall to the China Room.

Always the China Room, I thought. Just once I'd like something truly happy to take place here. The China Room was where I usually faced chastisement, and usually from members of the Secret Service. Baran wasn't an agent, even though he was now working with them. What the heck could the problem be now?

I stepped inside the gorgeous room that showcased White House china to find another man waiting for us.

Baran shut the door. "Ms. Paras, this is Agent Urlich. He's to be your bodyguard."

Another tall man, Urlich was at least five years older than I was. Sparse, pale hair, penetrating eyes, he gave the impression of being made of rippled muscle.

"Agent?" I repeated. "Secret Service?"

Baran explained. "Kalto also uses the appellation *agent* for our elite forces."

"Understood." I extended my hand, thinking about how that could get confusing. How would I keep the teams straight? "Nice to meet you, Agent Urlich."

"Likewise," he said.

"Agent Urlich has an update for you about your attack yesterday," Baran said. "From the Secret Service. They're coordinating with the local police."

Urlich turned to me. "Before we begin, Ms. Paras —"

"Call me Ollie, please."

"Yes, ma'am." He nodded. "Do you have any idea who might have pushed you, or why?"

I hesitated. Gav had warned me not to discuss the Ainsley Street murders with anyone. Not yet. I had to assume that meant my bodyguard as well. I shook my head and lied through my teeth. "I don't."

"That's fine. We didn't expect that you did. What's most important right now is that you know you're protected," Urlich said. "The head of the PPD, Agent MacKenzie, has been in contact with the police department, as Alec mentioned. The detectives there went over footage from the security cameras, but the homeless woman who pushed you kept her face averted, as though she knew the cameras were there. The police told Agent MacKenzie that the woman must have ditched her disguise before she escaped. Two bulky shopping bags, assorted pieces of clothing, and a dark head scarf were found tucked behind one of the kiosks. The security cameras, however, didn't pick up any of that."

"I think it was a younger person in disguise," I said. "She didn't move like an elderly woman."

Baran smiled, clearly eager to be on his way. "That's an interesting observation, and it could prove helpful. I can see you two will get along well, and I'll leave you now. Please let me know if there's anything else you need, Ms. Paras."

When he left, Urlich held out his hands. "A bit of housekeeping," he said. "In order for this to work, you and I need to coordinate our schedules."

"You can't possibly be on call twenty-four hours a day," I said, remembering other times I'd been under Secret Service scrutiny. "You'll have someone to relieve you?"

"Only when necessary."

"This has got to be an incredibly dull assignment for you."

He smiled. "I wouldn't say that. I've read your dossier."

I closed my eyes for the briefest moment. I'd known for a while that a security dossier had been assembled to document my activities, but that fact never ceased to amaze me. "I don't see the need for you to shadow me when Gav and I are together."

"Agent MacKenzie agrees. My orders are to protect you when you're out in public, alone. Special Agent Gavin is a well-respected member of the Secret Service. I am to escort you to and from the White House each day. While you're here, or in your apartment, I will see to duties elsewhere, but I expect you to let me know when there is any deviation to your schedule. Are we understood on this point?"

"Yes."

He went over a few more rules. He called them guidelines but we both knew better. "One question," I asked when he finished. "How long do we expect this threat to last? That is, how long are you stuck babysitting me?"

What looked like pain flashed across his expression so briefly I almost missed it. "I wish I knew."

"It was the worst." Back in the kitchen, I kept my voice low. Bucky and Cyan leaned in closer to hear me. "We've never had a tasting go so terribly wrong before." I explained about Virgil's adjustments to the menu and how everyone had been crowded together, bumping elbows as they sampled food, too close to have easy conversations, standing as they were, in a line along one side of the countertop.

Huddled close in the quiet space, I went into detail about it all, including Mrs. Hyden's comments to me as she left. Both Bucky and Cyan kept eyeing the doorways.

Reading their minds, I said, "He's gone home for the day. He left me a note, claiming exhaustion."

Bucky worked his lips. "I don't know. That guy is sneaky. I wouldn't put it above him to be hiding around the corner there, listening in."

"Did you let him know how much he screwed up?" Cyan asked.

"He thinks he's golden," I said. "Just as I was about to set him straight, I got called in to talk with my new bodyguard."

"Because of the Metro incident yesterday?" Cyan asked.

"Yeah. Looks like I have a buddy to watch over me. Again." I knew how much my close call bothered my colleagues. They'd been shocked and terrified at what had happened. At this point, I thought, the less I dwelled on it, the better. "By the time I got back to the kitchen, Virgil was gone."

Changing subjects, I asked, "How did your meeting with Sargeant go?"

"Great," Bucky said. He looked at Cyan.

She nodded. "Great."

I gave them both the evil eye. "What's wrong?"

"Nothing," they said in unison.

"Neither of you is a major fan of Sargeant's, yet you both went into this meeting without a complaint. You're back with smiles on your faces. Clearly, something is wrong."

"Not at all," Bucky said. He let out a theatrical sigh. "If you must know, we aired our grievances about Virgil."

"You did?" I turned to Cyan, who looked surprised by Bucky's statement.

"Mr. Sargeant was very open to hearing our concerns, wasn't he, Cyan?"

She'd recovered. "Very," she said. "Very open." Holding up a finger, she said, "I . . . uh . . . remembered something I forgot to do. See you later."

We watched her go.

"Bucky," I said quietly when we were alone. "Just as you suspected I was seeing someone — Gav — before I admitted to it, I know you're not being completely truthful with me about this Sargeant meeting."

He opened his mouth but I cut him off

before he could say a word.

"All I want to say is that I trust you. You've both earned that. Whatever the two of you really discussed with Sargeant is obviously something you're not ready to share with me. I want you to know that whenever you are, I'm ready to listen."

He grinned at that, which I thought was an odd response. "Yes, boss."

CHAPTER 18

New cell phone in hand, I wandered into the Butler's Pantry to try getting in touch with Gav. I'd called him immediately after my discussion with Urlich to let him know I had a bodyguard, but this time when I tried to reach him, his phone went directly to voice mail. I didn't leave a message but did send a text, asking him to get in touch when he had the chance.

When Urlich had told me about the police finding the purportedly homeless woman's disguise abandoned at the Metro station, something had clicked in the back of my brain. I needed to wait until my meeting with him was over to revisit that particular click. Now that I had, I couldn't wait to get in touch with Gav.

Back, mere moments before I'd been pushed, I'd recalled the homeless man Gav and I had encountered down the street from Evan's ministry. With all the excitement yesterday dodging the speeding train, and the relief at finally getting home, it had utterly flown from my brain. Before anything came up to cause me to forget again, I wanted to alert Gav.

I'd try again later. In the meantime, there was another matter I hoped to clear up.

Margaret sat outside Sargeant's office, tapping at her keyboard. She glanced up as I walked in. Sargeant's office door was open a crack. Enough for me to see that he was in. Still, I was nothing if not polite. "How are you today, Margaret?" I asked. "Do you think I could sneak in to talk with Mr. Sargeant for a few minutes?"

She gave me a bright "You're so clueless" smile. "I will be happy to ask Mr. Sargeant if he has any time for you, but I have to warn you, he's got a pretty busy schedule ahead of him." She gave the words *pretty* and *busy* a special little lilt to let me know she was serious. "In fact, he's on the telephone right now. Perhaps you'd like to have a seat and wait?" She gave a happy little shrug even though her eyes weren't smiling. "I have no idea how long he'll be."

"Instead, how about I set up a time to talk with him? I take it you're scheduling his appointments?"

"I am," she said, again with a happiness

that didn't reach her eyes. She turned to her computer monitor and clicked the mouse several times. "Let me see. . . ." Two more clicks. Then another. "Yes," she said triumphantly. "He has an opening here on August third."

"August?" What was this, a dentist's office? "No."

"That's the earliest I can schedule anything that isn't an emergency."

"That's unacceptable." I shook my head. "Please ask Mr. Sargeant to call me. He and I will work something out."

Her smile was wide. "I'll let him know you stopped by."

At that moment his office door opened. "Ms. Paras," he said. "I was just about to come see you. Would you have a moment?"

Margaret's mouth dropped open. "But Mr. Sargeant," she said in a plaintive little-girl voice, "I thought . . . I thought . . ."

"Ms. Paras rarely comes to see me unless there's a problem," he said with far less sarcasm than I would have expected. "If she's here, there must be good reason."

I felt the chill of Margaret's glare against my back as I followed him into his office. He shut the door behind us, for which I was grateful. The less Margaret was able to eavesdrop, the better. She looked like the kind of woman who kept her ears perked for juicy updates. Being that type of person myself, I recognized the trait immediately. "You said you were coming down to see me?" I asked.

He didn't go around his desk and take a seat the way I'd expected. Instead he faced me and spoke in low tones. Maybe he was afraid of Margaret's nosiness, too. "I heard about what happened on the Metro last night."

"Good news travels fast."

His familiar, squirrel-like stare was back. Anger rather than prickliness this time. "Do not joke about such things, Olivia. It isn't amusing, especially given your propensity for trouble."

Momentarily tongue-tied, I could only manage to agree. "You're right."

"Yes, I am." He sniffed. "Is there anything you need while the investigation is going on?" he asked. "I'm sure the police will have you come down to the station to identify the perpetrator. A woman, was it?" He clucked. "You may be required to be absent from your duties. . . ."

"Apparently the Secret Service is coordinating all that this time," I said. "I have a bodyguard." I waved a hand vaguely in the direction of the kitchen. "Again."

"I'm glad to hear it." Apparently that matter settled, he felt comfortable taking his seat. I lowered myself into the chair opposite him. "Do be careful."

That may have been one of the nicest things Sargeant had ever said to me. I was still reacting when he added, "It would be distressing to have to seek a replacement for your position. And heaven forbid we get saddled with Virgil in charge of the kitchen."

I tamped down a smile. Now *that* was the Sargeant I knew and sometimes loathed. "I'll do my best to stay alive. For your sake."

His eyes snapped up to meet mine. "You do that."

Changing subjects, I asked, "How's Thora?"

I got the precise reaction I'd hoped for. Sargeant's cheeks colored. He worked his lips several times before answering. "She's well."

Thora had assisted us with disguises when a group of us from the White House — Josh included — had set out on a field trip. The outgoing, statuesque woman had set her cap for our then-sensitivity director and didn't believe in wasting time. She'd asked me to act as intermediary between them, and from all accounts they'd become nearly inseparable ever since.

"That can't be why you came to see me," he said, resuming his expressionless stare. "I certainly hope not, at least."

"I came to see you about Virgil."

He shook his head.

"You don't even know what I'm going to say," I said.

"I do."

I leaned back, crossing my arms. "Then tell me."

Arching a brow, he sucked in his cheeks. He was either annoyed by my challenge, or rising to meet it.

"Let's see," he began with a smug cock of his head, "you're here to reiterate your reasons for naming Bucky as your second-in-command and you plan to attempt to do so by telling me how Virgil made a mockery of the First Lady's tasting earlier today." He held up a finger to keep me from interrupting. "Further, you're going to tell me that you haven't yet discussed this with Virgil." He shook his head. "Not entirely certain why not . . . my guess is that you haven't found the opportunity. Lastly, you would like me to speed up the process of giving Bucky the promotion you believe he so richly deserves. You're planning to ask how my talk went with Mrs. Hyden and if there's any chance of getting rid of Virgil." He waited a beat. "Am I close?"

As he spoke, I uncrossed my arms and now found myself leaning forward, one elbow on the edge of his desk. He eyed it as though he wanted me to remove it, but I ignored him. "Don't tell me you've installed a camera in the kitchen?"

Looking pleased with himself he said, "Mrs. Hyden came to see me."

"And she told you all that?"

"Most of it," he said. "The remainder I was able to deduce on my own."

My arms came up in frustration. "She must agree then, that Virgil is more a hindrance than a help."

"She does."

"So . . ." I strung the word out. "What does that mean for the kitchen? Any chance of crowbarring the diva out of our way?"

"Unfortunately, no. And unless something changes, no chance of promoting Bucky soon, either."

"Why not?"

"Because . . ." Lowering his head and his voice, he shot a look toward the door. "Oh, by the way, don't mind Margaret. She's a little aggressive, but I believe she'll be an effective gatekeeper."

"I'll say. She nearly bit my head off when I asked to meet with you."

He waved the air as though this was of no concern.

"Back to Virgil," I said. "Why can't we get rid of him? If Mrs. Hyden understands the chaos he brings, why in the world would she want to keep him?"

"As chief usher, I'm privy to information the rest of the staff never sees. I will thank you to keep what I'm about to tell you to yourself."

A muscle in Sargeant's cheek twitched.

"Tell me," I said.

"Virgil is family."

"No way."

He twisted his lips. "He's a cousin on the First Lady's side. Distant but related."

"The press has never gotten wind of this?"

"For all his spotlight seeking, Virgil has never once mentioned family. He clearly wants his career to be taken seriously, and nepotism isn't the most effective way to accomplish that." Sargeant shrugged. "Additionally, he is a quite distant cousin. A reporter would have to know what to look for in order to find this. Fortunately, there are some details the media doesn't choose to follow."

Thinking about Daniel Davies and *The People's Journal,* I almost said, "And some details the media gets wrong," but I let that slide. "What you're telling me is that we're stuck with him."

Sargeant nodded. "I'll continue to work toward promoting Bucky." He puckered his mouth as though he'd bitten into a bad persimmon. "What a ridiculous nickname for a man of his age. I do feel it necessary to warn you that Mrs. Hyden doesn't appear eager to move on promoting him very soon."

I pushed myself up from the chair. "Thanks for your time, Peter." As I made my way to the door, I pictured Margaret on the other side, still fuming from having her authority circumvented. I turned back to face Sargeant and thought about how, even after a very short time, Thora's influence had softened him ever so slightly. "Is Margaret single?" I asked.

Sargeant blinked in surprise. "I wouldn't know." He tilted his head one way, then the other, as though examining the question from different angles. "Based on some of our conversations, however, I believe she is. Why?"

I grinned. "Can't you picture the two of them together? Virgil and Margaret?"

"What a ludicrous notion, Ms. Paras," he chided. "I cannot believe you'd even suggest such a thing. This is the White House, not Staff-Match-dot-com."

I laughed. "I knew you had a sense of humor."

"Sense of humor?" He glared. "Ms. Paras, you wound me."

Gav met me outside the south exit after work. "Well, isn't this a nice surprise," I said. "When I didn't hear from you all day, I thought you may have been pulled in for questioning again."

"Not this time."

He nodded a greeting to Urlich, who said, "I'd planned to drive Ms. Paras home." The agent looked from me to Gav and back again. "Will you be accompanying her?"

"As a matter of fact, Ollie and I have dinner reservations."

Urlich gave me a quizzical look. "You didn't mention going out to dinner."

My turn to turn a curious stare to Gav. "I didn't know."

"Am I released for the evening then?" Urlich asked. "My understanding is that once you've —"

Gav cut him off. "I will not be able to see Ms. Paras home, unfortunately," he said. "Why don't you meet us back here in about an hour and a half? If that isn't a problem?"

Urlich scratched his head, clearly unsure

of how to proceed.

"We're going to a busy, public place, and then I will return Ms. Paras to the White House. I'd appreciate it if you could meet her here on our return. I'm very sorry to cause you inconvenience," Gav said, "but this can't be helped."

"No problem." Urlich shrugged. "Happens." To me, he said, "Please let me know when you're back. I'll be here."

We set out at a quick pace, considering Gav was still using the cane. "What's going on?" I asked him as soon as we were alone.

"I'd like the chance to talk where we won't be overheard."

We exited at the North West Gate and headed east on Pennsylvania Avenue. "We couldn't go back to my apartment? I'm sure we'd be safe talking there."

"I have to be back here in less than two hours. Too much to cover, not enough time. And we can't go over this inside the White House," he said. "Too many trained observers."

"That sounds ominous," I said. "Did something else happen?"

He smiled down at me. "Really, Ollie? Does anything more need to happen? You were nearly killed, remember? I'd say that's plenty."

"Okay," I said slowly, "then what's up with this unexpected dinner out and your comment about not being overheard? You're being very mysterious."

He glanced down at me with the saddest smile on his face. "Did you ever consider that maybe it isn't the secrets, the questions, or crime scenes I want to talk about? I just want to spend time with you."

My breath caught, and he looked away.

Gav took my hand. "I hope that's all right."

I smiled up at him. "It's perfect."

At the next intersection, the Walk light was about to change and I slowed my pace in advance. Without breaking stride and without letting go of my hand, Gav did a quick look both ways before starting across the street at a brisk pace, making me quicken my steps to keep up with him.

It did my heart good to see him getting around better. For the first few days after he'd been injured, I worried that he wouldn't be able to work in the field again. I knew that such concerns plagued him as well. Time was on our side, though. He still had several weeks of medical leave to recover.

Gav stopped in front of a popular local restaurant. "How's this?"

"Looks great," I said.

Inside, the hostess led us to a small table for two near the door, right in the middle of foot traffic. Gav pointed deeper inside the restaurant. "Do you have anything more quiet?"

"Of course." She led us to a cozy table in the far corner. Gav sat with his back to the wall and I with my back to the windows. Together we had a complete view of the room. We liked it that way.

It didn't take us long to decide what we wanted and once we'd placed our orders with the waitress, Gav turned to me. "You had something you wanted to talk about. What's up?"

I told him my idea about trying to contact the homeless man we'd encountered outside the Ainsley Street Ministry. "If you recall, he seemed spooked at the time. We brushed it off as mad ravings, but what if . . ."

"What if he saw something," Gav finished. "It's a long shot."

"It is."

"And he may be impossible to locate."

"True, too."

He skimmed the room and I followed his gaze. Dark paneling, gentle lighting, and linen tablecloths. This was the sort of restaurant where hushed conversations resulted in business deals and across-the-aisle cooperation. Our nearest dining neighbors — two men in suits — were three tables away, but the place was beginning to fill up. "Worth checking," he said.

"What did you find out about Jason Chaff?" I asked.

Gav took a deep drink of water, then shook his head as though he didn't believe what he was about to tell me. "I wasn't far off when I termed Chaff the invisible man."

He lowered his voice, and I scooched my chair closer to hear him.

"Listen carefully, Ollie," he said with a meaningful look, "because there are some details I can't share with you. Classified details that were shared with me. Got that?"

I nodded.

"What I *can* tell you are a few things I learned on my own."

The waitress came and dropped off uninspired salads with little pots of dressing on the side. The last thing I cared about right now was food. "Go on."

"Jason Chaff's real name was Jordan Campo," he said. "He used to be part of the Secret Service."

"Did you know him?"

Gav shook his head. "We may have met. I don't recall. I can tell you that I knew *of* him. He left to take a position with Kalto."

"Kalto," I repeated. "You mean the same company that's now working with the Secret Service at the White House? Alec Baran's company?"

"The same."

"Your friend Evan was part of the Secret Service at one point, too. Now they're both dead. Killed together. That can't be a coincidence."

"I'm sure it isn't."

I studied the look in his eyes, remembering how he'd warned me to listen closely. "You told me that Evan ministered to people on the fringes of society. Let me guess: Jordan wasn't one of those people. He's involved differently somehow, isn't he?"

"From what I could tell, Jordan was still an active member of Kalto. It's looking very likely that he and Evan were working together. Quietly, though. As though they were afraid of being found out."

"What about the other three victims?"

"Collateral damage," he said with obvious sadness. "They must have been at the ministry that day seeking help. Whoever took Evan and Jordan out didn't care that three other men were killed along with them."

"That's terrible." I put my fork down, having barely touched my salad. "Who would have wanted Jordan and Evan dead?"

Gav held a finger up, not quite against his lips, but near enough. "That's one of the topics you and I cannot discuss."

"But *you* know who it might be."

"Let's say this: I know who I can trust. There aren't many of us, but we're working together. The difficulty lies in not knowing who we *can't* trust. Can't say a word beyond that, except to warn you that you need to be on your toes, always. We both do."

"Fair enough," I said trying to come across braver than I felt after his ominous pronouncement. "Have you found out how Tyree, Larsen, and the rest of them knew to storm into Evan's place just then? How they knew to wear gas masks? That's some pretty specific intelligence for a quiet D.C. street."

"Believe it or not, that I *can* tell you."

The waitress placed a platter of steaming pasta primavera in front of me and a sausage and pepper plate in front of Gav. "Is there anything else you need right now?" she asked as she picked up my half-finished salad.

"Would you mind wrapping that up?" I asked. "I hate to waste."

"No problem," she said cheerily.

245

As soon as she was gone, I turned back to Gav. "Well?"

He sliced a piece of sausage. "Sorry, I'm starving," he said as he popped it into his mouth. "Haven't had very much to eat all day."

"Don't let me stop you," I said. "I'll probably just pick." Even as I started in on my dinner, I knew I'd barely put a dent in it. When the waitress dropped off my boxed salad, I was tempted to have her wrap my dinner up right away, too. I was so focused on our conversation that the food in front of me held no appeal.

"Tyree and his team knew to investigate Evan's place based on — wait for it — an anonymous tip."

I put my fork down with a clatter. "No way."

He speared another piece of sausage. "I kid you not. Apparently the tipster was quite precise, and shared information that lent credence to his claim."

"Why alert the authorities?" I asked. "Why kill those men? Who had the motive?"

Gav continued eating. We were dancing around that can't-share information again.

I pushed my plate forward a little and perched my elbows on the table. "Let me hypothesize," I said. "I know you can't confirm or deny, but let me throw out a few ideas here."

Between mouthfuls, he said, "I won't stop you."

"Among the five victims are two former Secret Service agents, one of whom called you recently for help." I shuddered to think what might have been had Gav decided to visit Evan earlier that day.

"Go ahead."

"Evan had retired a while ago, and Jason/Jordan had left the service to work for Kalto." Gav didn't interrupt as I scratched my forehead, piecing together the timeline with what I knew to be fact. "Kalto is one of the mercenary teams the United States has hired to keep peace in Durasi."

"Again," Gav said, "that is factual. Not a secret, nor classified in any way."

"The president recently put it on record that he intends to withdraw mercenary forces — including Kalto teams — from Durasi. Which has resulted in Kalto personnel being reassigned to positions here in Washington." Gav didn't say a word, but his stare grew more intense. "What if," I mused, "that makes someone unhappy?"

Gav remained silent.

"Who, though?" It was a rhetorical question. "If Jordan/Jason was a Kalto employee

247

working undercover with Evan Bonder, what were the two men trying to accomplish?" I picked up my fork and wound it around in my pasta, just to have something to do. I glanced up to see Gav watching me. "Or what were they trying to prevent?"

Gav had made it through his entire dinner in practically no time.

"I've always said you have good instincts, Ollie."

"The quick story in the newspaper about the deaths at the Ainsley Street Ministry — they characterized it as an accident, not a homicide. As you know, the reporter who wrote the article is the same guy who gave me a hard time at Sargeant's press conference. Tyree and Larsen were there, too."

"You believe there's a connection?" he asked.

"I'm not ready to rule it out."

Gav wiped his mouth with his napkin as the waitress cleared our plates. I was about to ask her to box mine up, but she gave me an understanding smile. "Got it," she said. "Not too hungry today, were you?"

When she'd left us again, Gav leaned forward. "Switching subjects, you know that our marriage license is almost ready to be picked up."

For the first time since we'd sat down, I

smiled. "Like I'd forget that."

He reached over to cover my hand with his. "Are you sure about this?"

"I've never been more sure of anything in my life."

He chuckled. "Considering how many times your certainties have put your life in jeopardy, that's saying something." Getting serious again, he went on, "We haven't had a chance to talk about plans. Not since Evan."

"No, we haven't."

"You'd want your mother and nana here if it were possible, wouldn't you?"

My words caught in my throat. "It would mean a lot to them. And to me."

"So even if we were able to find a minister willing to perform a marriage ceremony on short notice, you'd prefer to wait until we could get your family here, wouldn't you?"

I sighed. "That wasn't our agreement."

"I know that. But I'm asking you. If you could make all this work in the best way possible, how would you do it?"

Might as well admit it. "I'd want my family here."

He nodded, as though that settled it. "Eight weeks isn't so long," he said. "We can wait."

I twisted my hand under his and held tight

to his fingers. "You know I'd marry you today if I could."

He squeezed back. "I'll keep that in mind."

CHAPTER 19

"What is with the two of you today?" I asked Cyan the next afternoon.

She dropped an armload of shallots onto the workspace before her. "What are you talking about?"

Standing at the long stovetop, I raised the spoon I'd been using to check on the simmering chicken stock and gestured vaguely out the door. "You and Bucky have been the disappearing twins." I pointed the spoon at the shallots. "How long ago did you leave to get those?" I asked. "It should have taken you five minutes, tops. You were gone for at least a half hour."

Virgil leaned against the giant mixer, watching as its beater smoothed lumps from sweet potatoes. "About time you call the two of them out for slacking instead of always finding fault with me." He flashed an unpleasant smile. "Gets boring with only one whipping boy, you know."

I'd confronted Virgil this morning about his abrupt departure after the tasting, reminding him that I'd wanted to talk with him, and reprimanding him for taking off without telling me. He'd reacted with dismissive anger, claiming that I singled him out for censure. I was getting tired of his antics and attitude.

Cyan looked up at the clock. "Has it been that long?" She began sorting the shallots, examining the rose-colored bulbs one at a time, wrinkling her nose when she encountered the occasional moldy one and pushing those off to the side. "You sure?"

I was about to answer when Bucky returned, whistling. He gave me a grin as he pulled a fresh apron from the pile.

"You both remember that we have a state dinner in three days," I said. "It could be the most important state dinner President Hyden has ever hosted."

"I don't think anyone has forgotten that," Bucky said. He crossed the kitchen to peer over Virgil's shoulder. "The kitchen is running at full efficiency, isn't it?"

"Personal space, man. Personal space," Virgil said. "Back off."

Unruffled, Bucky gave a crooked grin. "Yep," he said. "Full efficiency given our" — he rolled his eyes, indicating Virgil —

"current resources."

"Hey," Virgil said, turning. "Ever since I agreed to help with this dinner, you and Miss Chameleon Eyes have been pretty scarce. All your work is falling on me."

That was an exaggeration if I'd ever heard one. Even though Bucky and Cyan had been out of the kitchen more often than usual, their work hadn't suffered because of it. I wondered if my including Virgil in the plans had upset them so much they couldn't stand to be in the same room with him anymore. Regret over my hasty decision was growing.

"Give me a break," Bucky said. "Except for the First Lady's tasting, which I heard was the worst run one in the history of this kitchen, you haven't done anything to move this state dinner further along."

"Oh yeah?" Virgil pointed. "I'm making these potatoes. Again." He pointed at me. "This time with the lame recipe she's making me use instead of with the special touch that made them interesting."

"Whoa! Be still my heart," Bucky said, grasping at his chest. "You're following directions? I don't know if I can handle the shock."

Virgil turned his back on the potatoes to face Bucky. "You're just afraid of me. Admit it. You know that the minute I take over the state dinners, you're on your way out."

The last thing I needed was for this to erupt into a brawl.

I was about to step in, but Bucky surprised me by saying, "You know what, Virgil, you have a point. Seems to me you're moving up so quickly here that Ollie's not going to need me anymore." He turned to me and winked. "Think I should update my resume?"

He had to be joking. "Bucky," I said. "Don't tease."

Virgil scowled. "I wouldn't want to get my hopes up."

"Stop this right now," I said. "We get far more accomplished when we work together. Agreed?"

Bucky was still grinning which always had the capacity to unnerve me. Although he'd proven to be a trustworthy ally, he was crusty and blunt. Smiling was not his face's natural state. Something was up. Something big. Virgil ignored me. Cyan was the only one to show solidarity when she said, "That's absolutely right."

I was about to thank her for her support, when she added, "Of course, we *are* ahead of schedule this time. We've been through so many state dinners we can afford to relax a little bit, can't we?" She gave me the sweetest smile, but I couldn't help feeling that she was patronizing me. "Don't worry, Ollie. We won't let you down."

I knew they wouldn't, yet I couldn't shake a vague feeling of unease. "Fair enough," I said. "We're all professionals here. And we're going to show President Hyden and his guests the best his White House kitchen has to offer. How's that?"

Virgil snorted.

I spun to face him, biting my tongue before a sharp retort flew. "Virgil." I fought to modulate my tone. The only reason we'd invited him to help was because I believed he needed to feel valued. Moments like this one, when he sneered at my authority, he chipped away at any goodwill I'd cultivated toward him. "When you agreed to help out with this state dinner, I expected you would do so with a decent attitude."

"*My* attitude isn't the issue here." He shot a vicious glare at Bucky.

For the second time in as many minutes, I held back. This was my fault. I'd been the one with the genius plan to get Virgil more involved. I'd been convinced that including him as part of the group would help turn him around. Suppressing my anger at Virgil's vehemence, I also chastised myself. We had a state dinner to prepare, and I'd committed myself and the kitchen. We would allow Virgil the opportunity to prove himself this one time. If this experiment failed, I would admit defeat and never try anything like this again.

Next to me, Cyan was at the computer, preparing to update a file. She had the monitor tuned to a local news channel.

Keeping calm, I said, "Let's all —"

Cyan shot an arm out, grabbing me. "Oh my gosh," she said. "Oh my gosh."

I turned to study the screen. "What?"

"Oh my gosh," she said again.

Virgil made a noise of disgust. "Wait, let me guess. They voted your favorite reality TV player off the show."

The video and the words were beginning to make sense to me. And yet it couldn't be true. "Be quiet, Virgil."

I didn't notice if he reacted. I didn't care. Bucky came up on Cyan's right, and the three of us formed a triangle, our attention fixed on the news playing before us.

Daniel Davies, the jerk reporter who'd had it in for me during Sargeant's press conference, was talking into a microphone. That was odd in itself. Davies was a print journalist.

"I'm here live, standing in for our regular

news anchor, outside the home of Theodore Cobault, the nation's Secretary of Defense." Even though it was clear that Davies was breaking bad news to the American public, he had a strange glint in his eye, as though secretly thrilled to be the one releasing this story. "Again, we have not received official confirmation from police nor from the Hyden administration, but eyewitness accounts suggest that the ambulance and police behind me were summoned when Secretary Cobault was found dead by his housekeeper."

"Oh my gosh," I said.

Virgil, who still hadn't come close enough to know what we were seeing, said, "Can't you come up with a more original expression than 'Oh my gosh'?"

I ignored him, addressing Cyan, Bucky, and the television. "How?"

Still talking, Davies answered me. "At this point we do not know details. We don't know what part of the house Secretary Cobault was found in, nor do we have any idea how long he was there before being discovered. Again — we can't stress this enough — we have not received official confirmation of the secretary's death."

"Then they shouldn't be announcing it," Bucky said. "They shouldn't say such things until there's official word. What is wrong with that guy? What kind of reporter is he?" His voice trembled. He was clearly shaken. As was I.

Secretary Cobault had been a frequent guest at the White House. Affable, polite, and genuinely warm, he was a popular member of the president's cabinet. Well-loved, well-respected.

"How can it be?" I said, almost to myself. Gav and I had been discussing him, just the other day, with regard to . . .

Involuntarily, I grabbed Cyan's shoulder, to steady myself.

Cyan misinterpreted my unsteady grip, and placed one of her hands over mine. "It's so sad. Such a nice man."

Bucky flung his hand toward the monitor, where Davies was repeating his announcement. "Maybe they're wrong. Maybe this reporter is full of it. He's the guy who went after you upstairs last week, isn't he?" Without waiting for a reply, he went on. "Can't trust people like that. There's got to be a mistake. I'll bet on it."

With that, Bucky turned his back to the monitor and stormed across the kitchen. He picked up two metal bowls, which had been left out. "Why haven't these been put away?" he asked, clearly dealing with anger the only way he knew how.

"See?" Virgil said. "Look at his attitude. And you complain about me?"

"Stop your whining," I said. "Leave Bucky alone."

Virgil returned his attention to the giant mixer without arguing, for once.

"How will this impact the Durasi state dinner?" Cyan asked.

I stood next to her, shaking my head. "I don't know."

After other news channels confirmed Secretary Cobault's death, I stopped by Sargeant's office, smiling at Margaret as she gave me an unpleasant once-over. Before I could even ask her if Sargeant was in his office, she said, "I know you work in the basement, so I'm not sure if you heard . . ."

Silently, I corrected her: *Ground floor. We work on the ground floor.*

"The secretary of defense is dead," she said, clearly tickled to deliver bad news. I had no idea where her spite came from. "If you're here to see Mr. Sargeant, all I can say is that he's a little bit busy with that. I doubt he'll have time to deal with your cooking problems."

I pulled in a slow, deep breath. "I think

we've gotten off on the wrong foot, Margaret."

She blinked. "What do you mean?"

"I don't know if you're this unfriendly to everyone who comes in here, but I get the distinct impression that you don't like me. The thing is, you don't know me well enough to have formed an opinion yet — unless I'm missing something. Enlighten me, please. What is it about me that annoys you so deeply?"

She worked her mouth, then gave a quick look around the small space to see whether there was anyone else in earshot. There wasn't. "It's not like I have anything against you, personally."

I waited for the rest of it.

Again the disdainful once-over. "I simply do not understand how you think it at all appropriate to be seen on the state room level in" — she pointed a finger at me, moving it up and down — "in kitchen garb. Can't you see how wholly inappropriate your appearance is up here?"

That took me aback. We in the kitchen took pains to ensure that — as much as possible — we weren't seen by the public unless we were in street clothes. I didn't, however, agree with her method of handling disapproval, which was to snarl and glare at me until I made the effort to ask what was bothering her.

"Unless the White House is entertaining guests," I said, "there's no need for your concern."

"You asked. I answered."

The fact that she was a newer employee didn't make her snippiness any more acceptable. I reminded myself to e-mail Sargeant in the future when I needed to speak with him. Working through his assistant was fast becoming a tedious endeavor. "When Mr. Sargeant is available, please let him know —"

"Ms. Paras," Sargeant said, as he opened his door. "You're here." Perhaps reading the tension between me and Margaret, he asked, "Is there a problem?"

"It's about the Durasi state dinner," I said before she could answer. "Now that Secretary Cobault's death has been confirmed, we're wondering what effect that will have on the event."

Sargeant tugged at an earlobe. He stepped back to allow me to enter his office. "Do you have a moment?"

I knew I should avoid eye contact with Margaret, but I couldn't help myself. I didn't smirk, didn't gloat, but I did get a happy thrill of victory at her glare of disapproval.

"Of course, Peter," I said.

Inside, door shut, he got straight to the point. "I was about to ask Margaret to call you," he said. "Sometimes your timing is uncanny."

"What's going on?" I asked. Sargeant's superior air had been replaced by one of grave concern.

"The president and his advisers are discussing the Durasi dinner right now," he began, "I expect a decision on that by the end of the day." He glanced up at the clock. "The timing of this couldn't be worse." He seemed to hear himself and amended, "Not that there is any good time, mind you. This dinner for the Durasi administration was to herald a new era of peace between our countries. Secretary Cobault was a big part of organizing these accords." Sargeant raised both hands. "There's no telling how this will impact the situation."

The intensity in Sargeant's face told me that he was feeling the pressure of this situation almost as though he were personally charged with negotiating peace with this foreign power. I understood that. Every one of us working here in the White House felt responsible for making certain that the administration's plans were carried out as well and as thoroughly as possible. None of us bore the burden the president did, but we all had our jobs to do and we all knew that when we performed well, it made President Hyden's job that much easier.

"What do you need from me?"

His expression shifted. Like he suddenly remembered I was there. "At the moment, nothing." He glanced at the door, as though to reassure himself that it was still closed. "About Secretary Cobault . . ."

I waited.

"He didn't die of natural causes."

I reacted as if struck by an electric charge. "What are you saying? On television —"

His withering look silenced me. We both knew, all too well, how broadcast updates didn't always square with the truth.

"That buffoon Daniel Davies is reporting that Secretary Cobault suffered a heart attack," Sargeant said. "That is inaccurate. The secretary was murdered."

I couldn't help myself. I repeated, "Murdered?"

"This is in confidence, Olivia. Secretary Cobault suffered two gunshots." Sargeant indicated a spot on his forehead, another at his heart.

"Who did it?"

"Isn't that the question? Right now we're

allowing the press to run with the heart attack information because we can't let this situation negatively impact negotiations with Durasi."

"Is that wise?"

"It's the directive I've been given," he said sharply. "The only staff members here who know the truth are you and I. The facts will be shared with the American public very soon, but not until the story can be better contained. Not that a story of this magnitude can be contained at all, mind you."

"Why tell me?"

For the briefest moment, Sargeant almost smiled. "Agent MacKenzie believes that it is in everyone's best interests. He was very clear on the fact that you and I are to share that information with no one else. There is a small circle of people who know what's going on. You're one of them."

"Got it."

Margaret knocked at the door, her pert features tight with apprehension. "Mr. Sargeant, your four o'clock appointment is here. Are you planning to make him wait?"

Sargeant stared up at her as though seeing her for the first time. "No, thank you. Ms. Paras and I are finished here. Please tell him I'll be with him momentarily."

I got up. "Thanks, Peter," I said. "I'll be

in touch."

I walked out of his office, nearly bumping into Sargent's next appointment — Alec Baran.

"Good afternoon, Olivia," he said. Perhaps assuming — correctly — the reason for my presence in Sargeant's office, he added, "Terrible news about Secretary Cobault."

"Yes, it is. The secretary was a lovely man. He will be missed."

"I'm sure he never saw it coming," Baran said, solemnly. "Such a shame."

As Sargeant welcomed Baran into his office, I wondered whether Baran knew the truth about Cobault's death. Sargeant had said that he and I were the only two on staff who would be trusted with the information. Baran, as head of Kalto, didn't *quite* qualify as staff. But he didn't quite qualify as Secret Service, either.

"Are you waiting for something?" Margaret asked, pulling me from my musings.

"Always." I excused myself and headed back to the kitchen.

CHAPTER 20

Urlich escorted me out of the White House that evening, walking me to the Southwest Appointment Gate, where Gav waited. The two men discussed my safety almost as though I wasn't there.

"You'll see Ms. Paras home this evening?" Urlich asked Gav.

"Absolutely," he answered. "I'll take over from here."

Urlich looked as though he was about to salute. "Very good," he said, and turned away.

When he was out of earshot, Gav turned to me. "You heard about Secretary Cobault?"

"I did," I said, wondering how much of what I knew I was allowed to share with Gav. As we walked to his car, and started on our way to try to find the homeless man we'd encountered near the Ainsley Street Ministry, it occurred to me that I hadn't ever been in a position to withhold information from him before. The sensation of keeping truth from him felt alien and wrong.

My discomfort was short-lived, thank goodness, when he added, "Tom told me that you and Sargeant are up to date on the details."

Like a giant breath of fresh air, relief whooshed out of me.

Gav took his eyes off the road long enough to give me a curious glance. "You weren't going to tell me, were you?" he asked. "If I didn't already know?"

I hesitated, but answered truthfully. "No, I wasn't."

He reached over to squeeze my hand. "That's my girl."

Not for the first time did it occur to me that we made the oddest of couples. We both regularly dealt with global leaders, hotshot politicians, and information not intended for public consumption. Gav and I trusted each other completely, but we both realized that we would occasionally encounter details that we couldn't share with the other. More often, this happened when Gav was unable to share with me. I got that; accepted and understood it, in fact. It was nice to know that sentiment ran both ways.

"Have you heard any more?" I asked.

"That is, are there any suspects?"

Though I watched him in profile, I could see his features tighten. "Nothing at the moment. Whoever killed Secretary Cobault knew what he or she was doing. We have to assume that Cobault was targeted specifically, because none of his valuables are missing and because his administrative assistant told us he'd planned to meet someone."

"Who?"

He gave me a sideways grimace. "If we knew that —" Drawing in a deep breath, he continued. "This all happened during the day in Cobault's home. That requires a level of sophistication. Whoever killed him was confident the secretary would be alone. Plus, the ballistics."

"What about them? Sargeant didn't say anything."

"I'm not surprised. He may not have been told about them. The bullets that were recovered were unusual."

"Unusual how?"

"They're still being examined, but preliminary reports suggest these were armor-piercing bullets." He took one hand off of the wheel long enough to hold up a finger. "That doesn't mean that these are impossible for the public to acquire, you understand. It does, however, support the hypothesis that this was a planned, professional attack."

"Who would want to kill Secretary Cobault?"

"Again, if we knew that, we'd be in better shape to solve the crime. In his position, Cobault's made plenty of enemies, both here at home and across the world. We need to narrow the pool of suspects, which won't be easy."

"The other day we talked about how Secretary Cobault was in favor of the president's withdrawal of mercenary forces from Durasi."

He nodded.

"Kalto forces are in Durasi, and they're being pulled."

Again, he nodded.

"We also know that Jason Chaff/Jordan Campo was working undercover for Kalto, and now he's dead in what also seems like a planned attack." I was putting things together as I spoke. "Could Secretary Cobault's killing be related to the mass murder at Evan's?"

Gav drew in another deep breath. "It's a worthy hypothesis."

"That's part of what you can't discuss with me," I said as realization hit. "Got it."

We rode in silence a little while longer and were still more than a mile from the turnoff for the Ainsley Street Ministry when Gav slowed down. "If the homeless man we met usually hangs out near Evan's, he could be anywhere in this area. Keep an eye out."

I'd already been watching the sidewalks and scanning the side streets. "We may need to go around a few times," I said. "It's hard to see all the way down when we're moving so fast."

He decreased the car's speed a little more, and engaged his hazard lights. A couple of cars behind us took the hint and passed on the left. When another straggler hung on our tail, Gav opened his window and waved it around.

As it passed, I chanced a look at the driver. An elderly woman wearing a bright-blue flowered hat and matching gloves, she was hunched over her steering wheel with hands primly at the ten and two positions, gaze fixed on the road. "She may have been happier behind us," Gav said when another car honked its horn because she didn't move fast enough to pass.

As the elderly woman signaled, then merged into our lane in front of us, the impatient driver passed. Frowning and mouthing words I didn't care to decipher, he was young, driving a sleek, black car with one of those expensive vehicle logos. When the lane ahead of him finally opened up, he roared away, as though trying to teach us all a lesson on how to drive.

"Nice guy," I said.

The brief interlude had drawn my attention from the street for less than fifteen seconds, but when I turned back, I caught sight of our quarry. "There," I said, pointing. "That's him."

The same man we'd encountered outside the Ainsley Street Ministry was walking on my side of the road, heading north, the same direction we were traveling. Even though I could only see his bare back, I had no doubt. He had the same stature, wore the same ripped jeans, and carried the same staff, which he used as a walking stick. He kept up a quick pace, the wind throwing his matted white beard over his left shoulder. As we cruised past him, I noticed he was muttering to himself. I hoped he'd be coherent enough to talk.

Gav slowed even more as we sought a parking spot. It took a full block and a half before we were able to pull over, but I kept my eyes on the man striding our way, and hoped he wouldn't choose that moment to veer away onto a new street or into a building.

Luck was with us. We slid into an empty spot and the minute the car was in Park, I got out to stare south. Gav came around to stand beside me. "Where did he go?" I asked. "I swear I didn't take my eyes off of him until I was opening the car door. How did he disappear so fast?"

"Come on," Gav said, and took off down the block. I noticed that he seemed to be relying less on the cane than he had been. He was looking better every day.

We'd gone about fifty steps when Gav and I stopped short. We'd both spotted our target at the exact same moment. He was sitting in the doorway of an abandoned storefront, his long legs stretched out in front of him, his staff tight in his wiry grip. It took him about three seconds to realize we'd stopped on his account.

"Get away from me," he said.

His accent-tinged voice was lower-pitched than I remembered. Or maybe it was his surprise at two strangers staring down at him. In either case, he got to his feet, with difficulty, using his staff for support. He was older than I remembered, too. Sun-browned skin was stretched paper-thin over pokey bones. His bottom teeth were mostly gone and when he finally stood up, he remained stooped. He smelled of body odor and hot, wet rags.

Gav took the lead. "We want to talk, that's all."

He made a deep sound in his throat, like a growl. "I am the Keeper. You don't belong here."

Gav and I exchanged a look. This may have been a futile endeavor, but I wasn't ready to give up.

"We just want to talk to you," I began. "You're the keeper? Of what?"

"Don't talk to cops."

"I'm a chef, not a cop."

That seemed to surprise him. "I keep the balance," he said. In a godlike move, he stamped his staff on the sidewalk, and I half expected the ground to tremble in response. If he'd been able to stand completely straight, he might have been taller than Gav. As it was, he had to stoop lower to make eye contact with me. His eyes were cloudy, but he didn't strike me as completely out of his head as much as reluctant to live in reality.

When he spoke again, it was a question. "You make food?"

"I do," I said, opting not to add that I did so for the president.

He waved the staff in front of himself. It was a defensive move, and it dawned on me that he could be afraid of us. In his position, I might be, too.

"Don't need your food. Don't want your charity. Have all I need. I am the Keeper."

Gav gave me a look that said he thought I was doing fine. It encouraged me to continue. "I'm not here to try to convert you," I said, "and we know you wouldn't take charity." That was a guess, but it seemed to be the right thing to say to him. "What we're hoping to do is trade."

The sourness of his breathy laugh nearly choked me. He held his arms wide. "Got nothing to trade. Go away."

"You have information."

I got another full-face blast of that horrific laugh. Tapping his head with the top of his staff, he said, "First thing you said that's right. More information than anyone." He straightened again, extending his arms as though to encompass the world. The skin of his bare chest sagged from overexposure and age, but his voice was powerful. "I know everything. I am the Keeper."

Gav tried again. "We can trade. You share information and we can help you. What do you need?"

I expected him to ask for money. He

surprised me by saying, "Enlightenment is what I seek. What we should *all* seek. I have seen a mere glimpse of the light and the real. I know it and I wait to see it again."

That didn't really answer the question, but he wasn't finished yet.

"Your aura." He wiggled a finger at me. "It tells me you are on the path to enlightenment, too." He squinted at Gav, but didn't say anything.

That seemed as close to acceptance as we might get from him, and I took it as a positive sign. "I'd like to think we are," I said. "It's a long journey to enlightenment, though. A tough one."

He pointed his staff at me. "You speak truth!"

I didn't quite know how we'd get him to focus on what he might have seen at Evan's that day. Gav's lips were tight, and I could tell he was wondering the same thing. Maybe this had been a mistake. Yet I still wasn't ready to give up.

I had an idea. "Would you walk with us?" I asked. We were probably about six blocks, maybe less, from the Ainsley Street location. It would be far easier to question him about the events of that day if we were able to point to where the murders happened.

The homeless man squinted at me, suddenly suspicious.

"Mr. Keeper," I said. "May I call you that?"

He nodded.

"We had a friend who was searching for enlightenment." I was struggling to make the connection we needed. "He's gone now. Maybe you know where he went?"

I could tell the question confused him.

I tried again. "Maybe you could walk with us?" When the Keeper didn't respond, I extended my arms, the way he had. "He lived here, where you keep the balance." When he still seemed wary, I added, "We need your help to find enlightenment."

That did it. With a nod of acquiescence, he took a step forward. "Lead me and I will guide you."

The Keeper had no problems walking, and he kept a pace that most men his age probably wouldn't be able to manage for ten steps, let alone six blocks. By the time we got within a block of Evan's street, I was breathing a little harder. More than that, though, I was worried for Gav, but he gave me a reassuring glance that let me know he was fine. He whispered close to my ear, "You're doing great; keep it up."

When we reached the building next door to Evan's, I pointed ahead. "That's where my friend lived."

The Keeper froze, his eyes wide as he stared at Evan's vacant storefront. "The demon lives," he said. "Darkness." He raised the arm that held his staff and used it to shield his eyes. Turning around, he began walking back the way we'd come.

"Wait," I said, chasing after him, "what's wrong?"

He didn't stop. Didn't turn. "The demon," he said again.

Gav and I exchanged a look as we hurried to catch up. While I knew these could be the ravings of a madman, I had to believe that the Keeper had seen something important that day. "Stop, please," I said, touching his arm for the first time. Gently, very gently. "Please."

He obliged. He seemed shorter all of a sudden, stooping lower, almost as though trying to make himself small. He stared at me from beneath bushy brows.

"That was my friend's building," I said. "Evan. Did you know him?"

"Your friend is lost."

"I know," I said carefully. "Can you tell me what happened?"

The Keeper seemed to notice Gav again. "Don't talk to cops."

Gav kept his voice low. "Evan was my

277

friend, too."

The Keeper stared at the ground, running his hand down his beard several times. "Did he show you the path to enlightenment?" he finally asked.

Gav nodded. "He tried. He asked me for help. But I was too late."

The Keeper drew a breath so deep he shuddered. "Yes," he said.

Pulse pounding, my heart raced. "Go on," I said.

The Keeper's head came up. "Bonder," he said, speaking Evan's surname aloud. "His name was predestined. He was our bond. He was kind to me."

"You knew him, then?" Gav asked.

The Keeper looked as though he wanted to turn around to face the ministry again, but was afraid to. "He gave me coffee, bread. Once in a while, some meat. I was hungry. He was generous."

I forced myself to tamp down my fearful anticipation, but he had stopped talking again so I prompted him. "You went there, that day? The day he died?"

He nodded.

"What did you see?"

The Keeper positioned his staff directly in front of his body where he gripped it with both hands. His voice was soft, almost a

278

whisper. "The demon was there. *They* were there."

"They?" I asked.

When he looked at me, he didn't wear the uneasy glaze of a street-battered homeless man. He was angry. Furious, in fact. "Yin and yang," he said. If he hadn't looked so completely in control, I might have lost patience.

"Two halves, two equals." His gaze roamed over us and he used his index fingers to gesture. "Like you" — he pointed to me — "and you," he pointed to Gav, "but different."

"A man and a woman?" I asked.

He nodded.

"They killed Evan?" I asked.

"They killed them all."

Gav stiffened and I swallowed. "Could you recognize them?" I asked the Keeper. "If you saw them again?"

He took a long moment to stare at us both. "You will see them on your path to enlightenment. The demon fears you, will try to stop you." He pulled the staff to one side and began walking again, very quickly. "Go," he said when we followed. "Go, stop the darkness from spreading."

"Come with us," I said. "We can get you to a shelter. Get you food."

"I have all I need." Suddenly fearful, he glanced around. "Go. The demon must not see me here."

I followed his gaze across the street and up and down the block. Gav did the same. There were a number of pedestrians and the occasional car passing by, but no one seemed to be paying us any attention. "Please," I said again. "Let us take you somewhere more comfortable."

He wagged a finger in my face. "No more talk. Go. I will keep the balance here. You will find the demon. Destroy it. If you can."

When he took off again, we let him go. There didn't seem to be anything else we could do about it. "I worry for him," I said as we watched him disappear down the next corner.

"It looks like he's lived on the street for a very long time. He'll be all right."

"I wish we could do more."

"We can." Gav placed a hand on my shoulder. "You heard the man. Let's go find the demon."

CHAPTER 21

I stood next to the First Lady and Josh in the dish storage room in the subbasement.

"It seems wrong, doesn't it?" Mrs. Hyden asked me. "To be attending to details like choosing china so soon after tragic news?"

"I understand," I said. "This does seem trivial. But when you think about what's at stake, what Secretary Cobault stood for and how hard he worked to make this moment happen . . ." I let the thought hang for a few seconds. "I suppose that keeping the talks on schedule is the best we can do to honor his memory."

Late last night the news had broken that Secretary Cobault had not died of natural causes as was first reported, that he had been killed by an intruder. The White House press secretary had fielded an hour's worth of questions, but had avoided any mention of ballistics. The reporters had gone crazy with conspiracy theories, suggesting that someone unhappy with the Durasi peace accord may have been behind the shooting. The press secretary had repeated "No comment," more times than I could count.

Everyone in the White House had held their collective breath after the briefing, wondering if the Durasi delegates would cancel the dinner and peace talks. So far, so good. No such directive had come down. Sargeant had informed me that, unless things changed, the dinner was still on.

Mrs. Hyden wandered about the small area, trying to seem interested but I could tell her heart wasn't in the task. "What do you think, Ollie?" she asked. "You've been part of far more state dinners than we have."

All I could think of was that we needed clear sailing from this point forward if this dinner was to be a success. A new sensitivity director hadn't been appointed yet, and so Peter Sargeant was temporarily doing double duty. Had this dinner been arranged months instead of days in advance, or had Sargeant not been occupied by his new responsibilities as chief usher, he would have caught today's problem much sooner than he had.

The issue that brought us here this morning was that we'd never entertained dignitaries from Durasi in the White House before, and thus, hadn't known that the color red was wholly inappropriate for use with dinner plates. In their culture, red equated death.

We'd planned our entire dinner expecting to use the abundant Reagan china. I'd been pleased. First Lady Nancy Reagan had worked with the Lenox china company to design a rich-scarlet plate trimmed in gold, with the presidential seal in gold at its center.

Now, a mere two days before the event, the red was out and we had to decide what was in.

Josh wandered between the giant, gray bins that held each of the china collections. While we featured a sampling of every design in the ground floor China Room, it was here that we kept the actual pieces used for serving. He lifted one of the plastic covers and peered in. "I don't like this one," he said. "Who wants to eat dinner off of a giant pink flower?"

I peered over his shoulder. "That's the Grant pattern," I said as he frowned and moved to examine the next bin.

"I like plain," he said. "That way it doesn't change what the food looks like."

I tended to agree with him. The simpler the better, which was why we'd been so pleased that Mrs. Hyden had chosen the Reagan china. But lamenting the change wouldn't help anyone now. "We can eliminate most of the early china," I said. "We don't have enough pieces in any of those patterns, anyway. We'll have to focus on the newer collections. Those tend to be the bigger ones."

I guided them both over to the other side of the room. Big, gray, utilitarian, plastic squares were stacked like pallets on the shelves around us. These were giant glass and cup holders, much like the kind you see in restaurants where the management hopes you aren't looking.

Mrs. Hyden had started to uncover the Clinton service, a gorgeous, unusual pattern that featured White House architectural elements, when I had an idea. I walked over to a bin holding one of our other Lenox collections, the Truman china, and lifted the plastic protection. "What about this service?" I asked.

Josh hurried over and studied the simple plate with its pale jade border trimmed in gold. "Not bad," he said.

Mrs. Hyden tilted her head. "I like it."

"I'm thinking . . ." Although I was hesitant to push for one design over another, she *had* asked for my opinion. I decided to share my thoughts. "This dinner with the Durasi is to signify peace, right?"

Josh nodded.

"Yes," Mrs. Hyden said, and as she did, I saw in her eyes that she knew where I was going with this.

"Right after the end of World War II," I continued, "President Truman issued an executive order that permanently changed the presidential seal so that the eagle faced the olive branch, signifying peace, rather than the arrow, signifying war."

"And this was the first set of china to represent that change," Mrs. Hyden said.

Josh grinned. "That's a cool story. Is it true?"

Mrs. Hyden and I exchanged a look. "I'm pretty sure it is," I said.

"Do we have enough?" Mrs. Hyden asked.

I went over the numbers in my head. "I believe we do. It may be a squeaker, though. I'll have the staff count every piece to make sure. We'll do that today. If there's enough, do you want to use it?"

She nodded. "I think it's a great idea and sends exactly the right message. Thanks, Ollie."

Josh was still examining the set. "I think this will work really well," he said.

I smiled at him. "I'm happy you approve."

He looked up. "You didn't forget that I'm helping you for this dinner, did you?"

"How could I forget something as important as that?"

Mrs. Hyden put a hand on her son's shoulder. "Ollie is being generous, Josh. This dinner is very important to your father, and the kitchen staff is going to be stressed."

"That's why I'm there to help," he explained with a little impatience. "So they can be *less* stressed."

"I understand," she said with a pointed look at me. "But if Ollie needs you to get out from underfoot at any time, you'll do that, right?"

"Mom, I'll be there to help. I won't be underfoot even a little bit." Reading her expression he hastened to add, "But if Ollie asks me to leave, I will. I promise."

As much as I enjoyed having Josh hang out in the kitchen, having a child around during preparations for a state dinner could prove challenging. Still, I'd agreed when he'd first broached the subject. He was a tough kid to refuse. And the truth was, with his sister having recently vacated the house for a two-week summer camp, Josh was lonely, and not a little bit bored.

"I'm sure we'll do fine, won't we, Josh?" I said.

"It will be the best state dinner yet."

I grinned. "You know it."

I brought one of the Truman plates back to the kitchen with me. Bucky, Cyan, and Virgil were all busy in three different corners of the small area, and I caught Bucky stifling a yawn as he stirred a pot on the massive stovetop. Not for the first time did it occur to me that we were far more relaxed before this state dinner than we'd ever been in the past.

"Here we go," I announced.

They looked up as one. Cyan was nearest to me and for the first time since I'd known her, it wasn't the color of contact lenses she wore that I noticed first about her eyes, it was the fact that they were bloodshot.

"You okay?" I asked.

She pointed to the files in front of her. "You know how much paperwork is involved when bringing on new Service by Agreement chefs," she said. "Even though we've vetted all these people, there are still a dozen forms to fill out in triplicate for each of them before they step foot in here, every single time they show up."

That was an exaggeration, but I didn't call her on it. Her point was sound: Every step in planning this event was recorded in excruciating detail. That was simply the White House way.

"Plus I have to figure out which of these are our best choices." She blew out a breath. "They're all qualified; it's a pain to try to decide."

"An embarrassment of riches," I said. "It's a nice problem to have."

She chuckled. "I guess you're right."

Placing the plate to the countertop, I said, "Mrs. Hyden has chosen the Truman china for Thursday's dinner."

Virgil, chopping a mango for the First Family's lunch, leaned around to look. "That color is atrocious," he said. "Who would want to eat from a green plate? The red-bordered china is so much nicer. Why on earth would she choose *that* instead?"

"You didn't get the memo?" I asked, knowing full well that we'd discussed this matter earlier. "Red is inappropriate for serving dinner to citizens of Durasi."

Virgil fixed me with a look that didn't belong in the White House kitchen. "They are coming to the United States of America, where red is a perfectly fine color for dinnerware. That's the problem with countries like theirs. They expect us to bend to their every whim."

"Whether you want to believe it or not,

Virgil" — my voice practically hummed with anger — "we are here to provide the best meal we can for the president and his guests. Our job is not to impose our preferences on others."

Virgil's bottom lip slid sideways. "I think that if people are guests here, they ought to respect our customs."

"Red dinner plates aren't a 'custom,' " I corrected him. "They're simply one of the choices we have. What's wrong with being nice? What's wrong with taking your guests' sensibilities into account before making a decision?" My voice rose. "What's wrong with taking the high road once in a while?"

He made a smirky noise. "Like you're some kind of expert on that. You've been out to get me from the start. Don't give me any of that 'holier than thou' garbage. I say we keep the red and let them deal with it."

For the first time in a long time, I literally saw red. And it wasn't from the Reagan dinner plates. More like flashing lights framing the insides of my eyes and brain. My blood pressure had to be skyrocketing to create such a vivid shade of crimson. Peripherally, I was aware of Cyan and Bucky moving in closer as though to grab me before I did anything foolish. I waved them back. I was still in control. Barely.

This was it, I decided. We would have it out now, once and for all.

"I *have* taken the high road with you, Virgil," I said in a steady, warning voice. "More than you will ever know. You know why you're still here in this kitchen today? Because I wanted to give you a chance. I wanted to allow you to prove yourself. Unfortunately, you continue to do so in a way that is entirely inappropriate. You have no place here."

He put down the spoon and turned to face me fully. "I thought this was a free country. Don't I have a right to say what's on my mind?"

"Of course you do," I said, clenching both fists so hard my nails bit into my palms. "We all do. You do not have the right, however, to disrupt my kitchen with your rants." All of a sudden, I didn't care *who* he was related to. "You have a choice, Virgil."

Hands on hips, he towered over me. "And what choice is that?"

"I have protected Mrs. Hyden from your transgressions in the past — not for your sake, but for hers. This time my gloves are off. You don't second-guess matters of protocol here. You don't threaten to subvert *anything* in this house. Ever. I don't care what your personal feelings are toward the delegates, your job is to prepare the food. And you are to do so to the best of your ability. You obviously have no desire to work here under such conditions. You asked me what your choice is? You either turn in your resignation effective immediately, or I involve Sargeant to take this to Mrs. Hyden."

He laughed in my face.

Bucky and Cyan jerked back; I didn't know if they'd reacted to my threat, or to Virgil's response.

"You can't fire me," he said.

"Oh really?" I said, goading him now. Enjoying the moment of being able to unleash the anger I'd managed to control this long. My conscience chided me: *So much for taking the high road this time.* But I couldn't stop myself. "Last time I checked, I was the executive chef. The boss here." I held out my hands helplessly, purposely casual, which, I knew, would only serve to annoy him more. "Haven't we had this discussion before? I can toss you out of here anytime I want." I was on a roll, exhilarated by my anger. *Come on,* I thought, *try to fight back. Just try.*

"You can't fire me," he said again. His cheeks and forehead had grown bright pink, damp with sweat. His lips spread to reveal angry, yapping teeth.

"Oh no?" I asked, oh-so-sweetly. "And why not?"

He leaned back, eyes blazing. He was furious. More than that, he wanted to be right. He wanted, desperately, to put me in my place.

"Just what I thought," I said, purposely provoking him. "You have no response."

He stomped his foot.

Here it comes . . .

"Because," he said, with a triumphal burst, "Denise Hyden is my cousin."

Behind me, Bucky and Cyan gasped.

I waited a beat. "Yes," I said. "I know."

More gasps from behind me. This time from Virgil, too.

I'd be lying if I said that didn't give me a little thrill.

"What I also know," I said, "is that the president and Mrs. Hyden always put the country's best interests before their own." I pointed toward his chest. "And most certainly before yours. I have no doubt that Mrs. Hyden would toss you out in a heartbeat if she knew how you constantly sabotage our efforts here."

"And you would be absolutely correct, Ollie."

I turned, struck dumb by the appearance

of Mrs. Hyden in the doorway. I noticed three details in my half-second shocked stare across the room: She had her arms folded across her chest as though she'd been listening for quite a while; Bucky and Cyan were staring at her slack-jawed; and Margaret, Sargeant's assistant, was standing behind the First Lady, equally stricken.

"Mrs. Hyden," I said, at once apologetic and utterly mortified, "I am so sorry. You should never have seen this. No," I amended, hand to my forehead, "this should never have escalated. My fault."

She strode deeper into the kitchen. Margaret followed in her wake, eyes wide. Gesturing toward the Truman plate sitting on the countertop, Mrs. Hyden said, "I stopped by the chief usher's office to talk with him about our decision," she said, "and when Margaret offered to go get an item from the collection to show it to Mr. Sargeant, I thought I'd come down with her, to see if the change was causing you any problem." With her arms still tightly crossed, she said, "Apparently it has."

"Do you see what I have to put up with down here?" Virgil asked her. "We wouldn't have these outbursts if I were executive chef. We would run this kitchen like one of the best in the world."

I very much wanted to remind him that this *was* the best kitchen in the world, but this wasn't the time. I bit my tongue.

"Mrs. Hyden," I began again, "I apologize for my unprofessional behavior. I have no excuse, and I am beyond humiliated to have behaved so badly. My only consolation is that Josh wasn't with you. I don't think I could bear that."

"Yes," she said. "I'm glad he went back upstairs, too." She came to stand between me and Virgil.

Virgil softened his tone, relaxed his angry face. "Denise —"

She stopped him with her finger. "Don't say another word. This is clearly a bigger issue than I was aware of." To me, she said, "Ollie, I will expect you to meet with Mr. Sargeant on this matter. At your convenience, that is. I realize we have a state dinner to prepare."

"Yes, ma'am."

Virgil worked up a smile. "I've been trying to tell you what a dictator she is, but you and Parker never listen."

I cringed when he referred to the president by his first name. Distant cousin or no, it wasn't right coming from a member of the staff.

"You, Virgil, will accompany me to see Mr.

Sargeant right now." She turned to Margaret. "I'm sure our chief usher will be able to fit us in, won't he?"

Margaret reacted like a woman who'd won the lottery. She practically jumped in awkward delight at the prospect of being able to help. "Yes, of course." She took the Truman plate — with its peace-facing eagle — and scurried for the door. "I'll let him know immediately."

Mrs. Hyden turned to me again. "We will discuss this in depth, later."

When she left, my shoulders slumped and I put my head in my hands.

Bucky patted me on my shoulder. "We've got to work on your timing, Ace. That was the first time I've ever seen you let loose like that. I'm proud of you." Bucky let out a low whistle. "But did it have to be in front of the First Lady?"

Chapter 22

Urlich picked me up from my apartment Thursday morning. He wasn't the first bodyguard who'd been assigned to me, but he was one of the few who didn't object to me sitting up front in the passenger seat and didn't mind a little conversation on the commute to and from work. I'd learned several things about the man. He wasn't a foodie and didn't understand the need to experiment with flavors, textures, and ingredients. To him, food was fuel, nothing more. He didn't cook, didn't care to. Divorced, he currently lived alone and was in a relationship with a woman named Naomi.

Urlich had been working for Baran for four years, and while he completely disagreed with the president's decision to pull Kalto's forces from Durasi, Urlich was a good soldier who understood the chain of command.

"How does Alec Baran really feel about

these changes?" I asked him. "His bottom line is sure to take a big hit."

Urlich didn't take his eyes off the road. "Baran isn't pleased, I can tell you that much. There's not a whole lot he can do about it, though. When the government signed the contracts engaging Kalto forces, no one could have predicted these peace negotiations. We all thought that we'd be in Durasi for another ten years."

"The contract goes ten more years?" I couldn't prevent the distress in my voice. "You'll all be here for the duration?"

"You don't like us around much, do you?" he asked.

"It's not that," I said. "I like you personally —"

"Don't worry. I didn't take offense. And I didn't mean to alarm you. We've got another two years here. That's it. The current contract runs out after that. We were all pretty certain they'd be renewed, that's all."

I was glad to hear it. Changing subjects, I asked, "Have you served in Durasi?"

"Oh yeah," he said with a smile. "I'm sure you've heard about how the country is decades behind ours in terms of innovation and quality of life, but I like it there. Things are simpler. Can't wait to go back."

"Back?" I said. "I thought all forces were

297

being pulled out."

"They are," he said. "You know as well as I do, though, that things like this take time. I'll be in charge of overseeing troop recall operations."

"That sounds like a big job."

"I'm up for it," he said. "These peace talks have been in the works longer than people are letting on. Alec knew about them more than a week ago."

That was interesting. "And you said that Alec is against these changes."

"Very much against them. When he first heard that Kalto might be pulled from Durasi, he asked a few of us to return to the States to help him strategize a way around it." Urlich turned to me. "We did our best, but when the U.S. government decides something, little companies like Kalto are powerless against it."

"I'd hardly call Kalto little," I said, "or Alec Baran powerless."

He gave a sad chuckle. "In this case, he is. But I wouldn't count him down for long. People like Alec always manage to come out on top."

We fell into silence for a few blocks. "Do you have any idea how much longer you'll have to keep an eye on me?" I asked.

He kept his attention on the road, but

looked thoughtful. "I can't say, really. I will tell you that Agent MacKenzie has given me no further updates on the matter." He turned to me when we coasted to a red light. "Do you have nightmares because of what happened to you at the Metro?"

I thought about the night gremlins. Not quite the same. "I haven't, no," I said. "I wonder what that says about me."

"Sounds to me like you perform well under pressure."

"Necessity is more like it," I said. "Although this week, with the dinner plans and unexpected blowups, the pressure is most definitely on."

"I can only imagine." He waited a beat, then said, "I've heard a few stories about things you've been involved with in the past. Sounds to me as though you would have made an excellent Secret Service agent. Maybe even gotten a job at Kalto."

"You're making fun of me, right?" I asked.

"Not at all."

"Ha," I said. "First of all, I'm too short so I wouldn't make it past the application stage. Second, I love what I do and have the best job in the entire world. I wouldn't trade my life for anything." Thinking about Virgil, I added, "And I'd fight for the right to stay in this position for the rest of my life."

Urlich kept his eyes on the road, but he smiled at that. "I hear you. I feel the same way. But like I said, Alec always has a plan. I'm sure whatever comes next will be even more challenging."

We drove in silence until Urlich pulled up behind the White House. I was about to get out of the car when I remembered something. "I have an errand to run today," I said. "I hope that's not a terrible inconvenience."

"Where to?"

"The Moultrie Courthouse," I said.

"Traffic ticket?"

I was reluctant to tell him that I wanted to pick up the marriage license Gav and I had applied for. It seemed silly to want to go get it. Even though it would be ready today, it wouldn't do us much good for several weeks. Still, I wanted my hands on the document as soon as possible.

"I can go on my own," I said. "It's not part of my daily routine. I can't imagine anyone keeping tabs on me so closely that they'd even notice me leaving the White House."

"That's not our agreement. What time do you need to be there?"

"It's not an appointment so there's no set time. Today's going to be busy and if I am able to get out at all, it's going to be last-minute. Is that a problem?"

He scratched the top of his head. "Text me when you're ready. I'll do my best. If I can't make it, I'll find a replacement who will."

As I walked to the White House from his car, I considered the idea of visiting the courthouse on my own, sans escort. I knew deep in my heart that no one would follow me. That no one was hanging outside the White House gates, waiting for me to emerge. Whoever had tried to have me killed the other day had to have noticed by now that I was being guarded. I was in as safe a bubble as I'd ever been. Still, I hadn't stayed alive this long by being stupid. I huffed a sigh of disappointment. Urlich had asked me about nightmares. I didn't have them at night — they were part of my every waking day. And I couldn't wait for this one to be over.

Bucky and Cyan were hard at work in the kitchen when I walked in. "You guys have been getting in early all week," I said, glancing at the clock. "I'm usually here before you. What's up?" I took a closer look at what they were doing. "And why are you making breakfast?"

"Official word came down two minutes

ago. Didn't you get a text message from Sargeant?" Bucky asked.

I pulled up my phone. "No," I said, then one second later, the sound of a text arriving. From the chief usher's office. It read, "Call me."

"Something about the dinner?" My heart raced. "Wait, where's Virgil?"

Bucky and Cyan exchanged gleeful grins. "He's on administrative leave," Cyan fairly squeaked. "Woo-hoo!"

"Wait a minute, what?"

"Sargeant came down a few minutes ago. He was thrilled to see us in early," Bucky said. "He told us that Mrs. Hyden put Virgil on leave. She wants time to decide what to do with that situation."

"Whoa. This is news. And no, I haven't had a chance to talk with Sargeant yet." My phone registered another text.

Sargeant, again: "Call me now."

"Hang on," I said. "I'd better do this." I picked up the kitchen phone and dialed his office.

"Ms. Paras," he said when Margaret put me through. Uh-oh. He'd taken to calling me Olivia lately. Being back to "Ms. Paras" meant he had to be in a royal snit. "I can see you've arrived. I take it your staff has informed you of Virgil's situation?"

302

"Does this mean that the three of us are in charge of the family's meals again?"

"Until further notice, yes."

"Peter, I can't tell you how embarrassed I was to be caught arguing with Virgil."

"As well you should be." He made a peculiar *tsk*ing noise. "It seems, however, that our First Lady has taken your side on the matter."

"She has?"

"You act surprised. And yet, you're here. Virgil is not."

"Yes, but she could simply be moving combatants to separate corners, temporarily. At this point, the day before the Durasi dinner, it makes more sense to remove Virgil from the kitchen than it does me. She could easily come back next week with a completely different outlook."

"Not to put your mind at ease, Olivia, because you know that is not something I am wont to do. . . ."

I sensed good news in his reluctant pause. "Yes?"

"Mrs. Hyden did, indeed, take your side. She told me that she'd heard enough of your argument with Virgil to fire him on the spot. If he hadn't been family — a fact that she now knows he's shared with all of you — he would have been out on his delicate

303

rump last night. As it is, he's simply on administrative leave. Effective this morning."

Relief whooshed out of me. "Thank you."

"This was Mrs. Hyden's decision," he said. "Not mine."

"You disagree?"

"Really, Olivia, you must refrain from putting words in my mouth." I heard him sniff. "Good day. I trust you'll keep me informed if there are any changes to the Durasi dinner."

He hung up, and I stared at the handset before putting it down.

"Well," Cyan asked. "Are you in trouble, too, or is everything okay?"

"For once," I said, thinking about this turn of events with Virgil, Sargeant's almost-supportive response, and knowing I would be picking up the marriage license later today, "I think things are just fine. Really great, in fact."

That lighthearted feeling of bliss lasted for exactly three seconds. Until my cell phone rang. It was Gav.

"What's up?" I asked.

"There's been a shooting."

"Are you okay?"

"Not me," he said. His words were clipped. "The Keeper. The homeless man we talked with Tuesday night."

Blood rushed to my feet so quickly that I grabbed the nearest cabinet to steady myself. "No." I covered my eyes with my free hand. "Is he dead?"

"In surgery. Ollie, I don't need to tell you what this means." Gav took a quick breath.

I exhaled. Thank heavens the Keeper was still alive.

Cyan stared at me with wide eyes. Across the room, Bucky had stopped what he was doing to turn and listen. I was ever so grateful to be surrounded by friends right now.

"It's because of us, isn't it?" I asked, feeling as though the blood that had rushed downward had pooled into concrete, paralyzing my legs, making me weak.

"I'm convinced of it," Gav said. "No more on the phone, though. I'll pick you up after work."

Shaken, I agreed. "That poor man," I said. "I'm so sorry."

"Ollie," Gav said, "keep this to yourself."

"I will, but Bucky and Cyan are here." The two looked surprised to hear their names.

"Don't give them any specifics. Don't tell them who was shot. They'll keep whatever they've overheard to themselves, I know. What time can I pick you up?"

It took me a minute to corral my brain. "I don't think I can leave before six tonight. Maybe seven. I'll let you know."

"Don't tell anyone where we're going. Not a soul. I'll fill you in later."

I never thought I'd hear myself say it, but Virgil's departure couldn't have come at a worse time. The last few days before a state dinner were always crazed yet micromanaged with great precision down to the minute. That was how it worked most of the time when everything was arranged months in advance and every task accounted for. With the shortened lead time for the Durasi dinner, however, and the not-unwelcome but thoroughly unexpected extra responsibility of having to prepare the First Family's meals, we were strained to the breaking point.

"The problem is," Cyan said, "even though the menu Virgil planned is here on the schedule, the recipes he intended to follow are nowhere to be found." She spread her arms wide. "All his stuff is gone." She glanced at the clock. "We managed breakfast today because it was easy and pretty basic, but we have two and a half hours before lunch and no recipe for today's entrée. What do we do?"

"Hang on." I called up to Sargeant's office.

Margaret answered. "I'm sorry, Mr. Sargeant is tied up at the moment."

Unwilling to deal with her fussiness this morning, I kept it brief. "I need to talk with him, as soon as possible. I need to know if Virgil took anything with him when he left the White House."

"I can tell you that," she said. "Mr. Sargeant asked me to catalog everything Mr. Ballantine removed from the White House. There was an agent helping us, making sure everything went smoothly, too."

"Which agent?"

"I don't know," she said. "She was simply assigned to make sure Mr. Ballantine didn't take anything he wasn't supposed to."

I hadn't noticed anything missing this morning, but I decided to take a closer look around the kitchen as she continued. "So, what did he take?" I asked.

"A set of knives. He said they were his."

I checked the spot where Virgil usually kept his personal belongings. Empty. "They were. We all have our own knives."

"That's weird."

"No it isn't," I said, "but go on. Anything else?"

"A couple of binders with recipes. He said

they were his, too," she added with concern. "Weren't they?"

"I'm sure they were," I said. "All I want to do is double-check." I wandered to our bookshelf. We kept the bulk of our cookbooks in another room, due to space considerations, but we kept a few favorites handy. Mine were still in their usual spots but Virgil's binders were most definitely missing. "Did he take any cookbooks?"

"He did. Just one, though. The agent who was with us was particularly interested in that book. Said she'd been meaning to get a copy for herself."

In a heartbeat I realized which book Virgil had removed. It had been his, all right. I remembered the one time Cyan had asked to borrow it. She'd spilled tomato sauce on one of its pages as she prepared the dish. Virgil had blown up at her. Page fifty-three, if I remembered correctly. I think he'd complained about that spill for a week straight, always referencing the page number and hinting that Cyan should replace the book for him. I shook my head at the memory. Much-loved cookbooks always got winged. They were supposed to. I considered that part of the books' job description.

"I'm glad his departure went smoothly." Knowing Virgil, I would have expected him to leave in a far more wild and dramatic manner. "Thanks, Margaret."

With more eagerness than warranted, she asked, "Did he take something that didn't belong to him?"

Sorry to disappoint you. "No, it looks like everything is in order here. Thanks for your time." After I hung up, I turned to Bucky and Cyan. "He took his binders and one cookbook. How much you want to bet his secret recipes for today's meals are out of our reach?"

Cyan tapped a finger against her lip. "The salads and sides shouldn't be a problem."

Bucky leaned over her shoulder. "We can do this," he said. "So what if we put our own spin on things? For instance, here: Virgil planned on pork with mango and apricot chutney for dinner tonight. He doesn't specify a method of preparation for the pork, but we can improvise. No problem."

"You're okay with that?" I asked. "Even though we have a major dinner to prepare in less than forty-eight hours?"

"We three have been called upon to be miracle workers before," he said. "You have any doubt?"

"You know what?" I said, "I don't. Not a one."

CHAPTER 23

We finally wrapped things up for the day by about six-thirty in the evening. We'd worked later than we were accustomed to, but considering how much we'd gotten accomplished, it was an excellent use of our time.

While Virgil's absence necessitated extra effort on our parts, it also meant that Bucky, Cyan, and I were able to function more cleanly as a team. Long before Virgil had joined the kitchen, we'd established a rhythm that suited us all and resulted in meals prepared quickly, efficiently, and with minimal angst. We'd all fallen right back into that rhythm today without missing a step. Boy, it felt great.

I sprayed the center counter with disinfectant and wiped it dry. "Today was just like the old times, wasn't it?" I said.

Bucky peeled off his apron and wiped his brow with the back of his sleeve. He gave me a half grin. "Best work we've done in months."

"Even the SBA chefs we brought in for the pre-work today felt the difference. So much cheerier." Cyan gave a little shudder. "Do you remember last time, when Virgil made that girl cry?"

Bucky snorted. "Since he's been here, he's made at least a *dozen* of our SBA chefs cry. Some men, some women. I'll give him that, at least. He's an equal-opportunity bully."

"I wonder what will happen with him. 'Administrative leave' could mean anything," Cyan said.

"I vote we don't worry about it," Bucky said. He stood in the doorway, with his finger on the light switch. "You ready to close up for tonight?"

I threw the dish towel I'd been using into the laundry bin. "Tomorrow's the big day," I said, and my stomach reacted with a light tremble. "Showtime."

Cyan had grabbed her purse and I'd grabbed mine. Bucky shut off the lights. "What time are you both getting here in the morning?" he asked.

"Probably around four," I said. "Which reminds me, I'll have to let my favorite bodyguard know that he's got an early call."

"Is he meeting you out back tonight?"

Cyan asked as she and Bucky turned toward the East Entrance, while I headed for the South.

"No, I texted him earlier to let him know he's off duty this evening. I think he's a little pushed in the nose that I don't need him, again. Either that, or he suspects that I'm dodging him on purpose. I'm not, though. Gav is picking me up." I grinned. "Thank goodness the Secret Service isn't insisting we be chaperoned."

"Hey, that's right, weren't you planning to pick up your marriage license this afternoon?"

I shook my head. "The only time I could get out, Urlich was busy, and vice versa. With the dinner tomorrow night, I know I won't be able to get out there tomorrow, either. Maybe Monday."

"Bummer," Cyan said. "Do you and Gav have a romantic evening planned for tonight? It must be so much fun making plans about your future together."

A trip to the hospital to visit a homeless man who'd been shot earlier in the day probably wouldn't qualify as romantic or fun in Cyan's mind, but I winked anyway. "You know it."

Bucky gave me a shrewd look before walking out the door. "See you tomorrow, Chief.

Be careful."

"How did you find out about the keeper getting shot?" I asked Gav as we sped toward the hospital. We were in a government-issue vehicle tonight, rather than Gav's personal car. When I'd asked him how he'd managed to snag one while he was still on medical leave, he'd shrugged and told me that Tom had arranged for it.

"He and I are working together on this with a very small group of high-ranking people. We've all agreed that we can't trust anyone else with what we know so far. Not yet," he said. "Officially, I'm consulting. In fact, they called me in as soon as the Keeper was rushed to the hospital."

"That doesn't make any sense. Why would anybody even think to call you? How does anyone know that you and I talked with him?"

"They don't." Gav kept his eyes on the road, and it occurred to me that we'd had most of our important conversations in a car lately. We'd spent precious little time together doing anything except talking about the five dead men at Evan's place and the parts we unwittingly played in its investigation. "No one knows, and it's important we keep it that way."

"Then why did they call you — ?"

"Because of the ballistics."

My stomach jerked sideways. "I don't understand."

"Remember me telling you about the bullets that killed Secretary Cobault?"

Pulse beats throbbed inside my ears. This couldn't be good. "Yes."

"They're the same kind that were used to shoot the Keeper."

"But . . . but . . ."

"I know," he said. "What does that tell you?"

Little clicks of understanding sounded in my brain, like itty-bitty magnets that clack together one at time, creating an instant column of comprehension. "Whoever shot the Keeper knew that we'd talked to him, didn't they?" I didn't wait for Gav to answer before continuing to build. "Which means that they must know what he told us. Or . . . at the very least, they have to suspect that we learned something from him." I stared at Gav's profile. "The timing is too perfect to be coincidence."

"Yeah," he said without turning.

"We were followed." Suddenly wary, I looked out all the windows. "Do you think we're being followed now?"

"That's one of the reasons I opted for this

314

car instead of my own. You didn't tell anyone where we're going, right?"

"No one."

"As I said, Tom MacKenzie is fully apprised." He shot a quick glance at me. "He's doing what he can to look into the five deaths at Evan's without raising any suspicions. Other than Tom, several members of the president's cabinet, and the president himself, no one else knows what's going on. And we're doing our level best to keep it that way."

"Sargeant?"

"We have not told him anything about the Ainsley Street murders."

"What about Tyree and Larsen? And the other people who rushed in with gas masks?" I asked. "Surely they *have* to know what's going on."

"They do not. The decision has been made to insulate all the different factions."

I considered that. "I get it. The fewer people who know the whole story, the better chance of noticing when the guilty party inadvertently blurts a piece of information they shouldn't know."

"Exactly."

"The thing is" — fear slowed my words, but I had to ask — "this new ballistics information means that whoever killed the men at the Ainsley Street Ministry is trying to keep the Keeper quiet, too. Worse, it sounds as though you, Tom, and these shadowy, high-ranking officials are fairly certain that whoever is behind all this is someone on the inside."

"That's the theory we're working with."

Reasoning aloud helped me. "And the ballistics match means that whoever tried to kill the Keeper is the same person who killed Secretary Cobault —"

"Things have changed, Ollie. In a big way." He worked his jaw. "When Tyree and Larsen interrogated me, they told me things I couldn't tell you."

"I remember."

He shook his head. "At this point, I can't decide whether they lied to me, or they've been lied to themselves."

"I don't understand."

"I'm able to share some information with you now that I couldn't share before."

I waited.

"Tyree and Larsen inferred that a Durasi faction was behind the five murders."

"What would the Durasi hope to accomplish?" I tried getting my head around that information. "And don't political factions usually leap up in their eagerness to claim responsibility for things like that?"

"Exactly right. And, as you know, we haven't heard a peep from any political corner. That was my first inkling that Tyree and Larsen were lying to me."

"Or being lied to," I added.

"Right. Or that."

"What else?" I asked.

"Think about it." His voice was so low I had to lean close to hear him. "What do we know?" he asked. "Five men killed, and an anonymous tip sends the authorities storming in. We stumble on the scene and all of a sudden there's panic that we might know more than we're letting on."

"Go on."

"Who gave them that tip?" Gav made a right turn, keeping his attention on the road. "We find that out and I believe we'll find the person, or persons, who killed Evan and the other victims."

"Do you suspect someone in the Secret Service?"

"I suspect everyone," he said. "Present company excepted, of course."

"Something doesn't make sense," I said.

He looked at me as though he'd expected that response. "Go on."

"Two of the dead men at the Ainsley Street Ministry, Evan and Jason, were working with the Secret Service and Kalto. Why would someone in either organization want those men dead?"

"Tom and I firmly believe that Jason and Evan knew about the pullout of forces from Durasi a short while before that information was made public."

"Alec Baran knew at least a week ahead of time."

Gav nodded. "I'm not surprised. We think Jason and Evan became aware of an undercurrent, a plot, or a coup of some sort that would serve to discredit that decision. Whoever is behind this is trying, perhaps, to get that decision reversed."

"Who would benefit?" I asked. "Baran? He stands to lose millions once these contracts are up."

"Another thing you don't know is that several weeks ago, Tyree and Larsen were tagged by Baran to join Kalto. Once the decision was made to diminish forces, however, he pulled his offer of employment from both men."

"That's not enough to kill anyone over."

"I agree, but it's what we have so far." Gav pulled into a parking spot in the hospital's visitor's lot. "I hope our Keeper friend can tell us more."

The Keeper, who was being referred to as

"John Doe" because the hospital couldn't determine his real name, was in intensive care. A unit secretary at the fourth-floor desk checked our ID and consulted a list before we were allowed to visit. She leaned in close and spoke in a stage whisper. "Who *is* this patient? He's not a serial killer or anything, is he?"

Gav answered her with a smile. "Which way, please?"

Frowning, she stood up. "I'll take you." As she led us down the hall, she tried again. "His type doesn't usually get this kind of protection." Affecting a shudder, she said, "He looks like that Unabomber guy."

Gav didn't respond.

She walked us down the hall to the heart of intensive care, where a Metro police officer was stationed outside the second glass-walled cubicle on the right. "Here you are," she said, as though giving us one more chance to let her in on the man's identity. "Ten minutes. No more."

"Thank you." The moment she was gone, Gav conferred with the cop, who assured us that no one else had been by to visit and that only approved doctors and staff members had interacted with the patient.

Inside the small, brightly lit area, the Keeper looked like a shriveled version of

319

the man we'd spoken to a mere two days earlier. Even though his beard was gone — they'd shaved him clean — he was instantly recognizable. He had a thick, white dressing wrapped around his head, and an IV dripped into his bandaged left arm. His eyes were closed, and I could see his chest rise and fall beneath the flimsy, pastel-patterned hospital gown.

"I hate to wake him," I said.

One of the Keeper's eyes popped open. Then the other. His voice was raspy but clear. "Don't whisper. It's not polite."

"You're awake," I said, moving to his side. "How do you feel?"

"How do you think?" he asked, lifting his bandaged arm and tapping his head. "I'm in this hospital because some fool shot me."

I glanced over my shoulder at Gav, who looked as surprised as I felt. I hadn't expected the Keeper to be this lucid or this aware. I wondered now if he'd been under the influence of some chemical when we'd seen him last. Or maybe he was under the control of drugs now — ones that helped him maintain the balance he sought.

Not wanting to waste a minute I asked, "Who did it? Who shot you?"

The Keeper gave me a hard look, then switched his attention to Gav for a moment

320

before returning to me. "It was you two who came to talk to me, isn't it?"

"Yes," I said. "We asked you about the . . . um . . . demon. The one who killed Evan Bonder and his friends."

"They came back," he said. "The yin, the yang. The man, the woman. They came back." He rubbed his hand against his bare chin, grimaced, then pointed straight at me. "They asked about you."

"What did you tell them?"

His bushy brows came together. "I told them nothing." If he had been stronger, his voice would have reverberated in the small area. As it was, it shook with fragile passion. "They are the demon. You are the enlightened. I see your shining auras, just as I saw their shadowy ones. I told them nothing. Nothing."

"It's okay." I patted his arm. "Thank you for not telling them we came to see you. They asked about us?" I asked. "Specifically?"

"Isn't that what I just said?" In emphasis, he tried to sit up, then sucked in a gasp of pain before settling back with a small groan. "You left, they came. Talked to me. I pretended not to recognize them. Pretended I didn't understand. I thought they would leave." He tried to shift again, but changed his mind. "When I turned my back, they shot me. Left me for dead."

Gav spoke quietly. "Another homeless person found him bleeding on the street. The man flagged down a police car and they called for an ambulance."

"I'm so sorry," I said to the Keeper.

"Fooled them, though, didn't I?" He grinned showing yellow, uneven teeth. "My time isn't up yet. Not until balance is restored."

"Do you know their names?" I asked.

He shook his head.

"Can you tell me what they looked like?"

His right hand, tethered to an oxygen meter, came up a second time to stroke his nonexistent beard. When his bony fingers came up empty, he grumbled. "Wondered why it was so cold in here." He gave a wet, phlegmy cough.

"What do they look like?" I asked.

"Good thing they shot me in the head," he said, knocking into it with his right hand. "Doctor told me that the bullet skimmed along my skull and stopped right about here." He pointed to a spot just above his ear. "Got lucky."

I knew our time with him was running out, so I tried a different approach. "If you tell us as much as you can about them, we might be able to catch who did this."

"Demons are wily," he said. "They look like us. Ordinary. They blend right in."

"What did she look like?" I asked.

"Tried to hide what she looked like."

"I don't understand."

He smiled. "Of course you don't. You aren't used to seeing demons."

A nurse stepped in behind Gav. "Time's up. The patient needs his rest."

"Please," I said to the Keeper. "What do you mean?"

"Young face. Young body." He shook his head. "I remember blue. Flowers, I think. She dressed old."

I thought about the woman who'd pushed me on the train platform. She'd disguised herself to look old, but had moved like a younger woman. Would I be able to recognize her again?

"What about the man?" I asked.

The Keeper coughed again, this time deeply.

"It's time for you to leave," the nurse said. "Now."

"But —" I said.

"We'll take good care of him for you, I promise," she said as she patted me and Gav to the door. "Come back tomorrow."

I knew with the Durasi state dinner that I

wouldn't be back tomorrow. "Don't let anything happen to him," I said.

She smiled. "He's in good hands here. There's nothing to worry about."

CHAPTER 24

When Urlich picked me up the next morning, the sky was still black. "Sorry," I said as I got in. "I know this is ridiculously early."

"Don't sweat it," he said. "I have a lot on my plate today and I appreciate the early start."

"I know you're one of the people giving speeches tonight," I said. "What else do you have going?"

"I have two important errands." He held up a finger. "I need to meet with Alec this morning." Urlich shot me a look. "He's a great boss, but a fierce micromanager. Not that I'm not nervous enough as it is. I swear he's going to send me over the edge."

I smiled. "I'm sure you'll do fine."

He nodded, holding up a second finger. "More important, however, when I'm finished with Alec, I need to connect with a colleague of ours who's helping with our speeches. That meeting is essential before the event tonight."

I didn't understand. "Your colleague is helping with your speeches, but isn't meeting with Alec, too?"

Urlich made a face. "Like I said, Alec is a great boss. But that doesn't mean he's particularly easy to work with."

Bucky and Cyan were in before me, again. "Good morning," I said when I pulled off the light jacket I'd worn against the early morning chill. "I expected to be here alone for a while."

Bucky downed whatever was left of his coffee. "Is that a complaint?" he asked, raising the mug in greeting.

"The opposite. I'm delighted. Confused, though. You two are never in this early."

Cyan pointed to the clock. "You said you would be here by four. It's four."

"Yeah." I'd been about to say that my being in at four usually meant that they showed up by 4:30, but decided to let it go. With Virgil out of the picture and the dinner scheduled for tonight, we'd be squeezing blood out of every single minute today. I was glad to have them here.

We'd already blocked out our tasks for the day, divvying up the temporary chefs among ourselves to get everything done on time.

As executive chef I had minimal food-making responsibilities. What I needed to do was ensure that everyone else was staying on task, that the courses were being prepared correctly, and that the presentation of each was perfect.

Most of the frantic work would happen in those last hours before we began to serve. And even though the stress wouldn't diminish until the last plate was carried out the door, I always loved every minute of it.

"Josh promised to be down here around noon," I said.

"Wow. That's early," Bucky said. "Won't it be a long day for him . . . and for us?"

"Could be," I admitted. "I think he'll do fine, though. He's a tenacious soul."

Cyan elbowed me. "No wonder you two get along so well."

Urlich poked his head into the kitchen later that morning.

"I didn't expect to see you today," I said.

"Change in plan. Alec needs me to meet him at the office, pronto."

"Has something happened?"

Urlich grimaced. "I don't know," he said with a burst of frustration. "Clearly something is up, but he isn't telling me what it is. He claims he wants to go over our presentations again, but there must be more to it. He warned me that he'll need me there for the rest of the day. What could possibly keep me busy that long?"

It was a rhetorical question, so I didn't answer. Urlich's exasperation with his boss, though evident, still didn't explain what he was doing here in the kitchen. As if reading my mind, he said, "I'm here to ask if you need to go anywhere today. I can arrange for a backup bodyguard if you do."

Surrounded by fresh, soaking-wet spinach leaves, I almost laughed out loud. "I think it's highly unlikely I'll leave this kitchen at all today," I said. "You're safe."

"Thanks," he said. "Uh . . . Your errand yesterday to the courthouse . . . did you ever get out there?"

"No, couldn't make it. Business got in the way. If I don't have a chance later, let me wish you good luck with your speech tonight. Excited about that?"

His eyes roved the kitchen, but it seemed as though he wasn't seeing anything. "Nervous is more like it. Alec wants to go over every word, every nuance. He says that our speeches tonight will go down in history."

"I thought you said you needed to connect with a colleague who was helping you with your speeches."

"Yeah," he said with more than a little anger. "That was the original plan. Thanks to Alec, however, everything has been turned on its head." He shrugged. "What can I say?" With a final look around the kitchen, he sighed. "See you later, Ollie."

When he was gone, Cyan turned to me. "I didn't think that Urlich was all that cute at first. He's starting to grow on me."

I laughed. "Two things: He's got to be at least ten years older than you are, and he's seeing someone named . . . what is it? Naomi, I think. He mentioned it on one of our commutes."

Cyan wrinkled her nose. "Darn." She wiggled her finger toward the guest list we had tacked to the wall. "There are a couple of other cuties coming to dinner tonight. Have you met Tyree and Larsen?"

"Have you?"

"They came down here once when you were up talking with Sargeant," she said. "Very polite. Very deferential."

"What did they say or do?"

She shrugged. "Looked around a little. Asked a few questions. Nothing special, why?"

I shook my head, but Cyan wasn't finished with her wish list. Her finger stopped about halfway up. "What about Alec Baran? He's gorgeous."

"He's also rich and powerful," I said. "Nice pick."

"Not so rich after the president's dinner tonight," Bucky said. "Remember the big announcement and ceremony they have planned. Baran is supposed to give that speech about how he supports the president's decision to pull mercenary forces out of Durasi. I don't know that I believe him."

"I don't know that I do, either," I said. Alec's speech was one of many scheduled to start immediately after dinner was served. I should be excited, and yet if I put my finger on it, I'd have to say my mood was something else entirely. Terrified, maybe.

I felt as though I was missing an important kernel of truth, a key point, or some flash of inspiration that might help answer my myriad of questions. No matter how hard I tried, however, it was just beyond my reach.

The first wave of SBA chefs arrived right on time, and we put them to work. I had two women in charge of deboning dozens of pheasants and slicing pockets into the sides of the breasts — just so — to make room for the wild rice stuffing that was currently being put together by a team across the kitchen.

I'd provided precise instructions for every step of every process. Although I had no doubt these chefs had made dishes similar to this one before, I insisted on instructing them step-by-step on how I wanted tasks completed. Each and every breast had to be perfect, so that they would present uniformly when served.

I was pleased that one of the women was Agda. One of our favorite SBA chefs, she was tall, cheerful, and took to the task of deboning the pheasants with her customary speed and accuracy. She spoke little English, but she was one of the hardest-working chefs in the business. Every single one of the portions she worked on came out like a thing of beauty.

Another chef we'd used before, Samantha, was struggling to keep up with Agda. "Take your time," I said after she'd ruined three breasts by cutting the pocket too deep. "This isn't a race."

"Yes, Chef." Slightly chubby, with tightly fastened maroon hair, Samantha was about twenty-five. The last time she'd been here, Virgil had belittled her in front of the rest of the staff. I noticed how she glanced up in fear every time someone entered the kitchen. It wasn't hard to deduce the reason for her anxiety.

"By the way," I added, conversationally, "Chef Ballantine won't be here today."

"Was he fired?" she asked, pale eyes growing bigger, more fearful. "Last time I read about him in the paper it sounded like he still worked here."

"He's not here today," I said, unwilling to share any more than that. "You can relax a little. We're all on the same team."

She nodded eagerly. "Thank you, Chef."

We worked quickly and efficiently, and mostly quietly. The kitchen tension would build as serving time approached, and it would get louder down here. For now, as I walked among the many busy assistants making the magic happen, I appreciated the team's calm competence.

"I'm here," Josh announced in the doorway, right at noon. He had two Secret Service agents assigned to keep tabs on him while he worked in the kitchen with us.

"Wonderful," I said. I knew Bucky and Cyan weren't thrilled by the prospect of having a youngster traipsing about in our busy kitchen, but I knew how important this was to Josh. "Come on over here."

I placed my hands on the boy's shoulders and raised my voice to the room. "Attention, everyone."

Chopping, stirring, and rolling ceased. All

eyes turned to me.

"As you probably know, this is the president's son, Josh. He's going to be helping us here today in the kitchen and we'll be encouraging him to help some of you. He's very capable and he's eager to learn. Two rules: One, if you would like assistance and you believe Josh might be able to help, come to me and I'll decide whether to assign that task to him; and Two, under no circumstances are you to share any information about Josh, any stories about his presence here in the kitchen, or even that he *was* here, with anyone outside these walls. Like everything else in the White House, you will keep information you acquire here confidential. Failure to do so will result in you being blacklisted from our SBA lists. If anyone here believes they will be unable to comply, now's the time to speak up."

No one did.

"Great," I said. "Thank you, all." As they returned to their jobs, I spoke to Josh. "You know that things may get a little crazy here, right?"

"I know. I'll stay out of your way when that happens." For the first time since I'd agreed to have him here while we prepared dinner, his eager smile and nod worried me. I hoped I wouldn't regret the decision to include him.

"You know that this is a really important night for your dad, right?"

I thought Josh might have been tempted to roll his eyes. "That's all he's been talking about this week."

"We have a lot of work set aside for you. When you're chopping your hundredth carrot, it may not feel as though you're helping, but I promise, you are."

He gave me a very solemn look. Maybe that was his substitute for an eye roll. "I made dinner for my family before, remember?" he asked, so innocently. So confidently. "I think I can handle this."

I tamped down a smile. "I think you can, too. Let's get you started."

A little while later, Cyan sidled up to me. "I didn't realize the Secret Service was supposed to stay right next to him," she whispered, gesturing to where we'd gotten Josh settled dicing dried apricots. She gave a melodramatic glance around the room. "And we thought we were cramped before, huh?"

The two large men accompanying Josh remained quietly alert, but were not friendly in the least. They flanked the small boy, at all times keeping an eye on every movement in the kitchen.

"We have a bunch of chefs here within ten feet of the president's son, all handling sharp knives and hot implements," I said. "Granted, everyone here has been thoroughly vetted, but they're not taking any chances. I don't blame them. Besides, you and I both know that we've worked under more challenging circumstances. Compared to a few of our other situations, this one is nothing."

She hefted the two containers of molasses she'd brought in from storage. "True that."

I did a quick check of Josh's progress. His pile of chopped dried apricots was growing. "Getting bored yet?" I asked.

"No way," he said. "Will these really be used tonight? You're not going to have me chop up a bunch of stuff and not use it, will you?"

I put my hand over his, stopping him from working for a moment. "Would I do that to you?"

"I didn't think so. But I overheard a couple of other chefs talking about what happens to the food they're working on when they don't do something exactly right. It doesn't get served."

I directed his gaze toward the center work area, where Agda and Samantha were still slicing the pheasant breasts. "Those have to be exactly right. Exactly perfect. Every single one of them. I've put two of our more experienced chefs on that task because I know that they're going to be able to deliver the results we need, quickly." I put my face close to Josh's ear, while indicating Samantha. "One of the two chefs is newer, but she's very talented. I'm hoping that by giving her this job, we'll boost her confidence. It isn't hard work, but it is exacting."

Taking a few of the chopped apricots from Josh's pile, I continued. "You see how these are more or less uniform in size? That's perfect because then they'll cook evenly. We will use every single one of these apricots." I replaced the diced fruit I'd picked up and said, "You're doing an awesome job, Josh. Keep it up."

As I patted him on the shoulder, I could feel him straighten, looking a little more pleased with himself, a little prouder than he had been moments earlier. "Thanks, Ollie."

We worked quietly and efficiently until the next group of SBA chefs began to arrive. "Over there," I said to two of them, pointing to the corner where Bucky was directing his team. To Bucky, I said, "Bring them up to speed on Josh."

Three other temporary team members

waited to be told what to do — two men, one woman, all in their twenties, eager and excited to be cooking in the White House. I recognized all of them as having worked with us before, but as I led them through to the pantry, I went over a few general rules, in case any of them needed a reminder.

As we moved from one area to the next, I caught sight of Margaret coming into the kitchen from the other side.

"Over here," I said to the chefs in my charge, indicating the wide workspace we'd opened up for these three, "is where we're going to have you stuff the pheasant breasts."

Wearing a bright-blue skirt suit and an expression of unease, Margaret held a book against her chest, both hands wrapped around the back of it, looking like a schoolgirl who was late and trying to sneak into class. If she hadn't been wearing such a vivid color she may have managed to get in and out without my seeing her. There were more bodies in the kitchen this afternoon than usual, and as the new people got settled, the place clattered, and chattered, and hummed.

She made her way across the kitchen, dodging chefs who were moving back and forth laden with trays and doing their best to avoid the woman. I kept talking to my group, delivering all the updates these young chefs needed, including my warnings about not sharing information about Josh's presence in the kitchen, but my curiosity about Margaret's presence was piqued.

I answered a few questions the young chefs had for me about how I wanted specific steps completed. Once I was able to leave the three alone to settle themselves at their stations, I set out to find what Margaret was up to.

CHAPTER 25

The kitchen was a sea of stainless steel and white. The decibel level of discussion here had grown over the past hour or so, and the din of clanking pots and pans was almost deafening.

I peered around the many bodies bustling about my kitchen, but couldn't catch a flash of the blue that Margaret had been wearing. Where was she?

"Cyan." I tapped her on the arm. "What's up with Margaret?"

My assistant half turned, halting tomato slicing as she looked around the kitchen. "Margaret?" she asked. "Is that one of our SBA chefs?"

"Sargeant's assistant," I said. "What was she doing down here?"

"Beats me," Cyan said, returning to her task. "I didn't even see her."

Bucky had no more light to shed, either. "I caught a glimpse of her and before I could say 'Boo,' she was gone again."

"That's odd," I said to myself. The noise level in the kitchen was too high for me to make a phone call from my regular workstation. As I made my way around to find a quieter spot, I checked on Josh. "How is it going?"

"I'm almost done," he said. "Take a look."

He wasn't kidding. "That's wonderful," I said sincerely. I'd expected the task to take him another twenty minutes, at least. "As soon as I get back, I'll get you started on the next part, how does that sound?"

"I'm ready," he said.

The two Secret Service agents flanking him didn't react, and didn't say a word.

I addressed them anyway. "Be back in a flash."

Having made a full circuit of the kitchen, I returned to the pantry, where I'd left the three young chefs who'd most recently arrived. They seemed surprised to see me back so soon. I waved a hand, dispelling their obvious concern, and picked up the nearest telephone.

"Margaret," I said when she answered, "this is Ollie — Olivia Paras — from the kitchen."

"Mr. Sargeant is not in his office at the moment," she said before I could get another word out. "He's quite tied up today, as you might imagine."

"It's you I wanted to talk with," I said. "Were you down here in the kitchen a few moments ago?"

"I'll say I was," she answered. "I barely made it out with my life. All those sharp knives and angry people." Even over the phone line I could practically hear her shudder. "How do you stand it?"

"What were you doing down here?" I asked. "I saw you hurry in, but when I looked for you, you were gone."

"I wasn't trying to hide what I was doing, I was simply returning a cookbook," she said.

I didn't understand. "As a general rule we don't lend out the kitchen's cookbooks. You borrowed one?"

"Of course not. I was returning the cookbook that Virgil took home by mistake. Apparently you were wrong. He did take one that didn't belong to him. He thought you needed it for today's dinner, so he sent it back."

Virgil deluding himself that we needed something of his for this dinner when, in actuality, we had everything under control was believable. Him being thoughtful enough to provide what we needed, was not.

"Slow down," I said. "Explain. You talked with him? He actually said that?"

"I didn't speak with him directly, no. He sent the book back with one of our agents. She brought it to me a little while ago and stressed that Virgil insisted that it be returned to you today. I knew you'd be busy and I remembered where he'd taken it from, so I slipped in and put it back on the shelf."

Speechless, I covered my eyes with one hand and tried to understand why Virgil would do such a thing. "Thank you, Margaret."

"Anytime," she said, and hung up.

"Ollie," Cyan called when I replaced the handset. "Got a minute?"

A half hour later, I'd finished working with Cyan only to find that Josh was ready for his next task. "You are a delight," I said to him.

"You mean I'm not getting underfoot like my mom thought I would?"

"You're a valuable member of today's team," I said. "Now, let's get you started with shallots. Are you going to be able to handle these?" I provided him with a face mask to help shield against tears that inevitably arose when chopping these bulbs. Although they were kinder, gentler cousins of the mighty onion, they still held the power to make us cry if we weren't careful.

Once he was settled again, I took another walk around the kitchen. Dinner was at 7, and we were closing in on 5. I needed to ensure that we were staying on schedule first. Then, I'd have a look at the cookbook Margaret had brought back to the kitchen.

I finally made it to the shelf about fifteen minutes later. My gaze skipped over the colorful spines, hurrying past the familiar titles to find Virgil's cookbook. Two seconds later, I had it in my hands and began paging through.

"What's up, Ollie?" Bucky asked me quietly. "Is there a problem?"

I smiled up at him, in a hurry to reassure. He had to be shocked to find me poring through a cookbook so close to showtime. At this point there should be no second-guessing, no referencing of recipes. We had every step for every dish printed out and posted across the kitchen, affixed to our appliances and stainless steel cabinets with powerful magnets. All at eye height.

I couldn't blame Bucky for worrying. The last thing one of us should be doing was double-checking that we'd gotten everything right. That moment had come and gone. "Not at all," I said. I held up Virgil's book so that Bucky could see the dust jacket. "Margaret brought this back to the kitchen a little while ago. She said that Virgil thought we'd need it today."

The look on Bucky's face mirrored my own disbelief. "That's crazy."

"You think?" I asked. "Not only is that not Virgil's personality, he'd have to know we wouldn't be bothering with this book today. Why did he send it back? Why did he insist Margaret get it to us immediately?"

"You've got me suspicious now." Bucky took a step back. "You think there's a bomb in it?"

"That's not funny," I said.

"Wasn't meant to be." Bucky shrugged. "But I can't see Virgil doing anything for us out of the kindness of his heart. That means something is up."

"I agree." I slapped the book shut and returned it to the shelf. "Do you think he believes that if he keeps his property here it will ensure his eventual return to duty?"

"Who knows what goes on in that head of his?" Bucky asked rhetorically. One of his chef assistants called to him just then. "Gotta run. Don't worry too much about it," he said. "It's just a cookbook."

When he left I started back into the activity around me, thinking about Bucky's "bomb" comment. A prickle of unease worked its way up the back of my neck, and I reached for the cookbook again. "Why are you here?" I asked it.

Again, I paged through the thick volume, turning the book on its side and shaking it, in case some handy-dandy clue might fall out.

Nothing.

The noise level behind me was growing and I knew I'd be pulled away any moment, but I couldn't put the book down; not yet. Not until I figured out what possible reason Virgil had for returning it.

I paged through again, more slowly this time. I wasn't seeing the words nor looking at the pictures, I was waiting for the answer to jump out at me. Paging faster, I realized what a ridiculous exercise this was, what a waste of time. I kept paging, however, through the thirties, the forties, and fifties —

Page fifty-three, I stopped. And stared.

"Cyan," I called over the busy din. "Do you have a minute?"

She was at my side a second later. "What's up?"

"Remember when you spilled on Virgil's book? This one?" I held it up for her to see the front dust cover.

345

"How could I forget? I don't think I'll ever get over my hatred of the number fifty-three."

"It was page fifty-three then, wasn't it?"

"Boy, was it ever. What's this about, Ollie?"

I held the book open and pointed. "Look."

She scanned the recipe, the entire page, up and down, her violet eyes straining to see what she knew had to be there. "What happened to the stain?"

"This isn't the same book," I said.

Creases formed between her brows. "Yeah," she said slowly. "I think you're right." After a quick glance over her shoulder, she said, "Not that I don't think this is weird and all, but right now my time is better spent elsewhere." She pointed to the clock. "Look how close we are."

"Five thirty," I said and my pulse quickened as the words came out. "You're right." I put the book back. Cyan returned to her team and I went to check on the young chefs in the pantry.

I couldn't get the cookbook out of my mind. Why would Virgil have sent a replacement? It made no sense. Again, I reminded myself that Virgil wasn't that thoughtful of a guy. Why would he do that? Unless . . .

Unless he *didn't*.

346

I froze in place.

"Chef?" One of the male assistants looked ready to grab me. Maybe he thought I was about to faint. "Is something wrong?"

I stopped my inspection of the stuffed pheasants. "Nothing," I said. "Nothing. Carry on."

I turned my heel on them and grabbed the book again. I hurried out, and made my way to the refrigeration area where I could find a quiet moment alone. I had to have faith that my team would be fine without me for five minutes.

This book had shown up on the day of the state dinner. Too much had been happening around today's event for me to consider it a coincidence. This book might mean nothing, but my gut told me differently. I stared at it a long moment. This time I didn't page through.

"Come on," I whispered to the book. "I know you've got something to tell me. Give it up."

CHAPTER 26

I held the book in both hands and concentrated. What could this mean? Who had brought this book to the White House? Why?

"Ollie?" Cyan called to me from outside the refrigeration area. "Josh needs another job."

"I'll be there in a minute," I said.

I turned the book over. The dust jacket featured an array of colorful vegetables and prepared entrées looking as though they were being served al fresco at a Tuscan villa. I had no idea why this particular title might be of any importance. I opened the front cover to see if any notes had been written inside.

That's when I noticed that the dust jacket had been fortified with clear tape. Someone had taken the time to ensure that the glossy cover wouldn't fall off.

My heart pounding, I eased the clear tape from the bottom flap, then from the top, releasing the dust jacket, which now hung from its hold on the back cover, swinging below the opened book. The weight of the loosened cover was not right. It was significantly heavier than it should have been.

Breath coming in quick gasps, I sat on the floor and turned the book over in my lap, flipping it to examine the dust jacket.

"Oh!" My hand flew to my mouth as I exclaimed my surprise. Attached to the inside of the dust jacket were several light-weight, folded sheets of paper.

I opened the first one and began to read.

In a hurry, I scanned it, then moved to the next. I couldn't do more than skim — I had a dinner to serve, after all — but in the forty-five seconds I allowed myself to study the documents, I understood what an explosive set of allegations I held in my hand.

"No," I said aloud.

The first document was a letter addressed to President Hyden, printed on Secretary of Defense Cobault's office stationery. Dated two days before Cobault's murder, the document warned the president not to remove mercenary forces from Durasi. Secretary Cobault's letter went on to express disappointment in the president's decision to withdraw, and further, advised him that if these changes were implemented,

"Consequences will be dire." Secretary Cobault also warned that if the president didn't reverse his plans immediately, he, Cobault, would bring "a certain unpleasant truth" to the American people. In very clear language that even I couldn't misinterpret, the secretary threatened that if this truth were to get out, President Hyden would likely face impeachment.

Perspiration shot out of my every pore. I held a hand against my face, feeling my whole body tremble. Hadn't Gav told me himself that Secretary Cobault had been wholly *against* the use of mercenary forces? This correspondence made it sound as though he'd taken the exact opposite position. What did this letter mean, and why was it here?

The second document read like a newspaper article. Without names, except for the byline: Daniel Davies. The article was a rough blueprint of an exposé claiming that President Hyden had ordered the murders of the five men at the Ainsley Street Ministry, that he'd ordered the murder of Secretary Cobault, and that he'd done all this to protect himself from allowing the truth to come out that Kalto had been the driving force behind peace in Durasi, and that pulling them from the area now was only being done to achieve the president's ambitious goal of securing a prominent place in history.

What? That makes no sense.

Kalto was characterized as the underdog, the highly respected, well-run organization that had done everything right, had played by the rules, and yet was now getting shafted by the president's directive. The president came across as a power-hungry dictator who would stop at nothing to have his way.

Scrawled across the top of the article, in script that had a woman's flourish, a quick note: "He's sitting on this until we give him the okay. Looks good, doesn't it?"

My hands were still shaking. This couldn't be right. None of this could be true, could it? The president I knew was an honorable man. He would never stoop to such activities. And yet, this letter from the secretary of defense . . .

Instinctively, I reached for my phone. I dialed Gav first, but the call went straight to voice mail. Fine. I'd find Tom. He had to be around here somewhere.

I stuffed the documents into my pocket, tucked the book under my arm, and raced back to the kitchen, where I was immediately besieged with questions. "Does this presentation look right?" "How often should we stir the potatoes?" "Josh is finished with the shallots, what should he do next?"

I faced each one in turn, giving staccato answers, assuring one of the assistants that I'd be over to help Josh soon and to ask the boy to sit tight and wait for me.

Bucky sidled up, keeping his voice low. "What's wrong, Ace? I've never seen you this stressed."

Still holding the book, I grabbed one of Bucky's hands. "You are in charge. You got that?"

"What happened?"

"Listen to me," I said, lowering my voice. "I don't have time to explain. You're in charge. Don't let me down."

The look on his face shifted from puzzlement to determination. "You got it, Chief. Go. Do whatever you need to do."

I took off with the book pulled close to my chest, much the way Margaret had held it when she'd carried it in. I hurried past my dumbfounded chefs to the spiral staircase, my feet thudding as I raced up the metallic steps. From above, I caught a whiff of the evening's dessert, Lemon Steamed Pudding, but didn't stop, even when the chefs on this level greeted me with surprised hellos.

I hurried across to cut through the Family Dining Room, where more of our SBA chefs were working at the final staging area before food was handed off to be served.

When I showed up in front of Margaret's desk, I thought she'd fall over from shock. "You told me you never allowed yourself to be seen when guests were present. We've got hundreds of people in the East Room at a black-tie affair."

"No one saw me," I snapped. "That's not important right now." I held out the book. "Who brought this to you? I need to know."

Though primly annoyed, she didn't hesitate to answer. "The agent who helped escort Virgil out, I told you." I could tell my abrupt manner and unexpected appearance was alarming her. "I don't know who she is, though. How would I know?"

"Where's Sargeant?" I asked.

Collecting herself, she gave me a "duh" look and said, "*Mr.* Sargeant is in the East Room, enjoying dinner. Which, I believe you" — she spiraled her index finger at me — "are supposed to be preparing." Cocking her head sideways, she said, "Or am I mistaken?"

"Is she here?" I asked. "The agent. Is the agent who gave you this book here tonight?"

Another wide-eyed look that told me she

believed I'd gone off my nut. "Of course she's here. How do you think she could have handed it to me otherwise?"

I dropped the book on her desk. "Come with me," I said. "Point her out."

"I will do no such thing," she said. "Mr. Sargeant expects me to stay right here, all night."

I placed my palms on her desk and leaned across. "Do you like your job?" I asked.

"What kind of question is —"

"You heard Sargeant the other day. I don't come to see him unless it's important. If you don't want him to fire you for refusing to help in an emergency . . . and he *will* fire you" — that was probably a stretch, but I desperately needed her cooperation right now — "you will show me who it was who brought this book to you."

Her manner shifted as she smelled gossip. "Has she done something wrong?"

"Yes," I said. "Now, you said this was an agent. Did she belong to the Secret Service or to Kalto?"

"How should I know? They're all agents to me."

"You're sure she's still here?" I asked.

"No, but I'd recognize her right away."

I grabbed her arm, intending to lead her out into the Entrance Hall. "Don't be obvious," I said.

"You're the one in the chef's outfit," she countered. "Which one of us is obvious?"

She had a point. "Tell you what. Go see if you can find her. If you do, come back and then we'll take it from there."

Margaret scurried across to peer into the East Room then made a quick circuit of the Entrance Hall. She was back in less than thirty seconds. "She's right outside the Blue Room, talking with another agent. I pretended I was looking for someone else and she didn't even give me a passing look. Is that un-obvious enough for you?"

Outside the Blue Room. That meant that if I circled around and peered out through the State Dining Room's doors, I'd get a good view of her. Problem was, the doors remained open between that room and the Family Dining Room where my stealth surveillance could raise eyebrows among the busy staff. "Come on," I said to Margaret. "This will be quick."

At each step, I expected one of the Secret Service agents on duty to stop me and question my presence here. Whether the Secret Service had gotten used to my eccentricities, or whether Tom had told them all to give me carte blanche, I didn't know. We made our way into the bustling Family Dining and into the semi-dark State Dining Room.

We crossed that large area to another doorway that led us into the Red Room and from there it wouldn't take long to get to the Blue Room. Thank goodness all these rooms were connected.

"Are you going to walk right up to her?" Margaret asked.

I shook my head. "It's dark in there and the agents are posted to keep people from getting into the State Rooms, not from coming out. We can sneak up to the doorway and take a look. With any luck, you'll be able to get a good view of her and point her out to me."

We tiptoed into the darkened, oval-shaped Blue Room. When we made our way across to the bright doorway that led to the Entrance Hall, I felt slow and clumsy, as though my feet were encased in twenty-pound boots.

"Right there," Margaret said before I even had a chance to ask. Pointing to a woman positioned a few feet outside the doorway, she said, "The one wearing the navy pants and jacket."

I studied the woman, thinking that I'd never seen her before. Who was she and why had she hidden information in my kitchen?

What role did she play that made her privy to such damaging information? She paced back and forth outside the room, as did several of the other agents, but almost as if she sensed me watching, she kept her back to me.

Taller than I was, she was slim with short hair. I didn't recognize her as a member of the Secret Service and I knew most of the female agents at the White House. She must belong to Kalto.

"Who is she?" Margaret asked.

"I don't know," I said. "I don't think I've ever seen her befo—"

I stopped myself as the woman glanced up toward the grand staircase, giving me a full view of her profile. My stomach lurched as recognition hit. The skeletal cheeks, the slightly bulbous nose.

It was her. This was the woman who'd pushed me from the train platform.

CHAPTER 27

I must have whispered an exclamation because Margaret nudged me. "You *do* recognize her. Who is she? Why are we watching her?"

At that moment the woman turned in our direction and I ducked out of the doorway, pulling Margaret with me. I started away, intending to return to the kitchen. "Wait," I said, deciding to push my luck a little. "I don't want to lose sight of her." I resumed my position at the door, again pulling Margaret with me.

"Why? What has she done?"

"Do you know who Tom MacKenzie is?"

Margaret adopted her snarly personality again. "Of course I do. How could I work for the chief usher and not know who —"

"Find him," I said, wondering what my next move should be if Margaret couldn't locate Tom quickly. I'd had no luck contacting Gav and the only other people in the know were too high ranking for me to get close to during dinner. I could just picture myself walking up to the president and trying to explain this to him as Secret Service agents took me down, kicking and screaming. Chef or no chef, one didn't simply walk up to the president without warning.

My only other option was Urlich, but I knew he was at dinner right now. If I asked one of the agents on duty to call him out, I could possibly talk with him. But how suspicious would that look to my would-be assassin? I wouldn't be able to tell Urlich much, except that I'd recognized the woman. He would know what to do.

I needed to do something and I couldn't do it here. I'd about resigned myself to leaving our surveillance spot when the female agent excused herself from the other agent she'd been talking with to meander a few steps away, where she pulled out her cell phone and studied it, as though she'd received a text. She kept her face impassive, but I thought I detected a ghost of a smile. She returned the phone to her pocket, looking for all purposes like she'd received very welcome news, indeed.

Margaret tugged at my arm, but I shushed her. I needed to know what the agent would do next. "Thirty seconds," I said, "give me thirty seconds."

We waited, Margaret constantly urging me to leave. So much for her rushing off to find Tom, I thought. "Okay," I said, finally, but as I was about to relinquish my spot, movement caught my eye.

Urlich had emerged from the East Room and was making his way toward the State Dining Room. Could there be more perfect timing? I wanted to alert him now, this minute, but I held back. Especially at a time like this, during a dinner with so many dignitaries present. I needed to operate in stealth. I waited for him to cross the hallway, trying to determine where he might be going. If his destination was the State Dining Room or beyond, then it might be possible to intercept him long enough to bring him up to speed.

The female agent had spotted him, too, and approached him.

No, I thought. *Not now.*

My body jerked, itching to do something to get Urlich's attention but the look on the female agent's face stopped me cold. She smiled. Not the kind of smile you give an acquaintance. Not the kind of smile you give your boss. This was a quiet, intimate smile.

When Urlich returned the warm expression, it hit me.

"That's Naomi!" I whispered.

"What?" Margaret asked.

I put my hand on her shoulder, silently shushing her.

Unaware of our scrutiny, Urlich and Naomi talked. From their body language, it seemed as though they were tense, but in a cheerful, excited way. And clearly together. Definitely together. She smirked as she spoke, checked to make sure none of the other agents were looking, and ran her fingers along his arm.

The Keeper's words echoed in my mind. The yin, the yang. The he and the she. Two made up the demon. At that moment, I knew. Deep down with every fiber of my being, I knew. The Keeper was right. I'd been on the path to enlightenment, all right. I just hadn't expected to come about it from this direction.

Unfortunately, I still had more of the journey ahead of me. Although I knew they were planning something, I had no idea what it could be.

"Come on," I said to Margaret as we hurried back into the Red Room. I shut the door to the Blue Room behind us and kept my voice low. I had to hurry. Urlich might come down to the kitchen at any moment. I had no doubt he was on his way to pick up the book with the notes Naomi had secreted inside.

"Listen carefully," I said. "Get back to your desk and hide the book. Get it out of sight. If anyone asks, tell them you put it in the kitchen. Don't let anyone know I asked you about it. You returned it to the kitchen shelf. That's all you know, got it? Don't breathe another word. Do you understand?"

Margaret's eyes were wide. "Mr. Sargeant told me you were difficult."

"You're getting a taste of it," I said. "Now go. I have to get downstairs fast. And please, find Tom MacKenzie. Tell him I need him now."

I hurried back through the State Dining Room and into the Family Dining Room, where I made a show of checking on our SBA chefs' progress. I retraced the steps I'd taken just five minutes earlier, backtracking through the pantry, taking the circular steps down as fast as I could to get to the kitchen before Urlich showed up.

My breath came fast and shallow. My head spun.

The busy kitchen staff was in the middle of plating the next course, covering dishes, loading the dumbwaiters. I took a quick glance at the clock. Seven twenty. Right on schedule.

Bucky stopped me as I crossed the Butler's Pantry. "What's going on?" he asked.

I grabbed both his forearms and stared him straight in the eye. "Tell me. Dinner. How is it going?" I asked.

"Very well," he said. "No problems."

I let go. "Thank goodness for that."

"What's wrong?"

How could I tell him that in my pocket were raging screeds that if made public — especially tonight, especially when peace negotiations with Durasi were within sight — could permanently ruin relations between our two countries? I couldn't.

From the moment I'd first read the documents in my pocket, I knew the allegations contained within them couldn't be true. Gav knew the secretary of defense's position on this matter. Gav had told me and I believed him.

Even if I doubted Gav — and I didn't — even if I thought it possible that the secretary of defense had had a change of heart, and the president could possibly be guilty of those despicable crimes, I knew better. I had proof now.

The woman who'd hidden these documents in my kitchen had been the one who'd tried to kill me. Which meant that she, working with Urlich, had killed the men at the Ainsley Street Ministry. Which further meant that they'd killed Secretary Cobault and attempted to kill the Keeper as well.

They were the bad guys.

A thought flashed through my brain, wondering why Urlich hadn't killed me when he'd had the chance. He had been my guardian, after all. Plenty of opportunity. There had to be a reason he'd allowed me to stay alive. This cookbook situation made me believe he'd kept me around because he needed a reason to have access to the kitchen. I shook my head — right now wasn't the time to ponder such things.

"I can't tell you," I said to Bucky, as I worked to corral the thoughts stampeding through my brain. The only thing that made sense to me at this moment was that the paperwork I'd found must have something to do with Urlich's scheduled speech tonight.

"What in the world have you gotten yourself into now?" Bucky asked. Hands up, he said, "Forget it. Don't answer, that was rhetorical."

I raised the back of my sleeve to my forehead, thinking about what a perfect storm of trouble these documents could cause if made public, especially tonight.

There were hundreds of guests and all sorts of media types swarming. It didn't matter that the allegations weren't true, Urlich could wreak havoc on the administration's careful plans for peace. I couldn't imagine the chaos that would result. Urlich apparently wanted to destroy all hope of negotiations with Durasi. What kind of person didn't want peace?

The only thing that made sense was that Urlich and Naomi had something to lose in this race. But what? Prominent jobs at Kalto? The position in Durasi that Urlich claimed to love? That hardly seemed worth all this effort. Again, I couldn't worry about this now. I had to find Gav or Tom.

The door opened behind Bucky, and Urlich came through, smiling as though delighted to see me. He raised a hand in greeting. Instinctively, I raised mine in return. "Keep everything running smoothly," I said to Bucky. "And don't say a word to anyone about this, okay?"

His face was grim. "You know I won't, Ollie. Go do what you need to do. We're covered here."

As Bucky turned away to oversee the remainder of the dinner preparation, Urlich reached my side. "You look upset. Anything wrong?"

I puffed up my cheeks. "You know how it is," I said. "Last-minute details are always the toughest to get straight."

He laughed even though there was no reason to. "Hey, do you mind if I hang down here for a few? I need to walk off my jitters. I've got a huge case of nerves." He managed a sheepish look. "I've never given a speech like this one before."

"I'll bet," I said.

He rubbed his stomach and attempted to look miserable. "I'm missing dinner but I can't eat. Too worked up. I'll just stay down here for a while."

"Fine," I lied, "but do me a favor and stay out of the main part of the kitchen." I gestured vaguely toward the busiest work area — the area where he'd have to go to find the book if, indeed, that's what he was here for. I worked up a heavy, overwrought sigh. "We have at least eight chefs shouting to be heard running around in that part of the kitchen. There are hot pans, high tempers, and delicate china. It's crazy in there and you could get hurt."

Darned right you could.

For one hopeful second, I held my breath. If he sauntered away without complaint, if he didn't attempt to look for that book, then I was wrong. I didn't think that was pos-

366

sible, but this was my last chance to be sure.

He scratched his head as though considering it. "I'll be quick. No bother at all. I'm only cutting through anyway," he said. "Look how much quieter it is on the other side. I'll go there." Ignoring my request, he took a step toward the kitchen.

"You'll be in the way." I put my hand on his arm, stopping him. "I'd really prefer you go around this time. In fact, I'm sure it will be quicker. Far less disruptive to my staff."

"Ollie," he said, his voice no longer quite so cheerful. "I need to get in there."

"No, you don't," I said. "This is my kitchen and I'm telling you to keep out."

Without another word, he started in again. I grabbed his arm, but this time he was ready for me. He shook me off, roughly.

"Don't touch me."

And with that, he bolted in, headed directly for the bookshelf.

Without Gav or Tom, without being able to trust anyone else to understand, let alone help me, I attempted to control my nerves enough to be able to come up with a plan. I had less than a minute before Urlich realized the book wasn't where it should be.

I crossed the room at a quick clip.

"Hey, Josh," I said, urging the boy away from his workspace and to the sink next to him. "It's time to wash your hands."

"I did that a few minutes ago."

"Josh," I said taking a tone with him he'd never heard from me before. "You need to wash your hands now. Come on."

The sink was about three steps away from Josh's workspace. Close enough for me to speak to him directly without the Secret Service agents overhearing. Keeping my back to the agents, with Josh in front of me, I acted as though I was helping the boy from over his shoulder. Dutifully, he began washing his hands.

Out of the corner of my eye I watched Urlich as he searched through the books on the shelf. *Gotcha,* I thought.

"What's wrong, Ollie?" Josh asked.

Keeping an eye on the renegade agent who'd begun pulling books out one at a time in an increasingly frantic search, I dug the secreted documents out of my pocket. "Dry up," I said. "Hurry."

As soon as he did and turned around, I stuffed the documents into Josh's hands. "I need your help," I said. "This is very important."

The little boy's eyes grew large. "What's the matter? Did I do something wrong?"

"Remember when you and I were in trouble together?" I whispered. As he nodded, I pushed the papers deeper into his fists. "This is like that."

He started to look down to see what he was holding.

"Don't," I said. "No one can see what we're doing. You need to take those papers to your dad. Now."

Josh looked confused. "He's at dinner," he said. "I'm not supposed to interrupt."

Using my body to shield our hands, I crouched to his level and covered the crumpled documents with his fingers as best I could. "Listen to me. This may be one of the most important jobs I ever give you."

He nodded.

"Nobody here can go see your dad without permission. Nobody. Except you." I waited until I saw that he understood. "They're in the East Room, you know that."

"Yeah."

"Go. Take these papers. Tell them he has to read them right now. Make sure he reads them *right away.* Don't let anyone stop you." I held his gaze. "Can you do that?"

The brave little boy I'd grown to love stared back with a combination of pride and resolve. "You can count on me, Ollie."

"I know I can. Don't let your escorts stop you. Tell them you have to see your dad. They *have* to listen to you. Got it?"

"Okay." Josh pushed the papers into his jeans' pockets and turned to his Secret Service guards. "I have to go upstairs now. I'm underfoot."

The two men acknowledged him and followed their young charge out the door. I watched them go, my heart thudding deep beats of fear. When I turned, Urlich was still at the bookshelf. Even though he remained in the way of everyone else in the kitchen, constantly buffeted by busy chefs hurrying in and out, he didn't budge. Anger and frustration twisted his features. Three cookbooks in the crook of his arm, he squatted to go eye level with the shelf as though to make sure his book hadn't fallen behind the others.

I walked over. "Agent Urlich," I said. "I told you before. You're in the way. You're going to have to leave my kitchen."

"I can't. Not yet."

When he looked up at me, I adopted the most convincing voice of concern I could manage. "What's wrong? What in the world are you looking for?"

"The chief usher's assistant," he asked. "Has she been down here today?"

"Margaret?" I asked, feigning innocence. "I haven't seen her in a while. Why would she come to the kitchen?"

Dropping the books to the floor, he turned away without answering.

I shot across the kitchen in the opposite direction, ripping off my apron and throwing it into the laundry bin as I ran past. I peeled off my white smock and dropped that in as well. I had on a gray T-shirt and navy slacks beneath my chef's whites. While hardly black-tie appropriate, my appearance couldn't be helped. No time to change.

I ran out into the ground-floor corridor, crossing it swiftly to take the stairs that led to a small space just outside the East Room. A quick right at the top of the steps and I'd be in.

Instead, I came face-to-face with an agent standing guard at the doorway. "Rosenow," I said.

She looked startled at my un-cheflike appearance. "Ollie, what are you doing —"

"No time to explain," I said, pointing into the adjacent East Room, where sounds of happy conversation, clinking crystal, and gentle dinner music floated by. "I need to get in there."

"Sorry." She blocked my path. "I can't allow you in."

"Agent Rosenow," I began, "I have no intention of causing any problems."

"No offense, Ollie, but you cause problems whether you intend to or not."

"Fine," I said eager to placate if that would get me what I needed, "let me have a look inside. I'll stay right here next to you and I swear I'll be unobtrusive."

She flexed her fingers, making her knuckles crack as she weighed my request. "Right here," she said, positioning herself close to, but still outside the doorway. "Right next to me. Don't move."

By the time I was able to see inside the room, Josh had already made his way across the expanse and was approaching the president's dais. A ripple of amusement made its way through the crowd, with exclamations of how cute the president's young son was. I held my breath as Josh and his two escorts made it to the front.

"What is Josh doing up here?" Rosenow asked.

I didn't answer.

The boy leaned over the fancy table to face his father, moving a silver candelabra to be able to perch on his elbows. A collective "Aww . . ." went up from the crowd.

Josh paid them no mind. He uncrumpled the folded papers, then handed them to his dad as my heart beat a terrified rhythm in my chest. I could see concern flash in President Hyden's face as Josh spoke. From this distance I couldn't hear a word they said, couldn't even see their lips to read them, but I could tell Josh was insistent. He poked a finger on the sheets more than once, and did his little-boy best to implore his dad to cooperate.

"Ollie, what's going on?" Rosenow asked.

I heard the tension in her voice, so this time I turned. "We were working in the kitchen together but he needed to take something to his dad," I answered vaguely. "I wanted to be sure he got up here safely."

That seemed to satisfy her. She stopped badgering me long enough to allow me to return my attention to the goings-on at the head table.

President Hyden stood, patted his son on the shoulder, and announced to all those gathered, "Just like being president, being a dad is also a twenty-four-hour-a-day job."

The audience laughed appreciably. President Hyden resumed his seat, smiling and joking with his tablemates. Josh hadn't moved. He waited for his dad's response, never budging from his perch across the table. His dad gave him a stern look, but finally nodded.

I watched President Hyden a moment longer. He unfolded the sheets, brought them to his lap below table height, and began scanning them. As he read, his posture grew more erect, his expression grim. Twice he glanced up into the crowd as though looking for someone, but returned immediately to reading once again.

The female agent, Naomi, had eased her way back into the room at some point. She studied Josh with a mixture of puzzlement and concern. She, too, began glancing around the room as though looking for someone.

When President Hyden stood and cleared his throat, the room went silent.

He ran a hand along his chin. "There's been a change in tonight's schedule," he said. Murmurs rose and the president held up both hands to quiet them.

"Nothing disastrous," he said with a forced smile. "And nothing wrong with the family." He leaned down to Josh and pointed to the door. "Go on upstairs. Upstairs, you understand."

Apparently unconvinced he'd done his job completely, Josh shook his head. The president pointed again. "Now, son."

This time, the boy complied.

I thanked Rosenow, wishing I knew whether Gav and Tom would trust this woman. I needed to confide in someone who would know what to do. But I didn't know, so I couldn't act. Spinning away, I hurried to meet Josh in the Entrance Hall, grabbing him by both arms. "Thank you," I said. "You were perfect. Now, like your dad said, you'd better go on upstairs."

"Dinner isn't over," he said. "I thought I was supposed to help the whole time."

"Josh," I said quickly and quietly. "Trust me. You helped more than anyone else tonight. This is a really big deal. But you have to go upstairs now. Right now you need to be where it's safe."

The word *safe* seemed to convince him. "Okay," he said slowly. "But I'll come back tomorrow, okay?"

"Can't wait," I said. Relief washed over me as he and his Secret Service team walked up the red-carpeted stairs to the private residence. He *was* safe. And maybe now the president would be as well.

CHAPTER 28

For the second time tonight, I hurried across the Entrance Hall's marble floor, intent on doubling back through the State Dining Room on my return route to the kitchen. Doing my best to appear sedate even though every ounce of me vibrated with tension, I tried to decide whether I should steal a few extra minutes to detour to the West Wing. Maybe I could find Tom on my own. Even if he wasn't there, someone in his office had to know where he'd gone. Heaven knows my impassioned plea to Margaret hadn't done the job.

At the cross hall, where a red runner covered the marble and softened my footfalls, I made a quick right and picked up my pace. Within seconds I was in the State Dining Room. It was still dark in here, more so than before because the door to the Family Dining Room had been shut. That was unexpected. And odd. I reached for the knob.

From the shadows behind me, "Where is it?"

I spun. "Agent Urlich," I said. "You startled me."

"Where is it?" he asked again.

As innocently as I could manage, I asked, "Where is what?"

Even in the dim light, I could see him study me, seeking evidence of deception. My being up here on the state level dressed in street clothes was certainly not in keeping with my executive chef duties, and I could read the hard suspicion on his face. I reminded myself that there were plenty of Secret Service agents around. Still, I took a wary step back.

His phone signaled a text; as he moved to answer it, I made for the door.

Urlich shot a hand out and grabbed my upper arm. "Where is the book? What did you do with it?"

"I don't know what you're talking about," I said, jerking away. "Get your hands off of me."

Noises from the food preparation going on in the adjacent Family Dining Room were too loud for anyone in there to be aware of activity, but a Secret Service agent standing in the hall had heard my exclamation.

He stepped into the room. "What's going on here?"

"Call Tom MacKenzie," I said to the agent. "Please."

Urlich waved the other man back and grabbed me again. "I need to take this woman in for questioning. She's caused a disturbance tonight."

I didn't recognize the newcomer, which meant he probably didn't recognize me. Without my chef's whites, I could be anyone. I could be a threat. I struggled to break free as the agent turned to speak into his microphone, holding up a hand in a gesture for Urlich to wait.

Before he could get a word out, Naomi strode into the room. Her sudden appearance was enough of a distraction to make the Secret Service agent glance up.

"Is there a problem here, gentlemen?" she asked.

The Secret Service agent was about to answer her, but at that same moment, Urlich let go of me long enough to whip a tube from his pocket. He shoved it beneath the agent's nose.

The quick, sickly smell made me clap a hand over my mouth. The agent never had that chance. His eyes rolled up for two long seconds before he toppled to the floor, the carpet deadening the sound of his fall.

I bolted, opening my mouth to scream, but the woman had anticipated my move. She grabbed hard, clamping a skinny, sweaty palm tight against my face, stifling my yell. In the same instant, she'd twisted one arm behind me so fiercely it brought tears in my eyes. I shook my head back and forth in an attempt to break free, but it was no use.

This Naomi might have been wiry, but she was strong. Even worse, she knew what she was doing. Every move I made resulted in her tightening her hold. I was forced to stop struggling before I lost consciousness from pain.

The Secret Service agent on the floor didn't moan, and didn't move. I couldn't tell if he was breathing. I hoped he was.

"What now?" Urlich asked the woman. With one hand still tight against my lips, maintaining dominance over my every excruciating move, she began yanking me toward the Red Room in violent, angry tugs. She ordered Urlich to grab the Secret Service agent and drag him, too.

I shouted against her sweaty fingers. Tried to bite. Straining for volume, I shouted again. I needed to alert the closest Secret Service agents. Where were they? Weren't we making enough noise for someone to notice?

We made it into the Red Room via the southernmost doors. They were keeping me as far away from the agents stationed in the hall as they could, given the circumstances. I fought with every scrap of strength I had. She was taller and far more muscular, but we were both sweating and I was beginning to slide out of her grasp. Trying my best to wriggle away, knowing my shouts were being stifled, I groaned as loudly as I could. Somebody was bound to hear that. They had to.

Urlich shut both sets of doors between the two rooms.

When he finished, Naomi thrust me into his arms. "Take her," she said. "She's tougher than she looks."

Again I started to scream, but they were ready for me. Urlich shoved fabric into my mouth — a wadded handkerchief — gagging me. He wrapped one arm around my middle, pinning my hands to my sides. I was suspended high enough that my toes barely touched the floor.

"Not another sound," he said.

I shook my head violently, pushing my

tongue against the fabric trying to force it out but it stuck to the inside of my mouth. A corner of the fabric slid down the back of my throat, making me gag. Even as I struggled, I tried to anticipate what might happen next. Tried to figure a way out.

Naomi quietly closed the doors from the Red Room to the Entrance Hall, cutting off my chance to alert Secret Service agents. What plan could these two possibly have? The documents they'd so carefully sequestered were now out of their reach. What would they try to do next?

Even if their only motivation right now was revenge, how could they expect to get me out of the White House to exact retribution? There was no way. No way at all. This residence was guarded like no other. I tried screaming and moaning again, but everything came out muted and low.

The two of them must have been thinking the same thing about escape because Urlich spun to face Naomi, his voice practically zinging with fury. "What now?"

"She ruined it," she said in a low voice that nearly broke with emotion. "Ruined it. All our plans."

Naomi shoved a fist under my chin, tilting my face up. "We can't get you out of here and we don't have much time. What we do have, however, is this." She pulled out a vial and held it aloft so that its shiny casing caught the light.

She gestured to Urlich, who manhandled me around the furniture, along the room's south wall, positioning me between the Red Room's tall windows. That way we wouldn't be seen in case an outside guard looked in, I supposed. I struggled, but Urlich was strong, much stronger than Naomi had been.

"You're not going to use that," he said to her.

Naomi's voice was shrill. "What choice do we have? Everything we'd planned is gone. We can't make those accusations stick without backup." She flung a hand backward behind herself. "Did you see what she did? She delivered our proof directly into the enemy's hands."

Urlich began to sweat, hard and fast. I twisted to see his face. "We can't." He shook his head. "It's suicide."

Naomi's eyes were bright. "The only thing we still have going for us is that no one knows who created those documents. They don't know you and I are behind this. Don't you see? The only way we get out of this is if she isn't around to tell tales." She glanced over her shoulder as though she'd heard something, then turned back to face us. "Hurry. Knock her out like you did the agent. We'll release the gas and leave the two of them here to die."

"We don't have our masks. We don't have any protective equipment," Urlich said with rising panic. "You saw what that stuff does. It'll get us, too."

"Not if we move fast enough." She spoke through gritted teeth. "Let's go, we're wasting time."

"Naomi, you know we can't get out *that* fast," Urlich said, almost pleading now. "You saw how quickly the stuff works."

"You have another idea?" She grabbed and twisted one of his lapels, bringing her face close enough for me to smell her angry breath. "What choice do we have? Think about it."

He didn't reply.

"Yeah, exactly," she said, letting go. "Hurry up."

When he reached into his pocket for what he'd used to disable the Secret Service agent — chloroform, I'd guess — I knew that in less than a minute I would be unconscious, too.

Naomi's voice was a ragged whisper. "Do it."

Urlich pulled a small bottle out, bringing

it close to my face. He had the disadvantage of having to unsnap its flip-top lid one-handed, and my heart pounded as he struggled. I thrashed against him, hoping for a chance. Any chance.

Naomi made her way toward the far doors that led to the State Dining Room. "As soon as she's unconscious, we'll release the gas and go out this way." She pointed, inching closer to the door. I got the feeling that if Urlich happened to succumb to the gas on his way out, she wouldn't stick around to try to save him.

Still talking, she said, "See? Straight in. All we'll have to do is settle ourselves in the next room, smile, and rejoin the party. No one will notice."

Urlich's bottle was almost to my nose. His pudgy hand was damp with sweat. Clamped tight around the bottle. Trembling.

I heard him suck in a deep breath and hold it. At the same time, he repositioned his thumb beneath the flip-top edge of the cap, ready to pop it open.

Gurgling my anger, I kicked backward like a donkey, landing my foot hard against his knee.

"Oof." He stutter-stepped to the side, but didn't fall, still holding tight to me. Thinking fast, I threw my weight against him, wrenching myself from his grasp as he stumbled.

In that frantic second of freedom, I fell to my hands and knees, managing to pull the handkerchief from my mouth. "Help," I cough-screamed.

Startled, Naomi took a precious second to react. With wildness in her eyes and a strangled cry in her throat, she tackled me on the floor, scratching to get a grip. I was not about to let her gain control over me again. I broke free long enough to fumble to my feet. She did, too, and we faced each other — angry combatants. I had nothing to use but my head. Literally. I crouched, ducking. With a cry born of adrenaline and desperation, I launched myself into her midsection, ramming hard.

She lost her balance with a *whoof* of surprise.

Her arms shot up as she went down. The vial flew into the air, away from my grasping hands. "No," I moaned as it spun away, out of my reach. "No."

Almost as though it hung suspended by an invisible thread, the vial twisted and turned, reaching a terrifying apex before it began to fall. The woman's eyes sparked with fear as the container landed softly on the floor, intact.

She was on her hands and knees. We both lunged for the deadly device and as I skidded to the floor, arms outstretched, I scratched, hit, and clawed at her, while blindly reaching where I thought the tube might have landed. My fingers wrapped around the cool, metallic container. I rolled away from her, up on my hands and knees now, screaming. "In here. Help. Help!"

Urlich had recovered enough to lunge at me. He latched on to me from behind and was doing his best to pry the vial from my fingers. I yelled as loudly as I could, gibberish probably. Anything to make myself heard.

Taller, bigger, and far stronger than I was, Urlich's face was hot next to mine, his sweat making his cheek slide as he gained leverage. Naomi leaped into the fray, the three of us on the floor, Urlich using his body weight to hold me down, Naomi reaching for the vial.

I was seconds away from losing my grip. With Naomi so close to sliding the tube from my right hand, I fisted my left and used it to punch Urlich in the face. He was breathing hard at this point, but barely registered the blow.

I stiffened the thumb of my left hand and, summoning every tiny bit of strength I could muster, jammed the appendage into his eye.

That got him. He toppled sideways, taking me with him, knocking Naomi to the ground alongside. His hold on me loosened long enough for me to tighten my grip on the vial and wriggle out of his arms.

On my back now, I used my legs to push away from him, knocking my head into one of the room's antique chairs. I scooched backward again, shoving the chair out of my way, hearing it topple to the floor. Urlich grabbed for my legs.

I was breathing like a marathon runner even though all this had taken no more than ten or fifteen seconds. "Get away from me," I shouted, giving Urlich another kick.

I was about to flip over onto my hands and knees when three Secret Service agents ran in, guns drawn. One of them was Rosenow. I stayed down on the floor, my hand still holding the toxic vial. The confused agents stared down at us, and even though they looked ready to shoot me where I lay, I couldn't have been happier.

"Thank you," I said.

I brought the vial to my chest where I held it with both hands, and let my head drop to the floor.

CHAPTER 29

Gav and Tom were on the scene within moments, but it wasn't until they'd personally vouched for me that I was finally allowed to get to my feet.

The Secret Service agents who'd rushed in seemed a little miffed, maybe even disappointed, not to be able to cart me away in chains. Well, except for Rosenow. As she holstered her weapon, she gave me a weary look and shook her head.

As soon as I steadied myself, I made my way over to Gav. From the look in his eyes, I could tell he wanted to pull me close and whisk me away from all this. He held back, of course. Not here, not now.

"Are you okay? What happened?" he asked.

"Careful with this." I handed him the vial. "I think this is the same stuff that killed Evan and the rest at the Ainsley Street Ministry."

"Hydrogen sulfide?" His expression shifted from concern to alarm, even as his grip tightened on the little tube. "How did you get —"

"Long story," I said, too weary to get into it all right now.

Tom took control. I heard more than one of his subordinates ask why I wasn't being hauled away. He didn't answer. All he said to each of them was, "You have your orders."

Agents swarmed, checking the Red Room and its neighbors for any other possible threats. Gav and I stood together, watching as Urlich and Naomi were searched for weapons, then handcuffed.

"He has a substance on him," I said, pointing to Urlich's pocket. "Chloroform would be my best guess."

The agent holding Urlich looked to Tom for guidance. He nodded. A moment later, after a more thorough search, the agent came up with not one, but two other vials, which they handed to Gav. I shuddered to think what else they'd been carrying.

As the guards herded the two toward the family elevator, I asked Gav, "Where are they taking them?"

"The ground floor and then out the back way," he said. "We'll try to keep this as quiet as possible, for now. Although the guests in the East Room are aware that something has gone down in here, no one quite knows what to make of it yet. Best to keep the excitement to a minimum until everyone has exited the building safely. No sense in starting a panic or giving the newshounds a bone to run with." He blew out a long breath. "Not yet, at least."

The White House doctor and one of his assistants had been summoned for the fallen Secret Service agent, who still lay motionless on the ground where Urlich had dropped him. The man was unconscious but at least he was alive. After a cursory examination, the doctor called Tom over to arrange to have the man transported to a hospital. From what I could tell, he was expected to make a complete recovery.

While they conversed, I asked Gav to bring me up to speed.

"Where's the president?" I asked.

Gav examined the vial I'd handed him. "We need to get this out of here." He pulled up a radio and spoke into it. "I need Hazmat in the Red Room, stat. Keep it quiet."

"Where's your cane?" I asked.

"You're worried about me? After all this?" He gave me an amused look. "I'm fine."

"What happens next?" I asked.

"We'll have to see how much the two rogue agents are willing to tell us." He reached, as though to take my hand, then stopped himself with a self-conscious glance around the room. "As far as the president goes, that was a brilliant plan to send Josh in with those documents. Absolutely brilliant. The president was able to excuse himself from dinner long enough to alert me and Tom. You provided the proof that someone was planning to sabotage tonight's dinner, but none of us knew who was behind it. The president is back in there now, telling the crowd that there will be music and dancing first, speeches later."

"That's going to be tough to explain."

"Fewer speeches?" One corner of Gav's mouth quirked up. "That roomful of guests will be forever grateful to you for sparing them, whether they know it or not."

Two Hazmat team members approached. They spoke with Gav briefly. He handed over the vials with a warning about what was inside.

"Here's what I don't get," Gav said. "How did you get your hands on those papers? How did you know who put them there? And how did you wind up here, in danger? Again?"

A butler walked by, wheeling a cart laden

with covered dinner plates. "I'll explain later," I said. "Right now I need to get back down to the kitchen."

"You can't be serious." This time he did take my hand. "Look, you're shaking."

I held tight to his fingers. "And the only way I'm going to feel safe again is if I can do my job. This is a major event, we're still serving, and I'm supposed to be the chef in charge. If you need me, you know where to find me."

"Ollie," he said quietly, "eight weeks can't come fast enough."

"You really think this sort of excitement will stop once we're married?" I squeezed his hand again as I glanced around the room. "Gosh, I hope so."

Even though Bucky had everything under control, he was relieved to see me when I made it back downstairs a few minutes later. "Where are we?" I asked.

SBA chefs were sending food up to the Butler's Pantry via dumbwaiter. Others, pushing rolling carts, waited patiently for the elevator to arrive.

"That," he said, pointing to the fourth cart in line, "is the last of the third course. There was a delay of some sort" — he glared at me, though not in anger — "that I suppose

I shouldn't ask you about. Once we were given the okay to start up again, we resumed serving." He glanced up at the clock. "The entire meal is running fifteen minutes later than we'd planned. They said the president left the dinner for an extended period of time. You wouldn't know anything about that, would you?"

I held up both hands. "Pleading the fifth."

"Figured," he said. "Anyway, we're about to get started plating the entrée."

"Excellent," I said. "I haven't missed it after all."

He pierced me with a look. "You okay?"

"Yeah," I said. "I am now."

Within minutes, I was fully immersed in the business of serving our guests, overseeing final touches and walking the kitchen, checking on uniformity and the beauty of each plate to be presented. I let Bucky know that I wanted him to continue managing and that I was there in a supportive role only. While I desperately craved taking control, I knew that to do so now would only confuse the staff. I didn't want to cause any further turmoil. What's more, Bucky had handled the dinner magnificently thus far. I didn't want to strip him of authority now. This had turned out to be his night.

SBA chefs were running up to him with

questions and concerns, and he treated each instance with more patience and quiet confidence than I might have expected of him. Bucky deserved to be named my first assistant. If Virgil remained out of the picture, he might even have a chance.

The pheasant breasts came out of the oven crispy and browned. I stepped aside as one of the chefs carried a tray of them past me. The room hummed with purpose, and I watched my team come together, creating gorgeous, delicious dinners. I smiled as the steaming breasts, sautéed spinach, sweet potatoes, and green beans with beets were lovingly placed on the Truman serving pieces.

Watching Bucky, Cyan, and the rest of the chefs work together in such harmony, knowing that the dinner upstairs had come close to being ruined, but had ultimately been saved, and knowing that I'd played a role in that happy outcome, made my heart swell.

"Chef Reed," Samantha called to Bucky, "the butlers want to know if we're ready for them."

He shot me a look, and caught me grinning. "We sure are. Let's roll."

CHAPTER 30

The weekend sped by with no more than dribbles of information coming our way. Gav, who had given up his cane completely, managed to glean a few more details to share with me Sunday night.

We were sitting at my kitchen table. Dinner was finished and we'd cleaned up. The sun had gone down and the only light on in my apartment was the one over the table, coating us in its warm glow. Being here with Gav was quiet and peaceful. For the first time in a long time, I felt myself relax.

Some of what Urlich had told me was true. What he hadn't told me was that he and Naomi had met as Kalto team members, working in Durasi. Their boss, Alec Baran, had no idea that his agents had been conspiring under his nose. He hadn't even realized they were a couple.

"When Baran was told, he was shocked," Gav said. "Not merely surprised. I think the fact that two of his employees could get as far as they did with their plans without him being aware has truly shaken his self-confidence."

"I'm sure they did their best to cover their tracks," I said. "And I'll bet he wasn't the only person they fooled."

"Yes, but Alec Baran's business is security. This is a devastating professional blow."

"I get it," I said. "He really had no idea?"

Gav shook his head. "Baran did have an inkling that something was amiss. I'll get to that in a minute. The thing is, he never suspected Urlich. He trusted him above all others. Believed the man to be not only his employee, but his friend."

"I need you to explain why Urlich and Naomi were plotting against the president. I can't believe it's simply because they'd lose their jobs, or because they might be assigned to boring details here in the States. That's hardly motive for murder."

Gav leaned forward on his elbows and as he spoke, I admired everything about the man: his unpretentious air, the set of his jaw, the concern in his eyes.

"Here's what happened: Urlich and Naomi met while working in Durasi. He was assigned to her division, and it didn't take long for her to tag him to help her run a business she'd established out there. From what we can tell, she's the mastermind behind all this. The brains of the outfit."

"What kind of business was she running?"

"Dealing black-market items: alcohol, fake IDs, some drugs. A thriving bookie enterprise. Even though Durasi is a relatively poor country, there are still people willing to gamble."

I couldn't believe it. "They managed to hide that kind of organization for four years? How was the Secret Service able to unearth the truth over the past couple of *days*?"

"Other authorities had jurisdiction up until now," he said. "And once we knew where to look, we were able to dig. That came thanks to you."

"So Urlich worked for Naomi?"

He made a so-so motion with his head. "Started out that way. They eventually became partners. Apparently her business grew faster than she'd anticipated. When Urlich arrived on the scene, she recognized him as a kindred spirit and quietly pulled him in. Together they've been running a multimillion-dollar empire."

"That means . . ." I began, reasoning aloud, "they couldn't have been very happy with the president's decision to pull Kalto's forces out of Durasi."

"That's the understatement of the year."

"Why didn't they simply resign from Kalto? Move to Durasi and keep their activities going without anyone being the wiser?"

"Ah, that's where it gets interesting," Gav said. "Durasi has strict laws about foreigners in the country. Individuals can't simply decide they want to live there. Not without jumping through a year's worth of hoops and winding their way through mountains of red tape. Even then, they risk being turned away."

"I'm starting to understand."

"The important point here is that the removal of Kalto's forces from Durasi meant the end of Urlich and Naomi's business out there. They were desperate to fight the president's initiative."

"But by the time of the Durasi dinner, this was a done deal. What did they hope to accomplish?"

Gav held up a finger. "Number one, they'd gotten rid of Secretary Cobault. He was probably the most anti-mercenary statesman in the country. Not only that, he had the president's ear. Urlich and Naomi cobbled this plan together quickly — remember, they didn't have much time and they were desperate for results. They believed that if they forged that letter, making it seem as though the secretary had advised the president to reverse his decision, they could silence Cobault and blame the president with one shot. Kill two birds with one stone."

"But their business was still lost to them."

"Which brings me to point two." He held up a second finger. "What Urlich and Naomi needed was for President Hyden's initiative to be blocked. With his approval ranks soaring, that wasn't about to happen. What they needed was a scandal — a big enough one to cast doubt on every decision the president had made. Possibly even getting him impeached."

"That couldn't happen," I said. "President Hyden is innocent. Surely the forensics and all the evidence would prove that."

Gav leaned forward a little bit more. "You've seen it as often as I have. We're supposed to be innocent until proven guilty. In the court of public opinion, however, that isn't always the case. Urlich and Naomi set out to ruin President Hyden. They were counting on the fact that plenty of people believe that, as an individual in power, he has hit men at his beck and call." He gave me a meaningful look. "There *are* people like that across the globe, no question about it. Our President Hyden, fortunately, is not one of them."

"Why kill your friend Evan and Jason Chaff? Why kill the other three men at the Ainsley Street Ministry?"

Gav nodded as though he'd planned to get to that point next. "As I mentioned, Alec Baran suspected that all was not right in his organization. There had been signs of trouble, hints of problems. He sent Jason undercover to investigate and report. Because Baran didn't know who in his organization he could trust, he approached the Secret Service, and they came up with the plan of Jason connecting with Evan to pass intelligence." Gav heaved a sigh. "Unfortunately for them, Baran trusted Urlich enough to tell him of the arrangement. Those men at the ministry were killed before the information could be properly conveyed."

I shuddered. I'd seen Urlich and Naomi's desperation and what they were capable of. I'd come way too close to sharing Evan's, Jason's, and the other men's fate.

"That reporter Daniel Davies?" Gav continued. "He was part of this, too. I can't quite call him innocent, but the worst thing he's guilty of is sitting on a story in the hopes of snagging an even bigger one."

"Are you saying that he reported the Ainsley Street murders as a carbon monoxide accident on purpose?"

Gav nodded. "Urlich recruited him. Told the young journalist that if he stayed tight and reported as directed, Urlich would hand him on a silver platter the story of all stories. And he'd have the full scoop before anyone else did."

"That scoop being that the president was behind Secretary Cobault's murder?"

Gav gave another nod. "Tyree and Larsen went to talk with Davies yesterday morning. The kid was practically in tears and gave them everything they asked for, including a copy of the mock-up article you found." He smiled at me. "Nice bit of detective work there, finding those pages secreted in the cookbook."

"Why on earth would they put them there?" I asked. "Why not just bring the documents in a purse or a pocket?"

"That's what Naomi did. She carried the paperwork into the White House with the intention of passing it to Urlich sometime in the afternoon before he made his speech. They ran into problems, however, when Alec kept Urlich busy all day, inadvertently putting a crimp in their plans. They had to find a way for her to get the documents to

Urlich."

"She couldn't simply hand them to him later?"

"They weren't certain they would see each other before the dinner started, so they had to come up with a plan for her to leave the documents in a place that would be safe, yet where Urlich could find them with relative ease. A dead drop. Hiding the pages in a cookbook seemed like a perfect choice — who would think to look there?" He chuckled. "They underestimated you, Ollie."

"What about the chloroform? And the poison? How did they get those in?"

"Tom and his team are currently looking into how they managed to get the hydrogen sulfide past security. The chloroform? Urlich stole some from the doctor's office earlier in the day."

I was blown away. "They came so close," I said. "Too close."

Gav wrapped his hand around mine. "Thank goodness you followed your instincts."

I could feel the mood shift. "How are you doing?" I asked. "You haven't been using your cane and you've been involved in this investigation a lot, even though you're still on medical leave. This can't be helping your recovery."

"Are you safe?" he asked.

I gave the room a quick glance, as though checking for bad guys. "Yeah, I think I am now."

"Then my life couldn't be better." He gave me a crooked smile. "Well, except for one thing."

"And I know exactly what that one thing is. We still have about seven weeks to wait."

"Maybe you're right; maybe your involvement in adventures like this won't stop even after we're married. Maybe I'm fooling myself into believing that once we say our vows, you'll be safe forever."

"Do you have any idea how superstitious that sounds?"

"Do you have any idea how much I hate that I think that way?" He reached over and grabbed my other hand. "Ollie, I will love you forever. These recent weeks have convinced me that I need to put these irrational fears behind me. You've reminded me time and again that you've been able to get yourself out of trouble. You've proved your point many times over. Time for me to get a grip."

At that moment, the little clock on my kitchen wall made a clicking sound that signaled the hour. Gav looked up. Eleven P.M. "It's late," he said. "I'd better go."

"It's not that late. You're still on leave and tomorrow's my day off."

"I thought you were going in."

"I've got a meeting with Sargeant at nine. After that, I want to connect with Bucky and Cyan and get a few things caught up in the kitchen. We haven't had a chance to do the event's postmortem yet. Josh said he'd like to be part of that, too."

"Still, I'd better go," he said. "We both need our rest."

I was sorry to see him leave, but I understood. These last few days had been taxing for him and as much as he hated to admit it, recovering from serious injuries was hard work.

"Okay," I said. When we got to my door, I asked, "See you tomorrow night?"

He cupped my chin and looked at me with the sweetest sparkle in his eyes. "Definitely."

CHAPTER 31

"What you're telling me, Peter," I said to Sargeant the next morning, "is that Virgil is definitely coming back? There's no way around it?"

We were seated across from one another in Sargeant's office. The fussy chief usher seemed particularly vexed by the news of Virgil's return. Either that or he was sitting on another big concern that he wasn't sharing with me.

"The First Lady has it in her mind that if Virgil apologizes to you and to the team, we can start fresh. She also insisted on him seeking help for his anger management issues. We don't know Virgil's reaction to her demands, however. He's incommunicado at the moment."

I scratched my head. "I take it that means Bucky is still in limbo where the promotion is concerned? I certainly hope the First Lady doesn't expect Virgil will make an instantaneous turnaround and become an exemplary employee just like that." I snapped my fingers.

"As a matter of fact, based on your recommendation and with the knowledge that he managed the dinner so well during your . . . er . . . absence, she's given me the green light to promote Bucky."

I sat up. "Really? You're not joking?"

"I do not joke, Olivia. How many times must I tell you that?"

"My mistake," I said with a smile. "Incidentally, Margaret was a very big help to me the other night." I'd discovered, after the fact, that Margaret had, indeed, tried to find Tom MacKenzie as I'd asked her to. It just happened that while she was looking for him, he'd been behind closed doors, at first talking with Gav and then with the president.

He sniffed. "So I've heard."

"I've thanked her personally, but I thought it was worth me mentioning it to you as well."

"Did you really threaten her with dismissal if she didn't cooperate?"

I felt my face flush. "I didn't believe she would appreciate the gravity of the situation otherwise."

"I realize how difficult it is for you to keep

out of trouble. Do you think it's possible to exercise restraint and avoid dragging my employees into these little escapades in the future?"

"I'll do my best."

"You're back," Bucky said when I returned to the kitchen.

I'd donned a white smock when I'd first arrived this morning. Now I pulled on an apron. "Yep, I'm back."

As I tied the apron behind my waist, he asked, "What's up with Sargeant?"

"Well," I said drawing out the word, "I have good news and bad news."

Cyan came around the corner looking harried, her eyes bright green today.

"You okay?" I asked.

"Oh yeah. Just a busy morning here."

I looked from one to the other. "Anything wrong? Should I have come in earlier?"

"Oh no," she said with a bit too much levity. "Bucky and I managed breakfast with no problem. I've got a few other things on my mind, that's all."

Bucky glared at her then returned his attention to me. "You mentioned something about good news and bad news?"

"Bad news first. Virgil is probably coming back."

Bucky and Cyan let out twin groans. "I'd hoped he was gone for good," Bucky said, rubbing his face. "So much for that."

"Want to hear the good news?" I asked.

"It had better be pretty good to run up against this Virgil news flash," he said.

"I'll let you decide whether it is or not." I stood directly in front of him and held out my hand. Instinctively, he shook it. Smiling, I said, "Buckminster Reed, congratulations. You have been promoted and you are now the first assistant chef in the White House kitchen."

His face transformed from a grousing frown to a bright, wide smile. "Are you kidding me?" he asked. "Of course you're not. You wouldn't kid about that." Grabbing me in a bear hug, he said, "Thank you, Ollie. Thank you."

When he released me I laughed. That had been one of the most emotional displays I'd ever seen from the man. "Thank yourself. It's your talent and hard work that got you here. I'm simply the messenger."

Agent Rosenow appeared in the doorway. "Ms. Paras?" she said. "Your presence is requested in the China Room."

We went from cheerful glee to unsettled silence in the space of a heartbeat.

I looked at Bucky and Cyan, silently com-

municating my "Not the China Room" fear
before asking the agent, "Who wants to see
me?"

"President Hyden."

I felt my jaw drop. My knee-jerk response
was to ask, "Am I in trouble?" but I thought
better of it and shut my mouth. "Yes, okay.
Right away." I untied my apron, tossed it on
the countertop and smoothed the front of
my chef's whites as I followed her out. When
I got to the doorway, I turned back to Bucky
and Cyan and mouthed, "What's up?"

Cyan shook her head, then turned to
Bucky, who held up both hands in a helpless gesture.

Rosenow led me into the corridor and
across the hall. Tours were finished for the
day so the area was quiet. The China Room
door was open. As we got closer I could see
the president pacing inside. He was alone.

"You can go right in," she said.

I blew out a breath of fear. "Are you coming, too?"

"No, my orders are to leave you here. I
have duties elsewhere," she said. "Good
luck."

Good luck. Was I going to need it?

"President Hyden?" I said as I entered the
room. "You wanted to see me?"

He turned. "I did, Ollie." He didn't offer

me a seat, even though there were several choices in the room. He didn't look relaxed, either. I had no idea what was coming next.

"As you're aware," he began, "there was a plan to undermine the Durasi peace initiatives and, more personally, to undermine me."

I didn't say anything.

"Although the circumstances have been explained to some extent, I'm still receiving reports. What I do know is that the guilty parties — trusted members of one of our mercenary teams — followed a peculiar, twisted logic in order to further their own interests, despite the fact that doing so involved killing innocent people."

I didn't think he was asking me a question, so I waited for him to continue.

"The reason I've called you in here today is, frankly, because I want to discuss your involvement in exposing this conspiracy. I'm shocked that the White House executive chef could so often be involved in situations that compromise the security of this country."

"I assure you, I never intended —"

"Ollie," he said, his voice a little softer than it had been a moment earlier. "I'm not here to berate you. I'm here to thank you. By sending me those papers when you did, the way you did, you helped avoid a major catastrophe, one that could have set back peace negotiations with Durasi for another fifty years."

My breath caught in my throat. "I don't know what to say."

"There's nothing for you to say. All I want you to know is that I'm grateful and your country is, too."

I had no words. "Thank you," was all I could manage.

"You have done us all a great favor, and I want you to know that if there's ever anything I can do for you, please allow me to be of service."

I smiled. Like I'd ever do that. "Thank you, that's very generous."

"I'm serious, Ollie. Is there anything on your mind that I could help you with? Anything at all?"

I was tempted for a split second to ask him to use his influence with the courts to allow me and Gav to get married sooner, but when I opened my mouth, I found I couldn't do it.

"Thank you," I said again, "but no."

Clasping his hands in front of his waist, he tilted his head. "You're absolutely sure there's nothing?"

The look in his eyes gave me the oddest

impression that he could read my mind. Still, there was no way I was going to ask the president of the United States to get on the phone with the Moultrie Courthouse so that his executive chef could move her wedding date up by a couple of weeks.

"I'm sure."

"Hmm," he said, massaging his chin. "Then perhaps you won't mind if we come up with an idea of our own?"

That was the moment I knew something was off.

From behind me, I heard, "Ollie?"

Cyan and Bucky were the first ones through the door, Bucky holding a bouquet of flowers. He crossed the room in five quick strides. "Here you go, Ace," he said handing the flowers to me and giving me a quick peck on the cheek.

"What's this for?" I asked.

Cyan held a chef's toque in her hands. When she pulled it up to place it on my head, I noticed that she'd affixed a veil to the back of it. "Blushing bride," she said.

"Wait. What's going on?"

They didn't answer.

I turned to glance back at the president, but his gaze was firmly on the door. I turned back and my heart skipped when Gav strode in, wearing his dark dress suit with a white

412

rose on his lapel. He joined me, taking my free hand in his. "Nicely done, Mr. President." To me he said, "Don't worry. It's legal. I picked up the license this morning."

I was beginning to understand, yet I couldn't believe. "How can we —" I turned to President Hyden. "Did you pull in a favor at the courthouse?"

"No," he said, "another of your friends helped out." He pointed to the doorway, where more people spilled in. This time Sargeant and Thora, accompanied by Margaret and a dark-haired, smartly dressed, bearded man I didn't recognize.

"Olivia," Sargeant said, as he joined our little group. "Allow me to introduce Frank Designa. He's authorized to perform wedding ceremonies here in Washington, D.C., and he's a personal friend of mine."

"Nice to meet you," I said. As soon as we shook, my hands flew to my face. "I can't believe all this."

Gav pointed to Cyan and Bucky, who were rearranging the China Room's regular furniture to make way for staffers, who were now setting up folding chairs. "It was Bucky and Cyan's idea," he said, "and Peter's." He nodded to Sargeant, who looked as though he was working very hard not to beam.

"You are a nosy person, Olivia," Sargeant

said. "All those questions about why Bucky and Cyan were meeting with me. *Tsk.*"

"I didn't know."

"And I suppose you didn't notice that they were coming in earlier each morning, so that we could work on plans before you arrived."

I smacked my forehead. "That's what's been going on."

Sargeant sniffed delicately. "And you call yourself an amateur sleuth." He placed a hand on Thora's back and led her away. "We'll take our seats now."

Gav was watching me closely. "As soon as Bucky and Cyan brought me in on the plans, I knew this was right." He squeezed my hand as more and more people began shouldering their way into the China Room. "This *is* right, isn't it?"

My heart was as full as it had ever been. I was about to answer him, to say, "Of course it's right," when I caught sight of two people in the doorway, escorted by Agent Rosenow.

I flew across the room, barely choking out, "Mom!" as I grabbed her and hugged. "How did you know?"

She hugged back, patting me and smoothing the back of my head, veil and all. "You think we'd miss seeing our girl get married?" she asked.

"I wouldn't. Not for the world," Nana said.

I hugged Nana, my throat thick with emotion. I couldn't trust myself to speak.

Gav had come up to greet my family. When he turned to me, he said, "Why do you think I left your apartment before midnight last night? It's bad luck for the groom to see the bride on her wedding day."

Mrs. Wentworth and Stanley were there. My heart skipped a beat when my former boss and mentor, Henry, strode in. It was too much to take in at once and I found myself breathless and grateful. Oh so grateful.

Josh came up to me, holding a little satin pillow. "My dad says that I can be the ring bearer if it's okay with you, Ollie."

"I am the luckiest person in the world today," I said. Crouching down to his level, I gave him a big hug. "There's nothing I'd like better."

Gav nudged me to look closer. "We have rings," he said. "I picked them out, but if there's a style you'd prefer . . ."

I shook my head. "I love them."

"I know it's the China Room," he said apologetically. "But due to other events going on today, it's the only room available."

I laughed. "You know what? This is perfect. Absolutely perfect."

Someone had remembered music. Soft, classical. I couldn't tell where it was coming from, but I didn't care. I took a look around the room and saw the faces of the people in this world I loved the most. As they got themselves settled, I struggled to get my emotions under control. I was rarely at a loss for words, but this time I had nothing but love in my heart, and no words were big enough or grand enough.

As Frank Designa called for the room to quiet down, Gav whispered, "Last chance, Ollie. Are you sure you want to marry me?"

I swallowed around the lump in my throat. "Oh, I do," I said. "I most definitely do."

RECIPES

BRAISED CHUCK ROAST

Serves 6

2 medium onions (optional)
2 pounds carrots
1 (3–4 lb.) beef chuck roast
3–4 tablespoons canola oil
4 cups beef broth

Preheat oven to 325F.

Cut onion into quarters, if using. Peel carrots and rough chop on the bias, leaving pieces 1 to 1 1/2 inches long.

In braising pan or heavy Dutch oven, heat oil until hot over medium-high heat, then brown roast on all sides. Add onion and carrots. Pour in beef broth (liquid should come at least halfway up the roast, but should not cover it completely). Cover, and transfer pan to oven.

Roast for 2 1/2 to 3 hours, or until meat is fork-tender.

Serve with mashed potatoes.

HERB-ROASTED PHEASANT WITH WILD RICE STUFFING
SERVED AT THE
INAUGURAL LUNCHEON, 2009

Serves 10

8 cups chicken stock or canned chicken
  broth
1 pound long-grain wild rice
10 boneless pheasant breasts, boneless,
  tenders removed and reserved for stuffing,
  and a small pocket cut into side of breast
  for stuffing
1/2 cup olive oil mixed with chopped rose-
  mary, thyme, and sage
1/2 onion, diced
2 carrots, diced
2 tablespoons garlic, roasted
1/2 cup dried apricot, diced
Salt and pepper to taste

Bring chicken stock to a boil. Add rice,

cover, reduce heat, and simmer until rice is tender and most of the liquid is gone, approximately 15 minutes.

Add onion, carrot, garlic, and apricot. Cook until vegetables are soft and all liquid has been absorbed, about 15 minutes. Refrigerate rice mixture until cold.

In a food processor, puree pheasant tenders to a paste consistency to use as a binder for rice mix.

When rice is cool, add the pheasant puree to the rice until well mixed. Adjust seasoning with salt and pepper and return to refrigerator until ready to stuff.

Preheat oven to 400F.

Divide rice into 10 portions, and shape each one into a football. Stuff each pheasant breast with one portion of rice, being careful not to overstuff the pheasant. Rub oil mixture on top and bottom of each pheasant breast, and season with salt and pepper. Place pheasant on a heavy-gauge roasting pan and bake for 8 to 10 minutes. Remove from oven and cover with lid or foil and allow to rest for 10 minutes. Serve over sautéed spinach.

Notes
Pheasant can be substituted with chicken.

SAUTÉED SPINACH
SERVED AT THE
INAUGURAL LUNCHEON, 2013

Serves 1

1/4 cup shallot, minced
1/2 tablespoon olive oil
8 ounces baby spinach
1 pinch sea salt
1 pinch cracked black pepper

Preheat a large, heavy-bottomed sauté pan on high heat. Sauté shallot in oil until tender.

Add baby spinach and season with salt and pepper, cooking only until spinach leaves are wilted. Remove from pan and keep warm.

Molasses Whipped Sweet Potatoes
Served at the Inaugural Luncheon, 2009

Makes 2 quarts

3 large sweet potatoes (about 3 pounds)
2 tablespoons unsalted butter
1 teaspoon kosher salt
1/4 cup orange juice
1/2 tablespoon brown sugar
1 teaspoon ground cumin
1 tablespoon molasses
2 tablespoons maple syrup

Preheat oven to 400F.

Place sweet potatoes on a baking sheet and roast until easily pierced with a fork, about 1 hour.

Peel the skin off of the sweet potatoes while still hot. By hand or mixer, smash potatoes until all large chunks are gone. Combine potatoes, butter, salt, orange juice, brown sugar, ground cumin, molasses, and maple syrup in a large bowl. Continue to mix all together until all lumps are gone. Adjust seasonings to your specific tastes.

Notes

Can be made 1 day before; keep refrigerated and reheat just before serving.

BABY GOLDEN BEETS AND GREEN BEANS
SERVED AT THE INAUGURAL LUNCHEON, 2013

Serves 4

8 cups water
Kosher salt
8 baby golden beets, peeled and cut in half
4 ounces green beans, ends snipped, cut on
  bias into 1-inch pieces
1/2 tablespoon extra virgin olive oil
1/2 tablespoon shallot, minced
1 pinch white pepper

Bring 2 quarts of water to a boil and add 1/2 tablespoon kosher salt.

Place beets into water gently and allow to cook for 5 minutes or until tender. Remove using a strainer, and set aside in a bowl.

Allow water to return to a boil and gently add the green beans for 3 to 4 minutes, until tender. Drain, and add to the bowl with the beets.

Place olive oil in a sauté pan on medium heat, add the shallots, and cook until tender. Add the beets and beans, and season with salt and pepper to taste.

LEMON STEAMED PUDDING
SERVED AT THE
INAUGURAL LUNCHEON, 2005

Serves 8–10

7 1/2 ounces patent flour
1/2 ounce baking powder
Salt
1 each lemon, zested
9 ounces butter
9 ounces white sugar
4 whole eggs
1 each egg yolk
2 1/2 ounces lemon juice

Sift dry ingredients together.

Cream butter and sugar until fluffy. Add eggs and little flour to keep mix from splitting. Add sifted dry ingredients. Slowly add liquid, and mix batter until smooth.

Divide batter among prepared pans, and cover each timbale with foil. Steam in water bath for 30 to 35 minutes.

Puddings are best removed from molds when completely cool.

Notes
Equipment: *timbale pans*

E

CPSIA information can be obtained
at www.ICGtesting.com
Printed in the USA
FFOW05n1410020714

9 781410 468